NICE

NICE

by

Charles Holdefer

THE PERMANENT PRESS
SAG HARBOR, NY 11963

Library of Congress Cataloging-in-Publication Data

Holdefer, Charles
Nice: a novel /by Charles Holdefer
p. cm.
ISBN 1-57962-038-8 (alk paper)
1. Social skills--Study and teaching--Fiction. 2. Married people--Fiction. 3. Self-employed--Fiction. I. Title

PS3558.0347746 N53 2001
813'.54--dc21 00-064275
CIP

THE PERMANENT PRESS
4170 Noyac Road
Sag Harbor, NY 11963

I was a derision to all my people; and their song all the day.

Lamentations 3:14

ONE

Where Have You Been?

One

THE COIN FELL with a *chink.*

"Hey thanks, mister," he said, looking up with bloodshot eyes.

"Take care."

Jerry Renfrow, alias Mr Nice Guy, walked homeward at a brisk pace, enjoying the sunshine on his face, the cupped palm of the sky and reflections off cars and signs and storefronts, his lungs swelling with spring air. What a day! Everybody, it seemed, was out tasting the afternoon. Glorious! Those who weren't squatting stuporously or lying on the pavement went about their business with springy steps as if readying for a race. At that instant he decided that he would change into his favorite celery-colored shorts and new sneakers and go for a trot in the park through its famed Woland Gardens.

> *"The future's gonna be* (he began to sing),
> *Home-made, Home-made . . ."*

Upon reaching his building, he bounded up the stairs, three flights, and, whistling, strode into the apartment where the breeze tossed a curtain at the open window and he saw his wife spread-eagled on the couch, her chin on a bony shoulder, bobbing, and a look of distant concentration in her eye . . .

Her fingers clasped air, her breaths came in puffs.

Then her gaze slowly focused on him: her eyes grew wide. She drummed her fist on the slim, happily rocking back.

"Huhh?"

The rocking stopped. A ruddy face with round, smooth cheeks looked at him. Now the face caved in with alarm.

"Excuse me," said Mr Nice Guy, hurrying past while the young man scurried off in search of his pants.

Suddenly breathless from the stairs, he went to the kitchen and groped in a special bottom drawer. But he didn't find what he was seeking. He grunted, his jaw working spasmodically, then remembered the top shelf of the cupboard. He reached high, waggled his fingers hopefully in a wicker basket, and came down with chicolo balls of mintgreen and bruisy plum. These he fingered into his mouth, one at a time, chewing meditatively as he looked around the kitchen. He decided to tidy up. On the countertop, the spine of an ice-cube tray lay in a tepid puddle, alongside lime rinds and a bottle of gin. He took a sponge and wiped the counter clean, put the bottle back under the sink and refilled the ice-cube tray, carefully sliding it into the freezer compartment without sloshing. He hated sloshing.

"Jerry?"

He turned around, where Barbara stood at the kitchen doorway, tying the string belt of her kimono.

"I'm sorry, baby. You came in so suddenly. Of course I wasn't expecting you. I'm so embarrassed. I'm sorry."

Mr Nice Guy rinsed out the sponge, then began to twist it dry.

"I hadn't planned to return early but they recessed us at the courthouse. Of course I had no idea, Raba. What bad timing!"

Barbara disappeared into the living room for a moment, then returned with a white carton, holding it out to him. "There's pizza here if you want some."

He looked at her. "Honey, I'm sorry for interrupting. I bet you didn't even get to come."

She opened the carton, a smell of basil and tomatoes wafting up as she reached inside and pulled him out a wedge, gooey strands of cheese stretching and resisting as she tuned them upwards till they broke, and presented him the slice.

"Here sweetheart. Well no, I didn't, but that's all right."

He blew on the pizza before biting it. "Drag, though," he said, chewing, traces of sauce in the corners of his mouth.

She kissed him. "It was just an accident, Jerry. He got scared badly. He was in such a hurry. I didn't even have time to pay him for the pizza."

She extracted a piece for herself and put the carton on the counter as she climbed up onto a stool.

"Well, next time I come home early," he told her, "I'll ring first."

When she sat on the stool, a gap appeared in the front of her kimono, shadowy and pink. She reached out and tenderly touched his cheek, shaking her head, whispering, "Listen, you're the only one I really want." After having run his tongue around his lips and wiped off his tomatoed fingers on a napkin, Mr Nice Guy responded by sliding his hand inside the gap. The gentle movement of his wrist made the opening larger till her belt came loose and the kimono fell open, her breasts and belly rounding the air. She leaned closer. "I'm still all tingly, Jerry."

The phone rang.

"Oh, gee whiz," he said. His hand stopped, he looked at her. Another ring, and he moved away to answer.

"Let it go," she told him, catching her balance, "we can let it go."

"Sorry, honey, but that could be my jury foreman. We're on call for instructions."

He plucked the receiver off the wall. "Yesss?"

Before the voice on the other end uttered a syllable, he knew that it was most definitely *not* the jury foreman. Over the line came high-pitched dog yapping, piercing squeals and whining. Then the rush of words:

"Jer, come on now, tell me the truth, just when are we gonna move on this deal? Me and the puppies can't hold out much longer. We're going apeshit. They're tearing the hell out of everything! They even eat linoleum! My couch is chewed down to the frame, man. Don't let me down!"

"Garson, you have to give me two more weeks."

The reply exploded out of the telephone receiver—Mr Nice Guy held it away from his ear.

"*Two weeks*! What am I supposed to do with them for *two weeks*? Walk them in the park twenty at a time? I can't believe what you're saying. You're jerkin' me around, man, that's what you're doing —"

"Now Garson," began Mr Nice Guy, as Barbara sighed and hopped down from the stool, reached into the carton for another slice of pizza, "these are exceptional circumstances. I have jury duty and there's no way to get out of it. Believe me! Why would I lie to you? This delay is costing me. Listen, I'll send you another 500 dollars, the check will go out today, I promise. That's more than enough for expenses. You can keep anything you don't spend."

"Six hundred, Jerry. Zap me with six hundred volts."

"All right then, six hundred."

"This is a favor Jer, you know that. You owe me big time now. Be informed that I am officially bummed to the max."

Mr Nice Guy consoled him in his best soothing telephone voice (both his mother and Barbara agreed, he could be masterful at this) till eventually Garson calmed down, though the dogs still wowed-wowed in the background. Finally he hung up the phone and turned to Barbara.

"Sorry, darling. Would you like to go to the bedroom? There are more conveniences."

She smiled, but before she could answer the doorbell rang.

"Oh, what now?" he exclaimed.

He trotted to answer the front door. When he opened it, the young man stepped back immediately, edging toward the stairwell.

"What is it?" asked Mr Nice Guy.

"I—uh—the keys to my motor scooter are on the coffee table. I got to have them. The scooter doesn't belong to me."

Mr Nice Guy went back and fetched the keys while the youth waited outside the door. He handed them across the threshold.

"There you go. And the pizza—how much do we owe you?"

Two

OF COURSE, PEOPLE don't know him as Mr Nice Guy. He's always Jerry Renfrow. His wife is Barbara Oliver. I'm the only one who calls him Mr Nice Guy—because he deserves it. I write this not to make fun of him but to give him his due. Though it might be hard to share his way of dealing with the world (as for myself, I'm not so nice), though plenty of his acquaintances could not understand his warmth or join in his delight, Mr Nice Guy was determined to shine.

He invited others to join him, too. Wanted them, please, to come to his side. Together they would mend human hearts. Together they would restore America's luster.

It wasn't his fault that most people ignored his call, but simply tried to position themselves in front of his happy beam. They treated his personality like some old-fashioned crank contraption of a nature no one had ever seen—a sunshine machine!—which, to their astonishment, actually worked, turning without a squeak of protest on the power of one man's hope and perseverance. To tell the truth, it felt delicious. Oh, they could smile, act superior if they wanted, but they had to admit that it was *very* comfortable to be in front of. In the right place at the right time, they basked.

Mr Nice Guy worked hard at it. He turned and twisted and cranked and turned. Only Barbara appreciated the sacrifices involved, understood that his inspiration was only fractionally good vibrations and significantly more pain and howling distress. The planet was in agony. How tired, sometimes, his arm grew! She loved him dearly, yet even she, who knew him better than anyone else, could not see the man completely. For she was too close!

Barbara's predicament was unique. The love letters she still found in her pockets. His reassuring hand on her shoulder as he brushed her hair. Rose petals in her underwear drawer. What about the cassette planted surreptitiously in her car?

If I ain't so smart
There's always heaven above.
You want pearls of wisdom.
You want pearls of love.

Barbara listened to this familiar voice sing a cappella on her way to work at the Secreast Museum, and though she laughed, she was also touched. With such devotion how could he not endear himself? His attentions also included her relatives, down to the smallest family details, such as the fact that Cousin Julie could sleep only with her head pointing north, Uncle Bruce was allergic to milk products, and Javanitos were Norbert's favorite cigars. The furniture was rearranged, the menu changed, the humidor stocked before people even walked through the door.

"Damn cat had kittens again," said Cousin Julie's husband, Mike, when they were visiting from the country. They were hippie farmers who raised rabbits and goats and hemp. Mike scratched at his knees. "We never get it spayed in time. Guess I'll have to drown them."

Mr Nice Guy flipped open his datebook. "Tuesday . . . Tuesday morning around 10 o'clock. How's that for you?"

Always ready to be of service! People were sometimes taken aback but they rarely ever said No.

Naturally he never forgot a birthday. For his ailing mother's 66th he did a magic show, pulled a basketball out of silk kerchiefs while she and her old teammates laughed and clapped (he'd summoned them from all corners of America for this moment, an unprecedented feat in itself, calculated for nothing less than keeping his mother alive): he sent the basketball with a bounce pass to Darlene Stevens, who tossed it to Connie King, who (with a plate of birthday cake balanced on her lap) whipped it over to Dee Dee Wilson, who threw it to Maureen Zeck, who gently passed it to his mother.

She struggled to her feet. "Let's put it in," and with voices rising, then blending into a single cheer, they cleared the way for her, helped her out the door to the basket above her driveway.

They were the Pantherettes. 1949 Iowa State Champions. The glory days of the six-girl teams. Over the years Mrs Renfrow had seen several of her teammates at school reunions, and had visited Margie Keats when she was dying of injuries from a supermarket shooting, but never had the entire team, the survivors, been reassembled. The idea of a surprise reunion came to her son one day while she was reminiscing about the '49 tournament final. "There were only six seconds left, and Maureen got the rebound. She passed it to me, I passed it to Connie. Then Connie, she never lost her cool—she threw it all the way cross court to Darlene, who was standing there by herself. You should've seen it—"

"A perfect strike," said Mr Nice Guy, bending over to unlace her shoes so he could rub her feet. Her diabetes gave her no end of problems with her extremities. Lately his visits consisted of little more than extended foot-rubbing sessions. She shifted in her lounger, which creaked under her weight. Mrs Renfrow was a big woman who favored loose print dresses and cooled herself with vigorous swoops of a lacquered Chinese fan.

"A perfect strike. Darlene just popped it in. Two points." His mother paused, as she always did at this part of the story, and the Chinese fan came to rest on her bosom. She sighed as his thumbs began to press and knead her arch. Despite her girth her lower legs were still shapely, and she was vain about them. "There was a kind of hush in the auditorium for a whole second, thousands of people. Then it sinks in what we'd done, that it's all over, 58 to 57, and the auditorium exploded! Amazing, Jerry."

"I'm sure it was."

"You know I haven't seen Connie in forty-six years . . ."

And now Connie caught the ball in the Renfrow driveway when his mother passed it, and she sent it, one more time, to Darlene. And Darlene looped in a left-handed lay-up.

Mr Nice Guy stood on the front yard grass and watched them, quick-handed gray ladies in pant-suits, talking loudly and happily and everyone at the same time. The ball arced through the air, skidded and thonked off the backboard. He could not help comparing his mother to the others, noticing how Maureen looked great, ready for a game right now, while his mother—not *old*, he told himself, not really—was struggling; disease was eating her, making her shaky. Even big fat Dee Dee was more spry, surprisingly so. The only one weaker than his mother was Darlene who, Mr Nice Guy knew from earlier reports, was still under radiation therapy. She soon left the others and sat on the front steps to watch, her chin on her fist, not far from Mr Nice Guy. He went inside and as he cleaned up the dishes, began to grieve for the 1949 Pantherettes.

Disease was one of those things that tortured Mr Nice Guy. Pain—where could he put it? Nothing could explain it away, and he knew it. Sometimes, when the horizon bore down on him too keenly, he could not hide his rage. Disease was a force that did not fit, that offended beyond words, that defied his intuitions and that in confusion he lashed out against. He had a problem with what some considered the most obvious truths, such as: people you loved died.

A part of your spirit, amputated. Friends, younger than himself, were already underground or their ashes dispersed. (*Wait!* he cried. *Hold on! Let's reconsider.*) They were already being forgotten by the living, by even their friends and family who claimed they would remember and maybe even believed it but it was not true, they *were* forgetting, at least several details of their loved one per day. A person did not merely die once, a person died over and over, not the same death, either, but a cumulative one, growing more and more dead as time passed.

Frankly, Mr Nice Guy would not stand for it. He would do what he could to stop this trend, take action, on all fronts. Since death was so huge and persistent, he would consecrate the small and ephemeral. Nothing would be ignored, for everything was vital. Life was in the details! One day, for instance, upon learning from a newspaper obituary of the death from cervical cancer of Nancy Rizzuti, whom he hadn't seen in 15 years but whom he still remembered clearly—his fifth grade girlfriend with unevenly spaced teeth and a green tongue from eating candy Zotz, a vaccination mark on her left arm which a school bully named Lyle Bishop had compared to the rear end of a cat—cervical cancer! Nancy hadn't even reached the age of 35. He found himself walking blindly through the park, voice straining as he spoke aloud to remember her better, resuscitate as many details as he could. "Father a mailman . . . her laughter, little hiccuping gasps . . . Willy, I think [the name of the cat] . . . " Saying these things, Mr Nice Guy looked and sounded like a crazy man. Occasionally his fists slashed at the air.

Oh, he would rub his mother's feet, rub them desperately, while longing to be able to do more. It was a ferocious battle. She couldn't have one foot in the grave, because he wouldn't let go.

Three

ONCE, WHEN HE was a young boy with noodle arms, his mother had shown him an envelope in which was a fibrous, brownish powder.

"What is it?" he asked.

She closed the envelope.

"It's your father's moustache. He shaved it off when he was stationed in Pensacola and sent it to me."

Young Mr Nice Guy's feet began to skitter under him. "Hey, let me see that again."

She lifted the flap once more, and he peeked inside.

"Someday I'll give it to you."

His feet stopped, and he looked up at her. "Gee."

There was something intensely personal in such a promise, the confidence seemed almost holy. His mother was always telling him how much he resembled his father, and when he thought of the man he felt conscious of a hole in himself, a hole big enough to put an adult fist through. One of his few memories of him was of sitting on his knees at the kitchen table as he described an explosion he'd witnessed when he was stationed in Nevada. He later learned it was one of his father's proudest achievements. "I had a front row seat, I volunteered, the most amazing thing that ever happened to me. *GaaaBOOOM!* Not Boom, but *GaaBOOOM!*" His fist struck the table twice, with increasing force; plates rattled, a cup jumped. "And the brilliance! I'll never forget that flash."

In fact, even when his bones were riddled with cancer and he lay immobile with tubes in his nose and penis (young Mr Nice Guy stood at the side of the bed, speechless), he returned to the subject, croaking in a voice as if he were choking on sand. "I'd be lying if I said the flash wasn't beautiful."

He was completely hairless. His eyes glinted, and there was a luster to his forefinger, too, as he pointed at the boy.

For years thereafter, his words would return to Mr Nice Guy and he would try to reassemble them into a satisfactory meaning, just as when a child he'd tried to reconstruct in his imagination the handsomest version of the disintegrated moustache and return it, lovingly, to his father's face. The words (were they an explanation? or advice? or maybe a warning?) were: "Son, you do whatever you can."

Four

HE WAS NO coward. For all his precautions and eagerness to please, no weakling. In fact, in his own impervious way, Mr Nice Guy could be fearless, such as the night he walked up to his employee Garson's cabin after Garson had drunk a bottle of pepper vodka and shot out all his lights and windows. The neighbors threatened to call the police, but Garson bawled out his shattered living room glass in a voice both belligerent and weary (his rifle barrel flashing, then disappearing, now flashing back) that if anybody dared call the cops he would come back and shoot whoever did it, if not tomorrow, then someday, they could count on it, he would never forget, he would come looking for that sonuvabitch.

This made the neighbors pause.

They called Mr Nice Guy instead.

So Mr Nice Guy found himself in front of Garson's cabin heading up a gravel path in the dark. At one point he stubbed his toe on a root and stumbled, almost lost his balance.

"Who is it?" Garson shouted. "Who's out there?"

Mr Nice Guy stopped.

"It's me. Jerry! Garson, what's going on in there? Why are you doing this?"

"That's nobody's goddamn business! Why don't people just leave me alone?"

"Garson, put that gun away."

There was a howl of anger, a splintering *screek* as the screen door was kicked open, then two sharp reports, yellow-red spurts in the dark. Mr Nice Guy felt the air move beside his left cheek, then the air closed over on itself, still again. Silence. He stood frozen, heart thumping in his chest.

Garson's voice came out small:

"I didn't hit you, did I, Jer? You still there?"

"Yes, I'm still here."

"You better go away. Stuff's happening. You could get hurt. Go away, Jer."

Mr Nice Guy was afraid, very afraid. But he knew Garson was in trouble. He edged up the path toward the door.

"Maybe you shouldn't be alone right now, Garson. Maybe you should tell me what's going on. I won't talk about it to anyone else. I promise."

"I don't want people messin' in my business."

"That's not what I mean. I won't mess in your business." He was at the foot of the steps now. "Here I am. You wouldn't turn down a guy in need of a beer, would you?"

Garson's craggy shape stood outlined in the doorframe. When Mr Nice Guy came up the steps, to his relief Garson handed him the gun without a murmur (he wouldn't have dared grab or wrestle for it the way he'd seen cops do in movies: many a time he'd seen Garson effortlessly crack open walnuts by clasping his hands as if to pray). They went inside.

"I can't see anything," said Mr Nice Guy. The stock of the gun was damp with Garson's sweat, the barrel still warm. Garson flicked on his cigarette lighter and led Mr Nice Guy into his living room where the air was acrid with smoke from spent cartridges. As he moved, Garson let his lighter go out several times when his thumb became too hot; he bumped into upturned furniture and cursed. Mr Nice Guy groped his way onto a broken recliner and settled in, with the gun across his lap.

"How can you do this to your place?" he asked him. "I'm surprised at you." He knew that Garson was proud of his cabin, an American Classics model which he'd constructed himself from a kit.

"I can fix it! What's it to you, anyway? Why you asking? Is that any of your business?"

"Nope, nope, it isn't!" said Mr Nice Guy quickly. "That's not what I meant."

"I got candles here somewhere," Garson grunted, fumbling. "The wiring shorted out except for the TV fuse, so I had light from the TV for a while, until I shot the TV. It was attracting skeeters."

Eventually he found a stubby red Christmas candle that he lit and placed on the corner of the table where it cast flickering light against the log walls. Mr Nice Guy's eyes adjusted to take in the pockmarks on the ceiling, the shattered glass. Garson dropped heavily on the splayed couch, his face looming momentarily over the candle, bloated crimson and calf-like, his eyes looking out through tangles of long, greasy hair.

Then, to Mr Nice Guy's alarm, Garson, grunting, bent over and pulled out another gun from beneath the couch, slapping and snapping the clip into place. He reached under the couch again and came up with a box of shells.

"Your automatic might be a handsome motherfucker but this Emerson packs the real kick-ass power." He laughed low and leaned to peer out the window. "It's Howdy Doody time, Jerry. They ain't never gonna take us now."

Mr Nice Guy shifted in his chair, his temples pounding, and fished a pack of gum out of his pocket from which, with two flicks of his wrist, he shook out a stick. This he folded into his mouth. His jaws worked quickly, methodically.

"Garson—umm—how about that beer?"

"Don't got any. No more vodka, either, or Colorado White. I'm down to the schnapps."

"Well, get me a schnapps then."

While Garson hunted for the bottle amid sticky trays of finished microwave dinners, back issues of *Boy Eats Girl,* Mr Nice Guy tried to think of a way to disarm him. As delicate a moment as he'd ever encountered! He helped himself to an additional stick of gum, his mind racing, his jaws masticating madly. Now, where could he find an opening? Unlikely he could get his hands on Garson's weapon unnoticed, and even if he could accomplish such a thing, he wasn't sure how to go about unloading, how to work the clip and the levery gizmo. (Mr Nice Guy wasn't versed in firearms.) By the time Garson returned he'd decided that his only option was to stall, and drink schnapps with him: keep him distracted.

There was 3/4 of a bottle, and he didn't like hard stuff, but they went for it heavily, Mr Nice Guy even encouraging the process, drinking snort after snort. He forced Garson to converse, occasionally tried to reason with him and then adeptly changed course whenever Garson riled. He knew when he had to back off and assume another tack, meander around a subject till eventually he could zero in again. "But why? Why do you do this? You're only hurting yourself."

By now Garson had found other candles, which he fixed upright in puddles of wax. The entire cabin was rosy, aflicker. He took a big hit of schnapps, then shook his hair back, his face beetlike in this light. He slammed his fist down.

"What's wrong with a guy doin' what he wants to do? Why's it anybody's goddamn business? Is this a free country or not?"

Politics *must* be avoided, Mr Nice Guy knew, but Garson was launched, he took another slug, then rose to his feet, lumbered toward Mr Nice Guy, his lips curling into a snarl. "We're talking unalienable rights here, fundamental freedoms, you nimble little fuckface. Got it? I don't take orders from nobody, understand? You do understand?"

"I do!" Mr Nice Guy nodded briskly, "I gotcha one hundred per cent!"

Garson glared, weighing the words which, despite their capitulation, seemed to disappoint him. "Listen, I'm gonna have it all. I'm gonna—" He staggered back, sat down with a crash.

In the hours that Mr Nice Guy was there, risking his life, not another shot was fired. An alcohol flush rose to his face, then spread down his neck and eventually felt like warm hands pressing on his chest. The danger passed when Garson stopped quarreling and became ill. The schnapps was too much on top of everything else he'd consumed, and suddenly he was down on the floorboards, crawling on his hands and knees, groaning, inquiring why God treated him so. Then, racked with violent spasms, he was stupendously sick. That harrowing, pinkly candlelit moment would return to Mr Nice Guy's mind—against his will!—for years afterward. Garson's effusions went on, and on, and on. When he was finally finished, his eyes rolled back. He collapsed in a heap in front of his gaping TV.

Mr Nice Guy stood up stiffly, dizzy, and covering his nose with his handkerchief, began to gather up all the ammunition he could see. He blew out the candles. “Good night!”

Five

WHEN IT'S SUB-ZERO cold and getting dark and your car battery's dead and you have no cables and everyone in the parking lot is in a hurry to go home, who's going to stop and roll down his window and ask if he can give you a jump start? You know who. Though he doesn't smoke himself, he always has a light. Who never forgets to flush a public toilet behind him? To squeeze the toothpaste from the bottom? Who, for his wife's sake, shaves not in the morning after rising but in the evening before going to bed, so as not to chafe her cheeks, or thighs? That's our man. And though it's true that he's not the life of the party, that his earnestness could convict him of a lack of hilarity, that he actually *liked* card tricks where you had to think of a number and count them into piles, then add your birthdate and divide by—oh, never mind—there was also that hopeful, teetering-on-glorious moment when people have eaten and drunk and the music comes up and your feet start to move, you just can't help it, and all of a sudden someone goes to work pushing aside the tables and clearing chairs to make room for everyone to dance—why, it's Mr Nice Guy! Everybody, everybody fall in!

Such impulses did more than win him personal appreciation; they also earned him a living. They were the spark of his business success. Mr Nice Guy not only took initiatives, he had that extra quality that made all the difference—he *anticipated.* He possessed the most potent form of American know-how: buttressed by know-*when.* That was Mr Nice Guy's inspiration: making the present blossom, then milking it for all it was worth.

Admittedly, he did not know how to go for the jugular, he lacked the claws necessary to become a fat cat. He would probably never join the club of the super-rich. But he could never come up empty-handed, either, since he noticed needs. In an economy of expanding services, he was at once a maverick and a traditionalist, an entrepreneur in human wishes, a free-lance pleaser with offices and a modem out of his fourth floor apartment. His company, Home-Made Services, was a pioneer in the personal duty market.

Anniversaries, birthdays, retirements, commemorations—these were his bread and butter. For a fee, you could register all your personal duty data in his Forget-Me-Not computer. A week before your Aunt Maggie's birthday, for instance, you would get a card or a phone call (your choice—or for both, add $1.25 to subscription price) reminding you: hey, you'd better write to your Auntie now!

For a slightly higher fee, you'd receive a draft letter, which you could adapt to your needs (Letter 42c, Female/*Retired/*Widowed/*High Blood Pressure) or, for $5 more, a custom-made letter. All you had to do was tell Mr Nice Guy over the phone (or leave your Sentiment Guidelines on his handy 24-hour 800 number):

> "*Uh, she's the one who lives in Cincinnati, and ever since Uncle Leon died she's just gotten more depressed and fatter and fatter, it stresses her out, she's all alone now in a cramped room and they've quit singing, I never know what to say to her* (click)."

Within 48 hours, you receive the following fax for you to copy out by hand:

Dear Aunt Maggie,

Another birthday! Isn't it remarkable! I want to take a moment to congratulate you. Perhaps you might believe that you've already seen too many birthdays but this is precisely the occasion for me to tell you what a place you have in this family, a place that I haven't put into words before. You are our grande dame and we are proud of you. Although I am sure that Leon's absence weighs heavily in times of solitude (when I think of you I think of him, too) you should know that on this special day we pay our respect to you, as you are now, with greatest affection,

Love

[sign here]

Hypocritical? Not at all, for Home-Made Services were sender-guaranteed. If the subscriber was unhappy with a draft, all he or she had to do was call Mr Nice Guy, let him know what the problem was, the sticking point ("Too serious—put in a joke somewhere" or "You forgot the canaries"), and a revised version would be faxed within hours. It often took several drafts to get it right, but it was precisely this process, helping people find what they wanted to say, that instilled loyalty in Mr Nice Guy's clientele, who gave him his best, word-of-mouth advertising. Hypocritical? How could it be, in the face of the toughest critics of all, the senders who would have to sign their name at the bottom, who wanted a good letter badly enough to pay for it? The real hypocrites could dash off any message, for either they didn't care enough to be picky, or on the contrary, they already knew exactly what they wanted, as only hypocrites can. No, Mr Nice Guy helped people who struggled sincerely for words of comfort or praise or condolence or affection, words from the heart and even deeper (a shared source beyond the mere individual, the *hearth*—that was how Mr Nice Guy thought of it), a desired Communion with the receiver. For lack of time or simply out of *fear*, many people could not find the words themselves. Or sadder still, circumstances had evolved so hearthlessly for some that they'd never been close enough to experience such words, feel them on their lips. Yet they still missed them for, somewhere inside, in a painful human inheritance, they ached to say them.

Mr Nice Guy stepped up from behind, whispered into their ear. (Via express mail or fax, or you could download on-line.) Discreet, comprehensive, and principled. He could've easily price-gouged on death condolences, for instance, the duty correspondence most in demand, the one people found hardest to do on their own. But for Mr Nice Guy's subscribers, death condolences were the same price, part of the same package deal, as St. Patrick's Day wishes and Congratulations Sore Knees! (For runners who had finished their marathons.) He prided himself on offering a full range of services.

On Arbor Day you needed an acorn, pronto? Where could you get your hands on a Guy Fawkes effigy, a roll of red carpet or a bona-fide Maypole? Who had a virtual monopoly in a four-state area on 100% biodegradable confetti?

He did one-shot gigs, too. Actually, this was the part of his job that he enjoyed best, found the most fulfilling. On an April day he leaped out of an airplane (thrilling at the sight of his planet rushing toward him: "Yes! Yes! Yes!") and tumbled neatly upon striking his destination, strode over with hand outstretched to a young woman whose mouth dropped open in amazement, for he proffered a diamond ring. A nervous fellow beside her swallowed profoundly, nodded at Mr Nice Guy, then took the woman's hand and began to propose marriage.

Or, in one of his higher-priced performances, Mr Nice Guy jumped out of a darkened stairwell, wearing a ski-mask and flashing a knife, and engaged in hand-to-hand combat with a client who was trying to impress his girlfriend. As prearranged, Mr Nice Guy lost the struggle to his manly rival. For his efforts he got several contusions, and $800.

His most satisfying work, though, came in reconciliations. Some of his pleading and promising letters had brought troubled couples back together:

. . . *I don't expect you to forgive me. But on the other hand I know you'll never forget that night on Wanamaker Island. Oh, choco! I pledge to respect that memory and if you'll only give me the chance, to make you feel that beautiful again* . . . (Etc., etc.)

In some cases, as a direct result of his letters, children were born. People wrote back to thank him. Men and women loved and made love because of Mr Nice Guy. To his mind he was following his father's advice, doing whatever he could. Perhaps no one knew better than Barbara.

Six

A PERSON SHOULDN'T be too quick to judge her. Blame—if blame you must—Mr Nice Guy. When it came to human desires he was nothing if not a facilitator. For the general public this was easy enough to live with, downright impressive, some thought, because to show graciousness in an increasingly mean and slovenly world, to cultivate civility made him the most up-to-date man of action, even a rebel.

But for Barbara it was different. For those whose fortune or burden it is to share life with a hero, it always is. She saw him in another, more modest light, less master planner than travel agent, one for whom her destination might be her most personal fantasy. And to his credit, his trips left no regrets, for with him you took off from a rock solid somewhere. Not for you a hippie goose chase to discover your True Self or the posturing of the sexual pilgrim, holding forth about spasmodic holy lands, gift shop enlightenments. No. Precious warmth and security were *already* in your most intimate possession, you could always click your heels and go back; wherever you ventured, your return reservation was already booked: *Home.*

Step back through the door: how wonderful it looked now! Put down your bag of unwashed laundry and maybe a few trophies, all those personal effects which had begun to seem heavy, even a burden, and go over and sit down in front of the fire with a happy grunt or a sigh of relief (maybe you're a little sore), and hold out your hands, feeling the welcoming light on your face.

"Bring you a cup of cocoa?" comes his cheerful voice.

The situation was this: in matters most personal, including sexual, Barbara was not much different from you. Yes, *you.* Mr Nice Guy wasn't naive about such things. He told himself: if Barbara finds someone attractive, the idea of standing closer to that person does not disturb her. One could bet that it causes neither disgust nor dread. And in certain circumstances, kisses are something she is very fond of. Something for which she feels an inclination. Like touching. And being touched. Why should she be deprived?

"Huh?" she'd said one day in bed shortly after they were married, and had just slid between the sheets, and he'd expressed this sentiment. She stopped plumping her pillow. "How's that, Jerry?"

"If you have extra needs, honey, that's okay. I want you to be as fulfilled as possible."

At first she didn't believe him. Thought he was joking. She shook her head. "I don't think I get it. What are you driving at?"

"I want you to be happy."

"Seems doubtful that's how. That kind of openness is usually a sham."

Barbara did not consider herself particularly adventurous, not anymore. Though Mr Nice Guy was only vaguely aware of this aspect of her past, in her younger days she'd experimented. Tried on different lives like tops in a shop. Yet that era seemed distant now, though it wasn't so long ago, really, that she'd left school and gone looking for a style that fit the shape of her aspirations; she'd rejected the West and moved to New York, which was the place to be when you were young and destined to be original (at least that's what everybody said). She shared a studio on Polsen Street and found work in a gallery selling aesthetic black-and-white postcards, where all the employees dressed in tight minimalist monochrome. She experienced the attentions of artistic younger men who were bored—much of being hip, she discovered, is being bored with your surroundings—and started getting high a lot, then more than a lot. She alternated between intense enjoyment and feeling sick. (Truth was, she never did get the hang of the cool and usual punishments.) The weather inside her grew very unpredictable. Early one morning, after a party at her place when the first rays of sunlight came slanting through the window, she stumbled into her bathroom with her head happily swimming and a pleasant prickling all over her skin and managed to find her way onto the toilet—then observed, in the bathtub next to her, a young man turning blue.

She thought he would die. He *was* dying, before her very eyes. She struggled to her feet, pulling up her panties, then dropped to her knees beside the tub and began shaking his shoulders, crying, telling him, "No, please! Stop! Stop!" She punched at him to wake up. Through the tears she also tried to pray, convinced that if she left him long enough to call an ambulance it would be too late when she came back. She could not let him die alone. "Oh God, please don't!"

She got him to sit up, and suddenly he bent forward, vomited between his knees, and ceased trembling; he turned his head and blinked at her.

Running the showerhead over the top of his scalp, on his chest and over his back, then holding his shoulders while he shivered and whimpered and became pink again—such a little manboy—Barbara felt miles and miles away.

Inside her, there was a momentary clearing in the weather, as when from a distance you can discern where you live. That morning her intentions shifted. Her doubts won out. For why pretend? She realized that she was indifferent to this place, to the local catechism, the way that everyone, whether a new arrival or to the city born, kept repeating to each other that this island was the mecca, the hippest locale on the entire planet and just by being here and walking the streets, some of its importance accrued to you. That's what made it OK to be less than what you knew or wanted. You could say you were important.

She realized how lonely, terribly lonely she was among these wishful and needy people. Earnest friends and true believers. She helped her guest to her mattress, threw a blanket over him and went to wash. Later she stepped out for a long walk which lasted the rest of the day. She wandered through the canyons of buildings which meant nothing to her, and every now and then looked up, thinking: how empty the would-be capital of the world, for when it comes to love, we are still hunters and gatherers.

That was it. She wanted love. As simple (*simple?*) as that, and she refused to apologize for it, wrap it up in a different guise. That was the only thing she cared about. The rest was . . . was . . . she would let other people decide for themselves what it was because to her it didn't matter, since she didn't want it anyway. Walking the streets that day, amid the honk and grind of Manhattan, she felt as light and unattached as a leaf flitting on the sidewalk.

So it happened easily that when the occasion presented itself, she left; expatriation seemed neither logical nor illogical but just another door, the next opening: she went to live in Paris. A place also distracted by itself but more broodingly, without the boosterism. Barbara liked that at first. Along with many others, she deluded herself for a time by thinking that she would find a real job, all the while scraping by with undeclared work. She taught English in a rich and wretched private preschool and proofread a surgeon's research articles on hip replacement. Her real achievement was in making friends, which culminated in sharing a rue Claude Bernard flat with a man who said he loved her, wanted to marry her, but when she hesitated Jean-Luc made a scene and forced her to leave; when she tried to come back he grew nasty; when she said in that case she would never see him again he tried to kill himself by jumping off a bridge but since his timing was bad he missed the Seine and landed instead on a boatload of upturned tourists' faces. He broke only his wrist but put four other people in the hospital, and would have gone to jail if the administration hadn't lost his dossier.

In the end, nervous about her own arrest (one night when they were drunk she and Jean-Luc had tried to fiddle with the date on her visa, but had done such a poor job that anyone could tell), Barbara came home. She'd had a bellyful. She returned to this alternately blazing and freezing Midwestern city on a hill, went back to school, and in three years earned two halves of two different college degrees (but not a whole). She did not fall in love, and did not try to; she pursued no lovers.

Then Mr Nice Guy came along.

She saw him first from a distance, on a warm sunny day when she could wear sandals and kids had their bikes out. A man running toward her. Nothing extraordinary, she'd assumed, just another jogger. But it turned out that this first meeting was the scene of an accident—his. Everything happened so fast, she didn't have time to cry out. He stepped off the curb, just as an ambulance came speeding around the corner. He tried to jump, get clear, and *Schlak!*—the impact made a slapping sound, like a child doing a belly-smacker at a swimming pool. The jogger sailed through the air, not quickly, but with a gentle arc like a badminton birdie, and landed on the sidewalk not two yards from her feet.

He quivered for a moment, then struggled as if to get up. "Don't move!" she told him, "Don't try it." His eyes blinked at her under his running cap's duckbill visor. The ambulance men arrived in seconds, rolling out the collapsible stretcher beside him. "Gee, that was fast," he gasped.

"You got hit by the ambulance," she told him, noticing a horrible, lumpy purple swelling in the process of appearing on his thigh.

"Well that's lucky," he murmured as they rolled him away.

And that might have been the end of it. If not for a friend who'd had a baby, whom she visited at the hospital the next day, she would have never troubled herself to call on him. Reception gave her the room number of an emergency admission that seemed to correspond to her description, and she checked it out. The door was part-way open. First she stuck only her head into the room, but he glanced up at that moment, startled. So she sheepishly walked in.

"I'm sorry," she said, coming to the chair at his bedside, "I didn't know your name, so I wasn't sure this was the right place."

He looked at her, directly in the eye.

"You probably don't remember me," she told him.

"Of course I do."

She didn't believe him, and explained how she'd witnessed the accident, what a frightening sight it had been, and that she wanted to see how he was doing.

"That's very considerate of you. To go out of your way to visit a hurt stranger. I'm impressed."

He gazed at her with such intensity that she stood up, and made a move as if to inspect the cast that protruded out of his bedsheet. She wasn't embarrassed or annoyed by his gaze (in fact she liked herself in this light) but she found it hard to look straight back into it.

"That's a lot of plaster there," she said. "What did the doctors find?"

"My ribs aren't broken, but they're mighty sore. My hipbone has a fissure. They say a side of me is cracked."

He asked her name. Then he asked her, please, to sit down again. His brown eyes never left her. They talked. He asked her where she worked, how she liked it, where she lived. Where she did her shopping, what she ate for lunch, the fabric content of that lovely blouse. Why her family had come to America. He wanted to know everything. When eventually she got up again he asked her if she would come back. She told him yes.

She meant what she said, but intended to let a couple of days pass. She did not want to appear pressing. But that night as she was fixing herself dinner the doorbell rang. A delivery of flowers, ordered from his hospital bed. She was surprised, and genuinely pleased.

Cutting the ends of the stems before putting them in a vase, she decided not to delay her return visit. Mr Nice Guy had entered her life. From that day, he simply never went away.

He was not insistent but persistent—an important distinction, as far as Barbara was concerned. He was not impressive as much as impressing: one detail at a time. That was how she fell in love with him, as the sum of his gentlenesses grew. Each offered like a single pearl. Even before he left the hospital she began to need his presence, and discovered his ready arms and the taste of his breath. She realized she wanted him.

The process of seduction was like a string of pearls that grew longer and longer and seemed to wrap around her and, when held up to the light, appeared curiously transparent. What were these pearls made of, really? What was their substance, if not love?

In her eyes he started looking better and better. Though not at first sight an obvious candidate for her fantasy Perfect Male (in her imagination, something of a walking menagerie: part lamb, part tiger, part stallion, with a bit of rabbit thrown in), though few men could live up to such a wonderful, albeit zoologically Frankensteinish standard, somehow he seemed to be guessing at her imagination and in her presence attempted a reasonable imitation of the monster.

When they made love, there was nothing to fix. No room for the past to fit between their bodies. No need to devise elaborate snares to writhe in. Let other people live for dreams they could not understand, advertise in magazines, get out the rubber truncheons. They felt no envy. The string of pearls wound round them tighter and tighter. They were in love.

So the conversation about "extra needs" came to Barbara as a surprise. When she realized he was serious, as he shifted in bed, getting ready to turn out the lights, she was stunned. For a moment she lay as if struck, so to speak, by an unseen ambulance. Then she sat up out of the blankets and drew close.

"You really mean that?"

"Sure, sweetie. I wouldn't say it if I didn't."

"Won't you feel jealous? What a thing to tell me. I mean, why wouldn't you feel jealous? Some people would say you must not really care for me."

She knew that she would feel jealous if he were with

someone else. The very thought stressed her. Naked, Mr Nice Guy was pinker than her ideal, but she had got used to it. With a proprietary air she often rested her hand on the small of his back; she found joy in the lank of his limbs.

"Do you doubt I care for you?" he asked, his eyes fixed on her with the intensity reserved only for her, while his hand came forward, his fingers gently raking her hair.

There were times, it was true, when she did not understand him. There were times when Barbara could hear herself speak or look in a mirror and not even recognize herself. But this was not one of those times. As his warmth reached her, as he caressed her, she stretched out her own hand, lightly touching his leg through the sheet, then running it along his body. She felt at this moment that she believed him completely, this man, this unusual man, who was her husband.

"No, Jerry." Her voice fell softer. "I don't doubt that."

"Good." He pulled closer, their legs pleasantly entangling. "That's the way it should be."

Even so, she did not intend to test him on his offer. For a long time, she did not believe she was interested. She liked married life, just as they knew it now, and desired nothing that reminded her of the folly of her divorced parents and their shabby new beginnings, her father with a big-cheeked moony woman and a doughy, disgusting little baby, her mother with a series of drippy boyfriends. Barbara thoroughly disapproved. Since the split both parties had moved to southern states, and in telephone conversations always tried to impress her with the temperature. "So that's what you've achieved?" Barbara wanted to scold into the receiver. "Suntans?"

No, that way was not for her. In her husband's arms she already traveled to the places she wanted to go. In any case she was so busy with her responsibilities at the Secreast Museum that even if she'd wished for an affair, where would she have found the time?

Any extra needs . . .

How was it that ideas began to pass through Barbara's

mind? Not plans, or discontent—just ideas. Actually it was not long after the first conversation. Was it really her fault? It was as if a seed had been planted. Possibilities which had always existed, regardless of her intentions, had been nudged closer to consciousness. By her husband himself.

"Excuse me," said a stranger, reaching over her at the supermarket to weigh his snow peas—surely he was doing it on purpose! And despite the lack of subtlety of this maneuver she admired his fine jaw, the agreeable blunt of his shoulders. She moved away. But in the car afterward, the image of him returned.

So what? she'd told herself. What's he to me?

"Give me the full tour," said a visitor at the Secreast Museum, "the works." This was much later, after many other overtures had been ignored. Barbara led the stranger through the rooms, then down the spiral staircase into the adjoining caverns and catwalks, from which she pointed out stalactite and stalagmite formations. But he looked not at where she was pointing but rather at her eyes. Or was he staring at her mouth?

No, she thought. Finish this and get upstairs.

Yet in the middle of her spiel she slowed down, let him interrupt with a question. And that's how it happened, the first time.

"Follow me," she said, unable to find other words but leading him toward a dimmer section, suspecting he would try to kiss her.

And she was right.

A kiss was all that happened, that day. All that she allowed.

Yet from then on, the line of fantasy was played with, twiddled; stretched further and further. Over time, during lunch and after hours in the museum or on a cool padded bench in the caverns (she preferred the safety of her own turf) she occasionally met chosen people, ready people with caresses and embraces and more; with kisses, especially—Barbara required many kisses. Sometimes small cries echoed in the caverns, and before the echo stopped, there was the next shiver and pulse, and they cried out again.

Seven

HE ASKED FOR trouble. That was his rub, the real reason behind these pages. After all, his Home-Made Services depended not only on sending glad tidings, on posting spill-proof cherry pies on Washington's birthday and pop-out cards saying *Guess-the-Weight-of-my-Newborn-Baby,* but also—and more often—on answering the cries of people at their miserable worst, cheering parents who found themselves in an empty house after the children had left home, consoling abandoned lovers, or saying Get Well Soon to the tumorously incurable. Disaster and distress were forces that drove demand. Mr Nice Guy trafficked in them every day.

Even a sweet deal could turn sticky. Only a few months earlier he'd landed his biggest Home-Made Services contract ever—what luck it had seemed at the time!—only to be saddled immediately after with jury duty, a major distraction when he needed to be operating at peak efficiency. Mr Nice Guy, a conscientious citizen, felt obligated to serve, but the timing couldn't have been worse.

The new contract was by any measure a plum: he was on hire to cater fun and good vibrations for the birthday gala of the daughter of the Sheik of Surimi. This young woman was a student at nearby Hughes College (a Presbyterian institution of liberal arts since 1862 but open to all persuasions); the Sheik was coming to the U.S. on an official visit which, according to the morning *Tribune*, would also allow time for a private birthday party. A restaurant and three floors of a hotel had already been rented for the occasion.

Zohra is a sophomore majoring in Communications and Earth Sciences, the article said, *she enjoys jazz dancing, tennis and adores animals. She loves America and her only regret is that she had to leave her apricot Labrador at home. No pets are allowed on campus, not even for the daughter of a Sheik. Sorry, Zohra!*

Mr Nice Guy, ever attuned to a transaction in goodwill, had put down his newspaper and picked up the telephone, called the local consulate, implored and wheedled as he was passed from office to office till at last he had the ear of a high-ranking Surimian official who was also Zohra's first cousin. Twenty minutes later, the idea was sold.

In three days, a $5,000 deposit check arrived in his mailbox.

The hotel management wasn't keen on Mr Nice Guy's idea, but they weren't about to ruffle the Sheik, either, so they tolerated the new arrangements: at the height of Zohra's party, a beribboned box as big as a baby-grand piano would be rolled out on dollies, and to Zohra's surprise, a trap door in the side would fall open: streaming out, tumbling over each other and yapping with joy, 20 pure-bred apricot Labrador puppies!

One gig like that, and Mr Nice Guy would turn $12,000 profit. Maybe $14,000, if expenses were kept down. Not a bad pay-off for reading up on world issues in the newspaper while asking the following question: how can I be of service?

Now, though, with the distraction of jury duty, and hampered by the tight-lipped paranoia of the Surimian consulate staff whose policy was to refuse to reveal the precise day and time of the party until the last minute, for security reasons, thereby forcing Mr Nice Guy to be on call to the consulate virtually 24 hours a day, he was seriously squeezed. "There's no doubt about it, I'm in a pickle," he told Barbara, his mouth assuming a grim cast. "There are limits to how much I can do."

More than ever before, he would have to count on Garson. This was an additional cause for worry.

"Get someone else!" Barbara urged. "You're just asking for trouble with that guy."

"He's doing better, you have to admit," Mr Nice Guy defended. "Look at the crack job he did in finding 20 apricot pups. I gave him a phony deadline one week earlier than the real one I'd set for the project, because I assumed he'd be late as usual. But look what happened, he was on time."

"That only makes things worse for you, Jerry."

"Yeah, but he doesn't know that. You have to give him credit. I think his attitude is improving."

Barbara shook her head. "We'll see. If you ask me, some people aren't employable, and he's one of them. I don't like the way he talks to you."

Mr Nice Guy knew that many people felt the same way about Garson, which was precisely the reason he had taken him under his wing; no one else wanted anything to do with him. And though it was true that his employee still had much to learn about interpersonal relations, especially with his boss (all too easily, Garson shouted), in the last two years he'd gotten to know the man well enough to develop a rapport. He could be frank with him, even scold him. For instance, one morning in the delivery van he'd told him, "You know I think you'd be happier, Garson, if you thought more of others. Worked on your social skills a little. It would be to your own benefit, I promise."

It was the week before Easter, and the Home-Made Services van was full of stacked crates of cheeping chicks. Every Easter Mr Nice Guy assured the delivery of thousands of chicks. Garson jammed down on the accelerator and the van lurched through another yellow light. His tongue pushed out his cheek from the inside. Mr Nice Guy was growing impatient with the fact that he couldn't take Garson into stores with him because Garson's presence hurt sales. Mr Nice Guy had to carry all the crates himself. "It's like you're in a bad mood all the time," he continued. "Why?"

Garson looked over at him. "Huh?"

"You're not even listening!"

"You got some aspirin, Jer?"

"If you're hung over all the time, it's no wonder you feel bad."

"I ain't hung over. Jesus, stop leaning on me, man. It's my toothaches. I need some aspirin."

"Why don't you see a dentist? Garson, that's another thing I've been meaning to talk to you about. Why don't you brush your teeth? It doesn't look good."

He went on to explain as they whizzed through intersections that attention to teeth could make a great difference in his life. Not just socially, but in more private ways, too. Mr Nice Guy hesitated, wondering if he should tell Garson of his own experience, of how *pleasurable* brushing his teeth had become over the years, probably due to the fact that he always brushed before going to bed while thinking of Barbara lying on the sheets, waiting for him. Somehow the act of brushing had become indissociable from a sexy anticipation of her. The ritual could trigger excitement. At first he wasn't conscious of the connection but gradually it dawned on him: his teeth had become erogenous.

A light turned red; Garson gunned the engine once, then decided he couldn't make it; he stomped on the brakes, the van screeched, and skidded to a stop. The top crate of chicks fell over, and the cheeping greatly intensified.

"Watch what you're doing!" exclaimed Mr Nice Guy. "They're upside down! They don't like that!"

He reached behind and tried to lift the crate back onto the stack. When he tilted the crate at an angle, the noise grew even louder. "CHEEP! CHEEP! CHEEP! CHEEP! CHEEP!" Garson beat one hand on the steering wheel, the other on the side of his head. "That noise, that noise! Damn!"

"It's your fault!" Mr Nice Guy told him, trying to brace the pile.

"I wish we were delivering snakes again," Garson moaned, "they're so much quieter."

He was referring to a recent job for a religious convention from Kentucky. That time, a young preacher had taken an interest in Garson, mistaking his curiosity as an indication that he was ripe for conversion; but the preacher had eventually lost patience with Garson because he teased the snakes.

The red light was a long one, and the chicks persisted, so Garson clapped his hands over his ears. Mr Nice Guy nudged him on the shoulder.

"Well?"

Garson turned to him. "Huh?"

"Why don't you go to the dentist? You could fix this problem. What about girls? I'm sure you'd like to be someone's heart-throb."

"Yeah, but I'd rather somebody was my dick-throb."

"You know what I mean! Why don't you take care of yourself?"

Garson drew in a deep breath. "I used to go to the dentist, he was always doing stuff, drilling on me, drilling all the time. I used to brush my teeth, too, but then the son-of-a-bitch would still drill on me anyway. So one day I says to myself, if that's the way my teeth are gonna be, then that's too bad for them. I'm not gonna worry and brush 'em anymore, if that's the way they're gonna be. I says to myself, Fuck them little fuckers."

"Garson, that's a mistake—"

"STOP, JER! STOP IT RIGHT NOW!" Suddenly he was breathing hard, sweat beaded on his face while behind them, the chicks still cheeped. Mr Nice Guy pulled over to the far edge of his seat, trying to create a safe distance in the event a fist shot out in his direction. "You're suffocating me, man," Garson said, rolling down his window, thrusting his head out. Horns began to sound.

Maybe Barbara's right, Mr Nice Guy thought with despair. Maybe he's too tough to crack.

In fact, Barbara hadn't even told her husband the main reason she mistrusted Garson. Generally she'd approved of efforts to help him, because although she had doubts about whether one could change the man, and believed that he was fairly immune to do-gooding, she also thought that Jerry might at least keep Garson occupied and thus from getting into serious trouble. That in itself would be a sort of success, a worthy thing to do. Her husband deserved some credit.

Still there was always a price to pay; she knew he had caught Garson siphoning gas out of the van, and Garson had never returned the refrigerator he borrowed. But these weren't really the reason, either.

Her leeriness stemmed from one day in particular. A time he and her husband had been working in the apartment, labeling bottles of Dew Dab. (One of the new and expensive sidelines of Home-Made Services, little bottles of pure dew to splash on your face in the morning, reputed by some to have special restorative powers and which Mr Nice Guy collected himself on dawn expeditions to clover and alfalfa meadows at Mike and Julie's farm—he avoided the marijuana—dragging linen sheets which he wrung out in a stainless steel vat. The idea had already been copied by other marketeers of green designer goods, and they were undercutting his price, probably, he suspected, by diluting their product.) Barbara came home one evening, and noticed that the underwear she'd hung out over the bathtub that morning after rinsing it in Dew Dab (her husband was experimenting with new applications) was gone.

She asked Mr Nice Guy if he'd taken the panties down. He said no, he hadn't touched them. He didn't know where they were.

"But I'm sure I hung them there . . ."

She said nothing else. But from then on she thought she noticed something different in the way Garson looked at her. Not flirting, exactly, but an insinuation. Sometimes he gazed and scratched one cheek of the narrow beard on his face of rounded features, chubbily Lincolnesque. She was no longer comfortable in the same room with him. He started with eye contact but his regard ended lower, much lower. She could almost hear the whir and clunk of his imagination.

Eight

AT THE COURTHOUSE for his jury duty, Mr Nice Guy found it hard to be himself.

People weren't nice there. He'd felt the tension from the start, during the tedious jury selection process: the prosecutor and the defense lawyer pretended to be polite but everyone could see they were snippy. And the judge was openly disdainful; he kept pulling off his glasses and rubbing red spots on his nose where the frames bit him, looking the other way, as if he didn't give a damn for the show. All the potential jurors reacted nervously to their questions—in the oaken courtroom, with the clock ever so slowly grinding on the wall, they felt on trial themselves. The ones who wanted to get out of serving had to justify why. And those who didn't want to get out of duty had to prove that they had no biases, that their mind was a blank slate. What at first seemed like ordinary statements, by the end of the examination sounded fishy. When one wrinkled woman with a back brace grew confused and started shaking her head and crying under questioning, her fingers twitching on her lap, they told her not to worry, she could come back and answer them all again tomorrow.

When it was Mr Nice Guy's turn, in response to whether he felt apt to serve in regard to the crime of homicide and would be in no way prejudiced or of compromised judgment or under the influence of outstanding religious conviction or of racial or gender presuppositions that might interfere with his ability to apply, if necessary, the penalty of death by electrocution or lethal injection, Mr Nice Guy paused.

Then he said, "I'm here because I hope to be a good citizen."

On the bench the judge's head jerked; he twisted his neck toward the jury box. The prosecutor hesitated, then turned to the defense counsel, a balding young man with pink rabbitish eyes who nervously licked his lips. The attorneys approached each other and began to murmur, occasionally casting glances in his direction.

The questions that followed were of a different order. Did Mr Renfrow hold a position in a political organization that might dictate his judgment? Did he actively contribute his time to any group that may be described as having a particular stand on judicial procedures, sanctions or appeals? Had he himself been tried or did he possess any contestatory notions about the courts, which, if he did, it would be illuminating if he communicated them now . . .

Mr Nice Guy shook his head. "No. I'm as busy as the next fellow but I just thought you people might need me."

The courtroom buzzed, and he wondered: What did I say? What did I say?

There were other questions (not too friendly, either), and during the lunch break in which the prospective jurors got a free chicken dinner in the courthouse cafeteria, he had the distinct impression that something had gone wrong, that he had failed a test and would not be selected. Oh, it's just as well, he told himself, what with Zohra's birthday coming up . . .

To his surprise, however, he *did* make the final cut, and arrived in the courtroom the first day of the trial with a mixture of anticipation and anxiety that he hadn't experienced for years: what would he see? Would he know how to act? It felt like the first day of school. Mr Nice Guy fingered the buttons of his jacket and noticed that he wasn't the only one to have dressed up. The other jurors, too, and especially the attorneys, had studied their appearance. The prosecutor wore a ruffled blouse under a gray wool suit, a confusingly sexy wide leather belt above her perfectly cylindrical skirt; the defense sported a blue three-piece suit with a subdued yet noticeably shiny burgundy silk tie, and thin-soled shoes with buckles: he looked like one of those clergymen who tried to appeal to young people.

Everyone stood when the judge entered, but the real excitement came after they sat down, and after some preliminary remarks, when the defendant arrived under police escort. Bulbs flashed, Mr Nice Guy blinked and saw blue sparkles—this was the only moment the judge had authorized cameras. All the jurors shifted their bottoms and craned their necks, trying to get a better look. This was the first time anyone had seen him except in the newspapers.

"The accused may be seated."

Randall "The Angel" Hutchinson was charged with murdering his mother with a hammer. The judge and the lawyers, of course, referred to him as Mr Hutchinson; it was the newspapers and television that had dubbed him The Angel, based on neighbors' accounts of his life.

Almost 40, Randall was a draftsman who'd divorced a few years earlier and subsequently moved back to live with his mother. Everyone who'd come into contact with the Hutchinsons commented on the son's consideration and devotion to her, including an elderly upstairs neighbor who'd told a Channel 8 Action-Cam reporter that until she'd learned that he'd been arrested on the charge of inflicting fatal blows to his mother's head with a hammer, she'd always thought he was "an angel."

And from then on, the name stuck. News headers proclaimed: "**The Angel of Death**" or "**(Really An?) Angel.**" Every detail about the Hutchinsons' lives together, about how he'd done all the shopping and washed her hair and gone to church with her (sometimes), about the surprise Christmas party two years previously (fudge baked himself), about his faithful fetching of his mother's prescriptions ("he was never late," the pharmacist was quoted as saying, "not once")—all these were paraded out in the days and weeks following his arrest, all these along with a question, formulated in many different ways but always the same: how could a man *do* this to his mother?

The judge and lawyers had warned the jury that they were supposed to forget anything they'd heard about him before the trial, and make their judgment solely on the basis of what they learned in the courtroom, which Mr Nice Guy sincerely intended to do, but try as he might, he couldn't get one detail out of his head: The Angel had always brought his mother, who had a sweet tooth, her favorite peanut brittle. Year round, no special occasion required, and from the same specialized candy store where Mr Nice Guy sometimes purchased imported chewing gum supplies. Maybe they'd passed each other in the shop without even knowing it! He'd read about The Angel's habit one day while scanning the newspaper columns, as was his custom, for inspiration about potential services he could render, and trivial though this detail was, it was precisely this piece of information that came to his mind during the hush as the defendant walked down the courtroom aisle. The best peanut brittle in town. Guilty or no, he thought, a *nice* gesture . . .

The Angel sat in the front row in a plain brown suit, a man with short curly hair and a round face which showed no emotion while the prosecutor, Mrs Madison, described the crime, the place, the time and the et cetera. Mr Nice Guy reminded himself that the accused *must* be presumed innocent, and once, when The Angel glanced at the jury, Mr Nice Guy smiled at him, for reassurance. He wasn't sure if The Angel noticed, but told himself: a fellow in his situation must feel pretty low. He should know that the jury isn't automatically rooting against him.

What the prosecutor recounted, though, sounded very bad. Confusing, too. According to the police, Mr Hutchinson had called them late on the evening of January 11 to inform them that he'd killed his mother. The police went to their address on Ingersoll Avenue and found the body of an elderly Caucasian female who Mr Hutchinson claimed was his mother (though neighbors and her church minister were unable to identify her the next day, due to the condition of her face). Subsequent tests and dental records confirmed within 48 hours that the deceased was indeed 73-year-old Mrs Charlene Hutchinson.

But at that point Randall Hutchinson changed his story. From his jail cell he suddenly proclaimed his innocence. The blood on his shirt and pants and shoes, and on the walls, he said, came from having cut himself while opening a can of peaches.

The courtroom had been silent except for Mrs Madison's voice and now, with each pause as she wrote dates and times with a squeaky magic marker on a white-board, the room grew, somehow, even more silent. Again the defendant looked over at the jury, and though it was harder now, Mr Nice Guy did his best to smile. This time The Angel noticed him. His chin jerked slightly, and he stared at Mr Nice Guy who, still smiling, redirected his gaze at the prosecutor, who said:

"Tests on the defendant's clothes confirmed, however, that the blood was not his own but the victim's. And upon being confronted with these facts, the accused changed his story *again*, admitted that he did commit this heinous act. The reasons he gives, as you will see, are as improbable as his previous excuses. We shall let the evidence speak for itself."

The prosecution's introductory remarks thus completed, Mrs Madison snapped the cap back on her magic marker, and they adjourned for lunch.

Nine

EACH NIGHT THAT week he went home to Barbara after hearing Mrs Madison interview police detectives, laboratory specialists and, finally, The Angel himself—who now claimed in a diffident, mysterious manner, "it was Mom's fault." Each time he said this, the prosecution cut him off. And each night, upon returning home, Mr Nice Guy expressed his perplexity to Barbara, who listened to his troubled questions. Such as, "How does a person get to that point? A *hammer*, honey, a *hammer*? A number seven ball-peen normally reserved for applying roofing tacks?"

Mr Nice Guy stopped himself short. The judge had lectured the jury that they weren't supposed to discuss the case while the trial was ongoing, at the risk of being sequestered, so even with Barbara he tried to limit what he divulged. She, however, was curious.

"And this guy acts normal, right? I mean, looking at him and hearing him speak, he would pass for, you know, ordinary?"

"Yes . . . I would say so." Mr Nice Guy decided not to mention an uncomfortable feeling he'd experienced lately. The last few days in the courtroom he'd had the distinct impression that The Angel was looking at him. Not staring openly, but pausing ever so slightly on him each time he cast his eyes in the direction of the jury box. When The Angel did this, Mr Nice Guy would smile, because it was his conviction that when things were going badly for someone, a dose of sunshine didn't hurt. Yet each time he did so, something flashed across The Angel's eyes; once, his feet shuffled under the defendant's table; another time, the fingers on one hand moved and the side of his mouth tightened.

Well, he's nervous, of course, Mr Nice Guy told himself. But now he asked Barbara, "Do you believe in Evil?"

He said this at the dinner table as he cut the chicken. Steam escaped his incisions as he worked his way around, then, with his guiding fork, gave a 30° tilt to sever a wing. One whack, it was off. Mr Nice Guy was deft at carving birds.

Barbara pointed. She always got to choose her piece first.

"Evil? Well, in the case of that guy, I'd say yes, I do. Killing your mother with a hammer ought to qualify if anything does."

He helped himself to a thigh, then sat down, shaking out a paper napkin.

"By the way," she said, "have you been putting coconut milk in my shampoo again?"

"Just a little, darling."

"But I've told you not to! It's a waste of money, I can live without *that*, and it comes running out of the bottle so fast it catches me by surprise and half of it goes down the drain anyway. Why do you sneak around in my things after I've expressly told you not to?" Barbara tweezered a serving from the salad bowl.

Mr Nice Guy tried to return to his subject. "Maybe there's a reason, Raba, for what The Angel did. It might sound weird but I *hope* there is. Maybe it's us, we just can't imagine it. But that doesn't mean there's not a reason."

"Oh Jerry," she said, "why should you cook up an excuse for everything? You must be the last person around, really. Haven't you noticed that everybody's fed up with excuses? People are drawing lines."

"Are those lines going to fix things?"

"Well—(she hesitated less than a second) *contain* them, maybe. You have to grant at least that much. Evil isn't just an old-fashioned idea. Look around you, it's really up-to-date. Some say it's actually the wave of the future."

This sort of talk triggered an instant reaction in Mr Nice Guy, set his fork waving in the air. He couldn't help himself. (Since childhood he'd experienced an attraction for chicken-and-egg dilemmas, for the sound of trees falling in the forest. When exactly did the refrigerator light come on?) "So you draw a line, put it in its *place,*" he replied. "Then what? Isn't making such a place like conceding that terrible things have to happen? A green light for misery? It's defeat before we even start. But are we really so helpless? Why all this giving up, throwing in the towel, this sourfaced morosity? Whatever happened to can-do Americans, that's what I want to know! Screwed up as things are, it's a wide-open field for goodness out there. Why can't we roll up our sleeves like our grandparents did? The eyes of the world are upon us! Why can't we get off our butts?"

She sighed. "We can. But that doesn't mean the Habers will speak to us."

She was referring to the couple across the hall. It was an unpleasant fact: the Renfrows didn't get along with their next-door neighbors. Mr Nice Guy could hardly believe this was happening to *him*. Yet everything he'd tried to improve the situation had failed. They were always busy when he invited them, and never asked him over to watch a ballgame or to feed their fish while they were away. His neighbors shunned him! Not so much as a little knock on the door for help opening a jar of pickles. He would've loved that.

Dan Haber hit his wife Becky. That was much of the trouble. Sometimes the Renfrows heard them fighting and once, when Becky began to scream, Barbara had called the police. "I can't stand it, I can't stand it," she exclaimed, clapping her hands on her head, tears leaking from her eyes. "We've got to stop it!" While waiting for the police to arrive she and her husband had pressed the Habers' buzzer, which after considerable delay was answered. "There's no problem," he'd retorted, then promptly closed the door. When the police came they could do nothing because Becky, through swollen lips, insisted the same. She did not wish to file a complaint.

This overture by the Renfrows poisoned all relations with their neighbors thereafter. The Habers even refused to acknowledge their greetings when they passed in the hallway or stairwell. Mr Nice Guy was determined to patch things up, all the more since the Habers were Jewish, and he recalled an incident which niggled in back of his mind, which he'd never told Barbara for she would say it had no bearing, concerning a time when he was a teenager and a bunch of guys had given their friend Sandy Ursel a joke birthday card. They'd signed it with names like Joe Maimonides, Saul McDonald and (his writing) Moses Renfrow. They'd thought it would be funny. But when Sandy opened the card, read the signatures, he didn't smile. He looked up at his friends and suddenly his face was different than it had ever appeared before. He laughed in an odd high voice—still without smiling—and abruptly left. Young Mr Nice Guy didn't see why. What was the big deal? Couldn't they have fun? But as an adult it was partly this memory that sent him to the Habers' door with fresh-baked oatmeal cookies on Rosh Hashanah.

"What?" said Dan Haber. "What do you mean?" He looked down at the plate that had been pushed into his hands.

"I just thought it would be nice for the holiday."

"Uh . . . oh." His forehead creased. "Well, thanks." He shrugged, then shut the door in Mr Nice Guy's face. Turning back to his wife, he said, "I don't get it. What the fuck?"

"Yeah," said Becky, watching him from the edge of the living room carpet, her hands on her hips. "Why can't they leave people alone?"

After the cookies, the Habers still didn't speak to the Renfrows in the hallway or stairwell.

"But he nods to me sometimes," Mr Nice Guy insisted. "She did too, last week."

Barbara threw up her hands. "Wow! What a breakthrough! In your case, Jerry, the more time passes, the more I think it's like you're fighting the force of gravity. Go ahead and try. Go on, jump as high as you like. But I have to tell you—in the end you're going to come down."

He smiled back at her. "My dear, gravity's on our side, it keeps us close to the sun." Affectionately, he ran his hand along the thin limb of the potted sapodilla he kept near the kitchen windows where it had the most light. "And the sun's good for us."

"Honey, you don't even know if that tree will survive."

He lavished much attention on his little sapodilla, spoke to it encouragingly, played it Vivaldi CD's and on occasion surprised it with treats of fresh chicken manure and mineral water. His aim was to tap its sap one day, sink his fingers in its beautiful white-gummy chicle. He'd always dreamed of making his own perfect blend.

Aside from moral dilemmas, chewing gum was Mr Nice Guy's chief vice. Though he regularly consumed commercial brands—a straight-on spearmint man, having long outgrown fruity flavors and inferior mints and the abomination of cinnamon (even if he did appreciate the occasional anise stick: the Italians made a good one)—he also spent hefty portions of his income on importing coagulated lumps of pure chicle resin from Mexico, Malaysia and Indonesia. These were special. These he took back to his room, hands trembling and saliva welling uncontrollably as he carefully unpeeled the foil, sliced off a piece and wrapped it in a freshly plucked mint leaf (he never, never cut his chicle with sugar), then bit down as hard as he could.

What joy! And *relief.* The joints of his knuckles, his innerdeep bowels, the outermost round of his kneecaps suddenly felt better. Soothed. He chewed and chewed. For a time the back of his neck prickled and the muscles relaxed so deliciously that his head tilted up, the world assumed a different angle, and he contemplated finer possibilities, the Optimal.

After considerable trouble and expense, he'd procured a sapodilla of his own—not just any sapodilla, but of the choicest chicle-producing region in the world, delicately transplanted by natives near Lake Hzá, Guatamala. He loved this little tree, watered it assiduously during what would have been the rainy season, and to approximate a more radiative climate, circled the tree's pot with the same reflective material as the underwear of astronauts. "Shine me a little more!" he had been heard to beseech his window, the world beyond.

Some lucky day, he believed, he would get to take his knife and bleed the tree.

After dinner that night Mr Nice Guy talked to his mother on the phone, attempting to persuade her to let him buy a whirlpool for her feet, and as soon as he hung up it rang under his hand; it was Garson calling to gripe about the dogs again. Barbara curled on the couch and scanned the newspaper, the freshest crimes and calamities, mysteries of severed hands being sent through the mail, the obituary of yet another jazz great. Where did they all come from? she wondered. There seemed to be so many. It would be a relief when they were all gone, and you didn't have to read about the death of another jazz great. With a snap she folded the newspaper, looked up—her husband was still talking—and reached for her book, *The Memoirs of Eli Secreast*. For her job she was trying to get through this tome, which was as fat as a brick and very slow going. Life on the American prairie with families of fourteen children eating corn mush. Blizzards, and feuds over rainwater. She began a chapter entitled "Locusts" but soon her thoughts drifted to her irritation at Mr Nice Guy's mother: how sick she was of hearing about that woman's feet! For God's sake, one of her toes received more attention than many a courtesan! Barbara remembered herself, tried to focus on the page, "*it was then that I began to fabricate my own toys out of the plentiful sod*", but soon her mind wandered again, this time to the image of a young colleague at the Secreast Museum. An eager one.

Reggie was his name. For his training period, he had asked to be assigned with her. Now he accompanied Barbara every day on her tours. That morning, while they were attaching themselves to an elastic leader to take a group of children into the caves, he had given a strange little performance. Barbara was explaining to the visitors how to hook the snap on their belt loops, when Reggie, who had also connected himself to the elastic band for the demonstration, added, "Make sure it's on good!" He stepped back, stretching the elastic, then reached out and plucked it. *Doingg.* "See? That's how it should be." The children laughed and affixed their belts, began stretching among themselves, giggling, testing, *doingg, doingg.* Reggie moved further away from Barbara, then further—he flashed a smile as she watched him, and took a little hop, stretched even more, now all the way across the room. She kept waiting for the SNAP, but it didn't come; with a nervous laugh, she plucked it once, too, as if to show him she didn't care: *Teek!* Very tight and high-pitched now. One more step . . .

"How about this one?" he called to her, smiling, and like a dare, plucked again: *Tik!*

At home that evening, reliving the events in her mind, Barbara suddenly felt nervous.

"Garson, everybody's counting on you," Mr Nice Guy was pleading on the phone, "come on, be a sport."

Barbara blinked once, then let the book slide to her knees, and closed her eyes.

In the years since her marriage to Mr Nice Guy and in her gradual enjoyment of his very understanding attitude, she'd had occasional crushes. She'd met men more handsome, or hotter, as well as richer, or more clever. Once she'd even surprised herself with an infatuation for a woman who sold Scandinavian furniture. In the last year or so, though, she'd decided to be with no one except him. It was a clear preference. Her curiosities satisfied, she knew with a certainty that some might have envied that the destinations she wanted most, she would find with her husband. (The pizza boy had been unplanned, an incident she regretted even as it was happening, and despite appearances it had little to do with sex: rather, it was about weakness, a way to indulge and spite herself at the same time, because for several weeks she had been trying to diet, trying heroically to take charge and lose some extra pounds she'd put on, but that afternoon had caved in to a craving for a Green Pepper and Onion Special, exactly what she *shouldn't* do. Suddenly she couldn't stop herself and when he delivered it and started flirting with her a little, in her broken state of mind she acted on an impulse and gave him more than he bargained for—all, however, part of the same irresistible downward spiral of abandonment to what she knew she *shouldn't*. Basically, the boy was just extra cheese.)

But Reggie was different. She couldn't put her finger on precisely why. It wasn't just the handsomeness of youth, though it was true that Reggie was as shiny as a new penny, with chestnut eyes, a mouth that was downright pretty, an angular build, and slender muscled buttocks. No, all that wasn't the reason. There were plenty of handsome men out there. (Well, not that many.) But it took more than that, much more.

With eyes shut she pictured him again, flirting with her in front of the schoolchildren. He literally pranced! She'd found herself laughing and staring: he showed off, flicked his brown hair, displayed not just a charm but a vanity, too, and a certain presumption (mature? certainly not!). She saw his limits. But somehow they didn't seem to matter so much. They even brought something appealing.

Barbara opened her eyes. Her husband's voice talked on and on. Trying to conciliate Garson. Its sincere tone reminded her of his song,

> *If I ain't so smart*
> *There's always heaven above . . .*

Actually she couldn't remember the last time she'd felt so apprehensive. I really do want one man, she told herself. Don't be stupid. Act on what you know.

Barbara believed that she'd learned the nature of her ability to love. Of love, period. She had tested limits. It was easy to enjoy someone's good side, but that had nothing to do with it. Love did not need only assets. Love was more than toleration of the other's maddening habits (and he had many of them!). No, the real measure was the endearment of faults. That was how she knew she loved Jerry, for indeed she did love what she believed to be his blindness about the world, his readiness to lose while doing whatever he could, and even his uncanny ability—*especially* that—not to notice that he'd lost.

Tears came to her eyes. Faults were the stuff of love, she thought.

Ten

NO MATTER HOW much Mr Nice Guy persisted, the consulate of Surimi continued to be purposefully vague about the exact date of Zohra's birthday party. It was a state secret. The precise time was going to be a surprise.

"But I read about it in the newspaper!" said Mr Nice Guy. "It's hardly a complete mystery."

"That was a most unfortunate excess on the part of your journalistic compatriots."

"But the party can't go on without me! I'm the apricot puppy caterer."

"When you need to know, we shall see to it that you find out."

The hotel management was almost as bad. Mr Sylvester of the Palais Royal believed the party would take place sometime during the week of May 22-29, for the hotel had been reserved for that period, but otherwise he was no better informed than Mr Nice Guy. And Mr Sylvester was extremely nervous, openly unsympathetic: "Absolutely no dogs on the premises till one hour before the festivities. Understand? Any damages or cleaning costs for carpets will *not* be assumed by us, that will be between you and the Sheik. Frankly, we disapprove of the entire idea. Puppies are notoriously leaky."

"An hour isn't much time for us to get ready—"

"An hour is all you've got."

Mr Nice Guy wanted to ask some of the Sheik's men to lean on Mr Sylvester, but the consulate stonewalled and he feared losing the whole contract. He found himself with precious little room to maneuver. His profit margin wasn't going to be so sweet after all, because on the other end Garson was gouging him. He'd had to buy his patience with another $400. And he worried about the puppies, too. They would turn wild if left too long under Garson's supervision. "Be sure to pet every one, every day," Mr Nice Guy had counseled. "Get some neighbor kid to help you."

"I don't like people coming on my place."

"Well, then pet them yourself."

"That's more up your line, Jer."

"You know I have jury duty! I'm tied up right now. Listen, I'm paying you good money to pet those puppies. Is that really so hard?"

So, like any self-run business, Home-Made Services brought with it plenty of headaches and there were no fixed hours. During recesses at the courthouse or during the jury's lunch breaks, Mr Nice Guy hustled to the Smoking Area (a narrow concrete strip outdoors marked with skull and cross-bones) and flipped open his cell phone to keep up on his affairs. He checked in with the Surimian consulate and Mr Sylvester at the Palais Royal. Then he folded his phone and whispered a prayer that Zohra's birthday party would take place on a weekend while the trial was not in session.

One Friday afternoon when he trotted out to make his calls after having wolfed down a glaucous pile on his lunch tray (the free menu was alternatingly turkey loaf or hamburger steak with mashed potatoes: afternoons the jury box could be unpleasantly malodorous, especially for the unfortunates who found themselves next to a juror named Mr Perry), Mr Nice Guy pulled out his phone and started punching out a number when, suddenly, a hand clamped on his shoulder. Turned him completely around. Mr Nice Guy's finger paused, suspended, his number sequence hanging unfinished in the air.

"Excuse me, Mr Renfrow. May I have a word with you?"

A tall man in a blue suit frowned down on him. He was one of those thin-mouthed individuals with what Barbara called razor lips—she didn't like people with razor lips.

"What is it?" Mr Nice Guy asked.

"You make a lot of phone calls, don't you?"

Mr Nice Guy stepped back.

"Well—some."

"You probably realize that this is a designated smoking area, not a phoning area. You could be disturbing people here."

Mr Nice Guy looked around and saw only one smoker, a man by the wall yawning and scratching his elbow until he saw they were staring at him. Then he hunched forward and glowered, puffing harder.

"I don't think I was bothering him," said Mr Nice Guy.

"Listen, any time you want to make a call, you just come in my office. You can used the phone there. You won't have to breathe all this smoke. How about that?"

"Well, I wouldn't want to be any trouble—"

"No trouble at all. You use the phone in my office. It's free. Nina here will always let you in if I'm not around."

A black policewoman with a walkie-talkie bulging on her leather belt stood several yards back, her arms folded across her chest, watching him.

So Mr Nice Guy followed him into the courthouse down a hallway into a lemon-scented office with gray cabinets bathed in fluorescent light. He sat obediently where the man pointed, in a swivel chair at a desk in front of a framed photograph showing two razor-lipped children. They wore matching turtleneck sweaters, clutched cloth rabbits, and looked as if they could devour nails. "Go ahead, call," the blue-suited man said. "I won't bother you. I'm going out for a cup of coffee. When you're finished, just tell Nina. She'll be waiting for you."

Mr Nice Guy found himself alone in front of the telephone and immediately shook out several sticks of gum, began chomping, trying to steady his nerves. Only yesterday the judge had lectured them about talking to outsiders, particularly the press; apparently a juror or jurors had made some unattributed comments about The Angel's unruffled calm and the effect produced the morning he'd worn a cherry bow-tie. But the leak was not Mr Nice Guy! He'd respected the rules. Now it was obvious, though, that they suspected him.

He looked at the telephone. Of course they would be listening in, he thought. But wouldn't they have been able to monitor his cell phone, too? *For some reason they want me to know.*

Sweat began to run down Mr Nice Guy's face. This was a test. He told himself: if I call the consulate or the hotel and they finally give me the date, the police will know where I am if I'm absent that day from jury duty. They might come looking for me. This could blow the whole deal! Twelve thousand bucks!

He put his hand on the telephone and looked around him. Maybe he was being watched, too. Oh, what a pickle! The longer he hesitated, each second that ticked by, the more suspicious he appeared.

He lifted up the receiver. He couldn't call home—at this hour it would be too obvious a ruse for reaching no one. For God's sake. Even the most innocent act looked guilty! Fingers shaking, he began to punch out Garson's number. Yes, Garson. You could count on him to know nothing.

He didn't even hear the phone ring. It must've been picked up instantly at the other end: an unmistakable chorus of yipping, squealing, whining. "Yeah?" Garson growled.

Mr Nice Guy swallowed. "Hu—hullo. This is Jerry."

"Jer! What's the scoop? Don't let me down, man."

Mind racing. Maybe this wasn't a good choice after all. What would be understood yet at the same time sound innocuous?

"As soon as we know the time of the party, Garson, you'll be invited."

"As soon as you know *the time*?"

"Yes," panted Mr Nice Guy. "I wanted to tell you."

"Well, that sucks shit, you know that, Jer?"

A terrible barking ruckus broke out, and yowling in the background. The phone dropped with a *chunk*, Garson was yelling, then the yowling stopped and he came back on the line. "They're fightin', man. I'm sick of this."

"You'll feel better after the party, I promise."

"Yeah but right now this sucks shit through a straw."

"Take care," said Mr Nice Guy.

"Fuck you, Jer."

After hanging up the phone he stepped gingerly into the hallway. Nina pointed with her chin. "They're waiting for you."

Mr Nice Guy looked at his watch. Past 1:30! The trial had resumed! He sped down the corridor and hurried through the side door into the courtroom, and the judge stopped speaking in the middle of a sentence, his glasses low on his nose. Heads turned as Mr Nice Guy trotted toward the jury box, toward the vacant spot in the upper row beside Mr Perry. He gave a little nod to the judge and then another to the defendant's table, where The Angel sat staring at him. Mr Nice Guy flashed a smile in his direction while Mr Perry's face tensed for a moment, then relaxed.

"Boy, I got here just in time," he whispered to his neighbor.

Eleven

DURING THE FOLLOWING weeks the defense took over the proceedings and the case became more complicated. Apparently, it was necessary to know all about The Angel's past in order to make sense of recent events, most notably his decision to administer a hammer to his mother's head . . .

"Objection," barked Mrs Madison.

"On what grounds?" asked the judge.

"One does not 'administer' a hammer. It's hardly first-aid. The word 'bludgeon' would be more appropriate."

The judge hesitated for a moment, and the defense lawyer countered, "This objection goes to the core of the problem. That might be the language of the *prosecution*, but it is not necessarily the language of the accused. He has his own way of constructing the situation, and it would be a sad day indeed for American free speech if his voice were, as a matter of course, denied. Is that a free society? Do we convict someone because they don't use the same dictionary? When I hear an objection like that, I become more than ever convinced of the source of my client's guilt: he is guilty of using a different language. This entire proceeding is a question of language! But is language grounds for judgment?"

The judge puffed out his cheeks. "Well—we'll see. Go on. Objection overruled."

On and on. It made for a very long afternoon indeed. Try as he might to follow their reasonings, Mr Nice Guy's attention lapsed and slipped into daydreams. He saw himself gliding through the Woland Gardens, so refreshing, good therapy for his bones, and the more he romped, even mentally, the limberer and cheerfuller he felt. He fantasized about the future of his business, of a glorious day when Home-Made Services expanded to international markets, seized a place in the burgeoning world economy. Mr Nice Guy was sure that these days an entrepreneur must think global. Home-Made Services would become . . . WorldServicesJR! (The final initials stood for Jerry Renfrow, of course, but dare he really?) What opportunities awaited his wares on the overseas trading floor, where he would meet consumers' demands while at the same time supplying—with the gentlest of invisible hands—for human needs? One particularly exciting project involved managing a cyberspace warehouse where donors could tax-deductibly dump their surpluses and spare grain futures. Then specialists in disaster areas serving the starving (or likely to starve, based on projections of specialized software) could back up their computers and pull out precisely what they needed (the beauty of instant inventory), no waste or bureaucracy getting in the way. The only thing missing from this idea was someone like himself to launch it. People everywhere, screenlight glowing on their faces, would be tapping out *@loaves&fishes.com.*

"A very friendly little boy," declared an elderly lady. Suddenly Mr Nice Guy snapped to attention. The Angel's second grade teacher paused to clear her throat. "Yes, I remember him very well."

Then psychiatrists were brought in and it became more complicated. Mr Nice Guy started taking notes on the little canary pad each juror had been authorized (which was kept under lock and key at night, and the number of pages checked, for no smuggling of impressions to the outside was allowed); he tried to keep up with the myriad details. Evidently, The Angel's mother had been very stern, a stickler for punctuality, and inclined to find things damp. And according to the psychiatrist, this couldn't be separated from the fact that when The Angel was a little boy, he had peed through his trunks while paddling in the McCorkleville public swimming pool. He had done it more than once.

(I used to do that too! thought Mr Nice Guy, scribbling. But only God knows.)

And then there was The Angel's humiliation at Cub Scouts, and a series of flat bicycle tires, and the day the baseball game got rained out, and how badly he'd wanted a dog . . . Mr Nice Guy stopped writing for a moment to rub his hand. (These guys weren't leaving anything out!) He looked over at The Angel, his usually impassive face now strained. A different psychiatrist, one who worked at three universities, was called to the witness stand.

After being sworn in, this new specialist of the mind, Doctor Brandon, pulled out a piece of paper which he unfolded with several jerks of his wrist.

"What I have here is a poem written by the adolescent Randall Hutchinson which I think should be shared with the public." He cleared his throat, fished a pair of glasses out of an inner jacket pocket, and balanced them on his nose. "The handwriting has been authenticated. There is no title marked on the document, but it is my professional opinion that 'First Love' would be an appropriate choice. May I?"

The defense attorney nodded grimly, and Mr Brandon read aloud,

I had a dog
His name was Rex.
Me and Rex
Had lots of sex.

His long red tongue
His floppy ears
We had some laughs
We drank some beers

But then one day
Rex went away
His letter said,
"I cannot stay.

"'Cause I'm a dog
And you're a man
It's too damn weird
Please understand."

So now I walk
The fields alone
In my pocket
Is a bone

I cry at night
And I miss Rex
We had some laughs
And lots of sex.

"Thank you, Mr Brandon."

A hush filled the courtroom. The Angel was invited to return to the witness stand, and a flurry of interrogation and counter-interrogation ensued; Mrs Madison of the prosecution zeroed in relentlessly. Question after question, with objections both sustained and overruled. Mr Nice Guy was riveted—it was just like in the movies! After an hour of testimony and considerable sifting of contradictions and facts, it emerged that the poem wasn't completely true; The Angel had indulged in artistic license. His dog's real name, it was revealed, was Sparky.

Mr Nice Guy went home that night with his head swimming. He climbed up the stairs with a bundle of asparagus in one hand, a pint of rum raisin ice cream in the other, anxious to discuss these developments in the trial over dinner with Barbara. Never mind his promise of confidentiality! If he was going to judge this case, he would need her help to sort things out.

"Raba! I'm here!"

(Just to give her warning . . .)

But Barbara wasn't home. He called from the kitchen where he threw the ice cream in the freezer, gave a leaf of the sapodilla a smile and greeting caress, then walked through the rooms of the apartment. He tapped on the bathroom door. "Hey-ho?"

No one. He looked at his watch. The museum had closed two hours ago. Something must have come up.

He checked the Home-Made Services fax machine, which had spat out three, checked his E-mail and listened to his telephone messages. Requests for letters to accompany birthday cards (piece of cake, Mr Nice Guy could crank those out in his sleep), three hospital get-wells (Singapore flu was making the rounds), a nursing home magic show and an after-dinner speech for an optometrists' convention. Plenty to keep him busy before he hit the hay tonight! He sighed, and returned to the kitchen to prepare dinner, racking his brain for some optometry humor. Fortunately, Mr Nice Guy had a respectable library of joke research, including rare back numbers of *Kneeslapper*, which he consulted often in the course of his work. (He wasn't too quick at making funnies himself, and relied heavily on secondary sources.) He did try his hand, though, at spinning limericks (he specialized in clean ones) for occasions both festive and sober:

"An optometrist from Manassas,
A Michelangelo of glasses . . ."

he mumbled, feeling his way around syllable, rhyme, as he reached deeply into the refrigerator for a tupperware container whose lid, when he pried, opened with a lazy kiss. He peered at the sirloin tips he'd set to marinate the night before. A surprise for Barbara.

. . . had lots of sex
with a dog named Rex

For Pete's sake! he told himself. Why can't I shake that trial from my mind? It's invading everywhere, taking over decent lives . . . He washed the asparagus and cut off the ends where woody. He stacked up the steamer.

Tonight he wanted dinner to be extra special. Romantic. The previous evening they had quarreled and he hoped to make it up to her. Barbara had been very touchy lately. It was a mystery to him why. All he'd done last night was allude to Wayne, but that was enough to put her in a bad mood and spoil the atmosphere. Wayne was a kitten she'd brought back from work a few months earlier, a sickly little clutch of fur and bones with festering eyes who cowered in a box by the kitchen window. As soon as he saw the animal, Mr Nice Guy was convinced that it would die; Barbara, too, expressed regrets that she'd accepted it. "He didn't look so bad in the dark," she told him. "Bringing this cat home is the sort of thing *you* would do." In fact, as Wayne's condition worsened Mr Nice Guy had the feeling that Barbara illogically revised her version of events, and believed *he* was somehow responsible. "But I didn't bring him!" he wanted to remind her. "Don't blame me."

But Wayne didn't die. He disappeared. It was very odd. One day, he was simply gone. Evaporated. "I don't get it," Mr Nice Guy said, poking round the shredded newspapers, searching under scraps. "He was too weak to crawl out of the box. Wayne?"

Barbara professed to know nothing. Mr Nice Guy peered on his hands and knees. "Wayne?"

"Maybe a big bird swooped through the window and carried him away," said Barbara. "Can't you see him mewing, disappearing into the sky?"

She laughed strangely. That was months ago. The sapodilla stood in place of Wayne's box now. From time to time Mr Nice Guy brought up the subject, but it always seemed to make Barbara edgy.

So tonight he wanted everything to be perfect. He had pine-scented candles, North Woods Delights, just as she liked. Blond asparagus was a favorite of hers, too. All the necessary ingredients were assembled, and he decided to lose no time in getting ready.

When it came to cooking, Mr Nice Guy was superstitious. Either he could wait for Barbara to arrive before preparing his dish or he could begin right away. If he waited, there was no telling what time they would finally sit down to eat. But if he started steaming the asparagus now—here Mr Nice Guy's superstition came in—she would arrive in time to eat it. This technique had worked on numerous occasions, the most impressive results from codfish in sour cream. As soon as sour cream entered the equation, the results were uncanny.

So he turned up the flame, pulled out knives and forks to set the table, and returned to mulling over The Angel—his past, his tribulations. Whatever the man's brutality (Mr Nice Guy suspected, based on the testimony so far, that he was guilty of having administered the hammer), there was a contemplative side to him, too. Poetic. He hadn't detected that until today. Squeezing the wine bottle between his knees, Mr Nice Guy twisted in a corkscrew. He pulled, grimacing—*pop.*

The doorbell rang.

Barbara! he told himself. Right on cue! Rubbing the bridge of his nose, he smiled.

But why would she ring the bell? he wondered. Had she forgotten her keys?

He put the bottle on the counter and went to answer the door. When he opened, an impeccably dressed olive-skinned man inquired, "Mr Renfrow?"

"Yes?"

"How do you do? I'm Mr Azid, cultural attaché for the Surimian consulate." He handed Mr Nice Guy an embossed card. "May I come in?"

"You surely may! Boy, am I glad to see you. Right this way."

Mr Azid took a seat on the couch and after the briefest of formalities announced that the party for the Princess would take place tomorrow evening at 8 o'clock sharp. The puppies should arrive in the ballroom between 8:15 and 8:20. Would he be ready?

"Oh, yes, you bet, Mr Azid. Don't worry about a thing. Home-Made Services guarantees satisfaction for every detail."

Mr Nice Guy felt like dancing. What luck! Not only was the mystery solved, but the celebration would take place late enough that he wouldn't have to miss jury duty, either.

He wouldn't have to lie to the judge. Moments like these, Mr Nice Guy suspected that fortune had a particular soft spot for him.

"Have a glass of wine, Mr Azid."

"No thank you."

"I got some chocolate milk. Are you a chocolate milk man?"

"No thank you, Mr Renfrow. For reasons of security, it is of capital importance that you keep this information to yourself. Do you understand?"

"Yes sir, no problem there. I only have to notify my assistant, that's all." (He imagined a smile erupting across Garson's jowls.)

The doorbell rang. Mr Azid sat up straight.

"I prefer that you not reveal my identity to whomever that may be."

Mr Nice Guy nodded, then went to answer. He opened to three policemen.

"Mr Renfrow?"

"Yes?"

"We hereby inform you that you are under arrest. We advise you to come peacefully."

Mr Nice Guy was stunned. Still, it didn't matter that he didn't know what to say or do, for the police took charge of the situation. They stepped into the apartment and informed him that he was charged with violating the state code with regard to cruelty to animals, as well as additional charges concerning sanitation infractions and criminal neglect. They handed him a search warrant which he was supposed to read but he couldn't concentrate, for he was still trying to grasp what they'd said. "*Why*?" he gasped. "*What*?"

"You may take some pajamas and a toothbrush," said one policeman while the other two filtered out through the apartment.

"Who are you?"

Mr Azid had been seated so quietly on the couch that at first no one had noticed him. He stood up suddenly.

"This situation is very unfortunate and I do not wish to

be in the way. My involvement is not possible. If you will excuse me . . ." he said, heading for the door.

"Who are you?" And then another voice: "FREEZE!"

Mr Nice Guy stopped in his tracks.

"I was just going to get my toothbrush, officer."

By then Mr Azid had been snatched by the arm, asked for identification; when he tried to free his arm he was jerked roughly, his tie flopped out of his jacket, and his shiny shoes struggled for traction on the carpet. The policeman gripped harder, repeated his request. Slowly, wiping his hair off his forehead, his eyes blazing at Mr Nice Guy, Mr Azid complied.

"Diplomatic corps, then? What's your relationship to Mr Renfrow?"

"I arrived only minutes ago, and have no relationship that would be of interest."

This answer didn't please his questioner, who suggested that Mr Azid come down to the station and they would see together just how interesting it was. This Mr Azid flatly refused, citing diplomatic immunity. Mr Nice Guy was enormously embarrassed and tried unsuccessfully to tell the police they were all wrong.

"No one's asking you, fella!" was the reply.

He had no pajamas to take to jail. He and Barbara always slept naked. (Sometimes he caught sore throats but since she preferred being nude he went along.)

Where was she, anyway?

The handcuffs flashed, then pinched down cold.

He barely had time to turn off the asparagus! He and Mr Azid were hustled out the door and down the stairs, pushed into the back of a police van. While Mr Azid glared at him in the grainy light, he looked up with disbelief at the darkened windows of the apartment, thinking with a pang of the dinner table, the places set, the unserved wine.

Twelve

I HAVE TO say that he was poorly prepared for certain problems in life, and serious criminal charges, incarceration, vilification in newspapers and on television, harassment by the United States State Department—these figured among them. Mr Nice Guy had never anticipated that such sea of troubles could affect *him*. Hadn't he, his entire life, tried his best to avoid making waves? He considered himself a law-abiding citizen, a straight-shooter, and so was now in a paroxysm of confusion. Barbara was disoriented, too, and despaired to their lawyer, Mr Vsalik, "He just wanted to be of service."

That first night in jail, he shared a cell with a young man fresh from a brawl whose hairline was a jamlike mess of drying blood, and two drunk drivers who argued loudly about their breath tests and urinated in the sink. He decided not to sleep naked. Oh, the stories! Except around Barbara, Mr Nice Guy was bashful about his body. He lay down in his clothes, spent a restless night cramped and sweating, and at dawn awoke terrified and disoriented when the young man with jammy hair stood over his bunk, shaking him roughly, his face looming then disappearing then looming again—his breath acrid—imploring, "Rich, Rich, is that you?"

"No! I'm not Rich," he blurted, sitting up suddenly in his bunk, arms flailing, wrestling free. "You've got the wrong man!"

His interrogator shuffled away, mumbling, and Mr Nice Guy dropped heavily on his thin mattress. At this hour he was stone tired, still in the sort of fuzzed consciousness where normally he might've told himself, "Ah, it was just a bad dream," then snugly drifted back into a deep sleep, after which he would awake entirely refreshed. Even for someone of Mr Nice Guy's disposition, being able to face the world required, at repairing intervals, the healing tonic of being unconscious of it. Momentarily he started to tell himself, "It was just—" then stopped. No. It *wasn't* a dream. I am in jail, he told himself, and experienced an unpleasant tingling in his forehead. In jail! He rose halfway at the waist, propped himself on his elbows, and looked round the gray light with blinking, stinging eyes. Steel bars and their shadows on cement. Huddled forms under blankets. In the cell across the corridor, someone farted fizzedly. *I'm in jail.*

He lay down again but couldn't go back to sleep. Pressure, then pain crept into the top of his skull. With eyes closed he listened to the sounds of the cell block, different registers of breathing, a low electric buzz somewhere. Permeating all was the smell of sweat. It originated, among other places, from right under him, his mattress. He lifted his hand to his face to block the smell with the scent of his own skin, and breathed hard, using his exhalations to snuff out other sounds. He thought of the previous night's events, how during the short time Mr Azid had spent with him in a holding pen of wire mesh like a giant chicken cage, the consular official had refused to speak, even to look at Mr Nice Guy. ("I'm very sorry about us getting arrested and all, sir, and I hope it won't affect our doing business together . . .") Not even a hint of eye contact, much less a parting handshake. Very unpromising . . .

After Mr Azid made his guaranteed phone call, it took only minutes for another man from the Surimian consulate to come and get him. By then a plainclothed policeman had arrived and apologized profusely, on behalf of the department and the county and the United States of America, and promised that the arresting officer would be disciplined.

"Goodbye, Mr Azid!" called Mr Nice Guy as the diplomat's steps echoed down the corridor. "I'll be in touch soon!"

When his turn came he'd tried to call Barbara but there was no answer after 14 rings. *Where was she?* Later, just before he went to sleep, they let him try again. This time she was home, and her voice sounded higher, strained.

"I'm so sorry I was late," she said. "I found the dinner you left out, I'm waiting for you. Jerry, where are you?"

He explained that he was in jail and that the amount of bail wouldn't be fixed till the next day, so there was nothing to do. She, like Mr Nice Guy, was dumbfounded by the charges.

"Where's Garson?" she wanted to know.

"I have no idea."

"How can they do this to you? What are they hiding from us?"

The public knew first. Even after Barbara went to the police station to answer questions and spoke to her husband in the visitor's section to tell him she did not have the $200,000 bail, she had no idea of the extent of charges, for they increased over the course of the day like ants accumulating on a piece of spat candy. She learned more when she saw his face flash on the television screen during the six o'clock news. She was working at the table, wading through accounts to see how much money they could raise, scarcely paying attention to the television, when suddenly her husband's face appeared. She froze, the pencil sliding out of her hand and rolling in a semi-circle on the floor. The station had used his driver's license photo, for which he'd given a big smile ("Your identity oughta be fun!" he'd always said)—now, though, with the news anchorman's voice behind the image, the grin was misplaced, almost sinister:

". . . *the owner and manager of the 'kennel from hell,' as one officer described it, is Jerry Renfrow, 34, of 525 East 81st Street.* (Here the image changed to their building, which gave Barbara an eerie feeling, as if television had succeeded in shrinking their lives: she was reduced to that box.) *At least four of the dogs are known to be dead, others were suffering from severe dehydration. Witnesses on the scene said that some were reduced to eating their own excrement, or the cadavers of other animals—all puppies. An employee of Renfrow, Garson Carter, 28, arrived at the scene while authorities were rescuing the animals. He broke into tears at the sight, and, according to Carter, his employer had left the dogs unattended during his vacation.* (The screen flashed a photo of Garson, all solemnity and beefy red cheeks.) *Carter was held for questioning, then released on his own recognizance. Renfrow is now under custody . . .*

"Garson, you son-of-a-bitch!" exclaimed Barbara, slamming her hand down on the table so hard that she hurt it, instantly bringing her palm to her mouth.

". . . *police searches also revealed an unspecified number of Renfrow aliases . . . .*"

"No, no!"

Barbara had already noticed that her husband's papers had been rifled through. Confetti had been tracked around the apartment. His calendars, birthstone inventory, mortuary newsletters were in disarray. Computer diskettes might be missing; she could not tell. At the police station that morning she'd tried to explain that the only reason he was writing letters using other people's names was that these same people paid him to do so; the sergeant who questioned her seemed skeptical and took many notes, for he'd never heard of Home-Made Services. Obviously, the media were still uninformed, too. "You've got it all wrong, all wrong!" she cried to the screen.

That her husband's arrest should take place the evening she and Reggie had gone out for a drink compounded her regret with guilt. Of all nights! This drink had prolonged itself into several: amber-colored Mexican beers with multiple wedges of lime which they squeezed, then dropped into their glasses—conversation paused as they watched the sleepy, sinking green—then conversation resumed, following sinuous paths and sometimes twisting agreeably over on itself. The beer tasted sweeter and sweeter. Usually Barbara wasn't fond of beer but she'd never mixed it with lime before. Reggie spoke of his plans of living in Mexico on the mountain island of Quiertolan; he dreamed of running a white-stucco pension. He described a world of shimmering blue skies, volcanic bluffs, bleached houses and boro-fish baked in yellow mud.

He gazed at her warmly. Any second now he would reach out and take her hand.

This realization made her sit up straight, shake herself into action. She excused herself by announcing flatly, "Well this is nice but my husband is waiting for me. I have to go."

He nodded slowly.

But the effect of these words was not as she'd intended. Reggie brought his glass to hers with a *tink,* then smiled as he lifted it to his lips, as if they shared a complicity.

"I'll see you tomorrow at work," he said. "But I'll be thinking of you tonight."

Now the memory of that smile competed with her husband's grin on the television screen. Barbara's hand rose to her throat when the newscast finished with images of trembly, rescued skeletal puppies yapping hoarsely, crawling toward bowls.

Thirteen

"A Dog-Eat-Dog World" proclaimed the Morning *Tribune*, and an editorial inquired,

How far will people go for profit? We might not like to look at the answer. From time to time an event makes us all pause, gives us the needed wake-up call.

After the newspaper vilification, public outcry was genuine. It quickly moved beyond the local level, for the report about Mr Nice Guy touched deep-rooted feelings. How do I explain? People were *hungry.* In a world where right and wrong were increasingly hard to get a grip on, where moral questions were vexed, compromised, or the local monopoly of a given group—suddenly everybody agreed about Mr Nice Guy. Only a bastard, pure and simple, could so mistreat a puppy! Who could say the contrary? Mr Nice Guy brought together people of all horizons, appalling everybody regardless of age, sex, religion, race, or political persuasion. He united them in disgust.

Indeed, if one believed public reaction, no rationalization or circumstances could excuse him.

I say, let him be locked up for a while with nothing to eat but his excrement, and see how he likes it!

was a typical letter to the editor, among the printable ones.

Garson was arrested a few days later on an unregistered weapons charge, but he was able to post bail. Meanwhile Mr Nice Guy saw *his* bail soar to $350,000, far out of reach. This increase was due in part to the public outcry, in part to zoning violations for kennel facilities, and in part to mysterious pressure from beyond the local police force.

"You should know that they brought the feds in," Mr Nice Guy's lawyer Roger Vsalik told him one morning, petting the head of a baby boy strapped to his chest. Vsalik often carried along his son Richie when he made the jail rounds. He was the court-appointed counsel and by all appearances a good dad. "Grapevine has it that the FBI has invited itself in, so now the District Attorney is flustered, trying to prove that he's on top of things. I'll tell you, Mr Renfrow, somebody high up is taking you mighty seriously." Vsalik leaned closer, lowering his voice, while Richie's head wobbled, his mouth a drooling rosebud. "Are you sure that there's nothing more to this case that you're not sharing with me? In *your* interest, I should know everything."

"But I've told you everything!" Mr Nice Guy moaned. "I've got nothing to hide."

"That machine in your garage?"

"It's for making confetti, I swear!"

Apparently this device had excited and intrigued investigating officers. But it was only a turn-of-the-century Meeber machine originally used for punching holes in shoe leather, which Mr Nice Guy had gotten for free in exchange for moving it out of a landlord's way. With Garson's help in adding a kerosene engine, he'd converted it for his own purposes. The thought of strangers tampering with it troubled Mr Nice Guy. "People shouldn't be fooling around the storage canisters without masks, confetti fiber dust is terrible for your lungs! Any party professional will tell you."

Vsalik scratched his chin. "It must be the Surimi connection," he mused.

And he was right—though he didn't suspect the gravity of the affair—that in the garage the authorities were looking for more than a methamphetamine laboratory or even a bomb factory, that for several days, in fact, under their very noses Mr Nice Guy had been under round-the-clock surveillance. A "car thief" transferred to share his jail cell was in truth a CIA operative. Was this man Renfrow an agent for a hostile foreign power? The abuse of Mr Azid's diplomatic status had come at a delicate time in U.S./Surimi relations. Though the general public was in the dark, at stake was a deal worth between 1.5 and 2 billion dollars, pending the

Sheik's purchase of F-16 fighter jets (also at stake was invaluable leverage in the strategic alliance). Was it only for the sake of some street cop's sloppy procedure that the Sheik might buy French, after all?

Actually, as soon as State Department policy analysts read intelligence reports about the birthday party and grasped the canine variable in the Surimi equation, they acted fast. A senior foreign officer hastily gave up his children's young labrador (code name Desmond) and shipped it to the Surimian consulate, a goodwill gesture that unfortunately backfired, for the consular employees didn't know what to do with the dog (they were hesitant to send Desmond back, in the event that the princess would come to claim him). The puppy took up residence in the consul's offices, a constant reminder and irritation to Mr Azid, chewing on his computer cables.

Roger Vsalik, with dark rings under his eyes and his baggy, wrinkled suit emanating a diapery stench, did not know any of these globally-charged particulars, but as a bleeding-ulcer liberal capable of sensing the whirl of outside forces, he warned,

"This is going to be a tough fight, Renfrow, I might as well level with you. There's pressure from above, *high* above, to make an example of you."

Their legal consultation always took place before lunch. Then Mr Nice Guy went to the prisoner's cafeteria to eat chili and mashed potatoes, and glumly spread margarine on floppy white bread while thinking of the carefree hours in his own kitchen with Barbara, of a salad recipe he was in the process of inventing that would use only the edible blossoms of flowers. There were so many rich vegetarians out there who would subscribe to an on-line Nouveaux Comestibles. Folding a piece of bleached bread into his dry mouth, tears welled in his eyes.

"What's the matter, Jerry?" said a gentle voice.

It was Carl Harvey, the grand theft auto specialist who shared his cell. He often came over to cheer him up, ask him how he felt and what was on his mind. His only friend in the place.

"Carl, I'm at the end of my rope . . ."

Mr Nice Guy told him everything, his legal woes and ache for Barbara (if only they could've had that romantic dinner before parting!), the ruin of his business and missed family obligations—he was expected at Cousin Mike's farm at 10 o'clock that very morning, he'd made an appointment—as well as his worries about his mother undergoing circulatory tests on her feet at the hospital, where she had little to do except lie in bed and watch television, including, of course, sensational reports about him. "To put that poor woman through this," he fretted, "when she's already had enough troubles —"

"Tell me more about that Mr Azid fellow," Carl Harvey interrupted, holding out a pack of spearmint gum. "Boy, he sure is interesting . . ."

Mr Nice Guy helped himself to a stick. "Gee, I don't know what else to say."

As he went over his story again, the image of his father's pale, almost translucent face returned to him as it sometimes did in moments of distress, and he recalled his words. *You do whatever you can.* Yet that advice was harder to follow now since he couldn't understand the situation. "Carl, help me figure this out. Please. What is it I've done?"

Fourteen

Mr Nice Guy stood in the dock, awaiting his sentence. He'd worn his best tie for the occasion, a silvery silk strip like the belly of a fish. For a moment he twisted his neck and met Barbara's gaze across the courtroom, noticing the tired, anxious lines around her mouth.

"*. . . it is the will of this court to hold you to the maximum sentence of three years for premeditated cruelty to animals . . .*"

Three years! thought Mr Nice Guy with despair, shaking his head, clenching the wooden railing before him.

"*. . . plus one year for violation of Code 117 regarding sanitary requirements for an agglomeration of animals . . .*"

Oh no! Four years!

"*. . . plus six months for operating said agglomeration without a Class C permit . . .*"

Dear God!

"*. . . plus six months for not filing for commercial authorization from the zoning board . . .*"

He clapped his hands to his cheeks, teetering.

"*. . . plus one month each for 20 counts of unlicensed domestic canines of which you were the proprietor . . .*"

Mr Nice Guy struggled to keep his balance.

"*. . . for a total of five years, eight months, with eligibility for parole not before a period of three years served.*"

There was a roar of approval from the rear of the courtroom where animal rights activists had camped since the beginning of the trial. They shook their fists and emitted coyote woo-woos. The judge pounded his mallet several times and Mr Nice Guy, blood booming in his head, caught himself again on the railing—he felt like a man at sea on the flimsiest of rafts, powerful forces buffeting him, pitching him toward a deep, unwanted place he could barely comprehend. At the sight of him Barbara let out a small cry, but this was lost in the commotion.

"Does the accused understand the sentence?" the judge asked.

Mr Nice Guy nodded, rocking amid cat-calls, hanging on with all his strength.

"Does the accused wish to make a statement?"

His ears popped as the light reflected off the judge's glasses, yet at the same time he experienced something terrifyingly calm and familiar. Suddenly he remembered another day and a different man at the railing. The Angel.

"I just try to do what I can, your honor."

Jeers and hisses erupted from the back of the courtroom, and the mallet came down again.

"Defense counsel?" the judge asked.

Roger Vsalik, his voice trembling with rage, told the judge that it was clear that the court had acted not only against the interest of justice but also with a brand of vindictiveness such as he had never seen in his 11 years of experience in the Seventh District. He would appeal this decision immediately. As he spoke his words came faster and faster, and carried along by his own fervor he made quite a speech. His tenor rose, his hands swam. "I've seen the future, and it's jerks!"

Later, in the rocking police van after the push and crush of reporters with microphones and flashbulbs (background hecklers taunted, "Puppy killer! Puppy killer!"), Roger Vsalik grew grim when Mr Nice Guy asked about his chances in an appeal.

"These people slammed you, they're not going to get any easier. But I don't think they have a leg to stand on for the license violations for the dead puppies. The code is applicable only to *live* animals. That'll knock four months off your sentence."

Mr Nice Guy held his head in his hands, gritting his teeth. "That's good news."

A moment later the sound of sobs filled the van. And for the rest of the ride there were words of comfort, as Mr Nice Guy tried to reassure, "It's all right, Roger. I'm not mad at you, I promise."

Fifteen

THAT NIGHT HE was allowed to call Barbara.

"As soon as I get my address at the penitentiary, I'll let you know."

She was crying, too. Never had he known such a miserable time. Never had he needed to console so many people outside of his job—and for a problem of which *he* was the source! "Oh Jerry, I feel so confused," she said. "How did we ever reach this day?"

He searched desperately for something to say. Something soothing. "Five years, eight months. Or if we get through my appeal, it'll be just five years, four months." He felt his chest tightening into knots. "I'll miss you. Dear God I'll miss you." Now his control was slipping away. "I guess this ruins our plans to go back to Billy Hare Lodge for Christmas."

Now he choked, and Barbara didn't make matters easier by telling him that she'd been looking forward to that trip with all her heart. The Billy Hare Lodge, in Hummel, Minnesota, was where he'd proposed marriage to her. A beautiful spot in a forest beside a lake like a melted diamond. When, if ever, would they get to meet there again? There was a silence on the line, then he collected himself to say,

"I might as well tell you that your birthday present is hidden behind the oak buffet, you don't have to wait until February. It's that salmon silk top you liked. And never mind the business. There's nothing I can do about it. This will spell the end of Home-Made Services."

"No, Jerry, don't say that! I know how much it means to you. We'll keep it afloat!"

"I don't see how."

"We'll find a way. I promise!"

Yet she didn't believe her own words. Ever since his incarceration, Mr Nice Guy's affairs had been sinking.

She'd tried to cover for him in her spare hours when she wasn't guiding senior citizens or the Bulgarian Navy Choir through the depths of the Secreast Caverns; and from the county jail, balancing his paper on his knee, Mr Nice Guy had whipped off letters by hand (though such output was small compared to what he could've accomplished at home with his computer and its Forget-Me-Not database). But these efforts were not enough. Inevitably, requests piled up. Phone messages went unanswered, deadlines were missed. Grandmamas and great uncles knew the pain of empty mailboxes on their birthdays. Lovers' roses went unsent. Condolences for parents of dead children did not arrive.

There was a time lag before these lapses were discovered, but now subscribers were beginning to exclaim with hurt, angry voices. Late last night a man had telephoned Barbara and rousted her out of bed. "Listen, you screw-ups, my Uncle Ted went ballistic, and it's not even my fault!" He threatened legal action.

"The calls are getting nasty," she admitted to Mr Nice Guy. "If I try to say we've been having a rough time, that's not good enough for them. The only thing that calms people is when I tell them you're already behind bars."

"Well, if that makes them feel better . . ."

"But you'll get time off for good behavior, won't you Jerry? If anybody can do it, you can."

Sixteen

GARSON FOUND A parking place directly across from the apartment building. He turned off the engine of his Cherokee and looked up at the glowing fourth floor windows. Yes, she was home.

Nervous but pleased, he gripped the steering wheel and took several deep breaths. His hair was still damp against the back of his neck; he was wearing a new blue-striped shirt which scratched on his chest, his nipples. He'd washed and waxed the Cherokee that afternoon. Proud he was of this almost-new machine. In fact, Garson was bursting. This vehicle had been the source of many of his woes, but now he felt it could bring him pleasure, too.

All the troubles of these last few months had started when he'd seen the ad for a barely-used turquoise Cherokee (perfect upholstery! less than 7000 miles!) for sale in St. Petersburg. They asked 16,000 volts. He'd called and the fellow who answered informed him that he wasn't the first prospective buyer, and that it would be sold, first come first served. Garson had no choice but to jump in his car and drive the 150 miles to check it out.

Jerry's dogs could fend for themselves for a day, he figured.

He'd saved up $16,742. His careful calculation for freedom. No one, certainly not the Renfrows, suspected how carefully he'd guarded his resources, how prudent he was with expenditures, how ready to sacrifice. His trollish self-sufficiency. Of course he could've lived in a nicer place than the cabin, which he'd bought as a kit and erected on the edge of township plumbing. Of course he could've allowed himself more comforts, a better car than his rusted-out Camaro, a bigger microwave and a VCR that wouldn't jam and a refrigerator that didn't leave pissy puddles on the floor. But he was saving up for something finer.

Beautiful Mobility. That's what Garson wanted. To go the way he pleased and with no constraints. That was his ideal. Not just transportation but a gorgeous, moveable *where,* a homestead on a chassis, in which he could sleep and eat and live, from sea to shining sea: free.

For years he'd longed for nothing else. He'd done his homework, studied automotive magazines and brochures, knew which models performed best. But it had to be beautiful, too, and he'd decided on either a candy apple red or a classy turquoise (just like the one in the ad!). He would travel West, maybe down to Mexico (and why not Guatamala? or Panama?—shove the nose of his steed into the Canal, so that the lower half of the world stretched before him, and all of North America balanced above: kissing *his* ass!).

He would depend on no one. No connections, no obligations. Just climb in back to sleep or, if the weather was fine, pull out a bedroll and stretch out under the stars. If he felt like it he could travel straight to the Utah mountains where people still prospected for gold. Try his hand at that for a while. His fingers blue in a stream, pines waving behind him and the occasional eagle or condor above, which he straightened to look at, tilting his head, listening to the water ripple, then lowering his gaze to the deep valley below that was so pretty it gave him a boner.

America, he warned, get ready! Garson's here.

But when he arrived in St. Petersburg, the Cherokee had disappeared. Fuck a duck. The owner's wife told him, "Don't ask me! You should try the Blue Bird Tap, my husband sometimes goes there with his high school bitch."

The Blue Bird Tap was easy enough to find, with its overhanging neon sign operating even by day, a blue bird flitting with motions that looked more like digestive spasms than flight, but with an effect that was somehow cheery nonetheless.

Inside the Blue Bird, he learned that he'd missed his man by minutes! In fact, the Cherokee had been the subject of conversation, its owner had been talking it up, looking for buyers in the bar. Garson stood at the rail and nervously gulped his beer (actually he wasn't very fond of the stuff but believed he needed the yeast) and tried to squeeze as much information as he could out of the bartender who, as soon as he saw that Garson was eager, gave out facts in tiny doses since watching a man suffer and squirm alleviated his daily boredom. Nearby a drunk with a hanging lower lip was trying valiantly to peel a hardboiled egg, while behind the bar a fish flashed momentarily in the dirtiest aquarium Garson had ever seen. Greenish black water and yes, there really was something moving in there. Garson felt himself in the presence of life forms that might not survive till tomorrow, or would survive the Apocalypse.

"Ain't seen you here before," said the bartender. "Least not Monday through Sunday."

"No, no. The vehicle is why I'm here," Garson reminded. "The Cherokee!" The bartender acted puzzled, as if he'd already forgotten.

"Vehicle? Oh yeah, those wheels. So you might be interested, huh? You're not from these parts, are you?"

Eventually, Garson found out that Kyle Pederson was splitting with his wife and wanted to unload the vehicle because he needed cash fast.

"And he hasn't found a buyer yet?" Garson asked, his voice so excited it came out in a squeak.

The bartender left him to help the drunk with his egg ("Focus, Johnny, focus!") and when that was accomplished, moved to the end of the bar and began transferring bottled beer to his cooler.

Garson repeated his question in a loud voice, not hiding his anger.

The bartender looked back over his shoulder. "Two plus two, Einstein? Think it over."

Garson fairly ran out of the Blue Bird. Thus began his search, his increasingly desperate attempts to track down the Arizona turquoise Cherokee. He didn't forget the labrador puppies back home, but his calculation was simple:

if he lost as much as six hours for the round trip to go feed them, the Cherokee might get snapped up by someone else. A deal like this was too good to pass up! The dogs could hang on by themselves for a while.

How could he have known it would take five days to find his man? Cruising St. Petersburg and nearby small towns in his Camaro, he followed a trail of Cherokee sightings all over the county, several times just missing it. Kyle Pederson was a self-employed electrician so it was impossible to track him to a particular workplace. The phone company had disconnected his Yellow Pages listing. He was on the run with his new girlfriend, Stacey, Garson discovered from people he questioned. They'd holed up someplace. But where?

This much was sure: once Garson decided a thing, he was not one to give up. Each night after a long day's search he crawled exhausted into the back seat of his Camaro where he slept badly, scrunched in a fetal position. (What a contrast it would be when he had his Cherokee!) Each new morning he crawled out from a litter of crushed beercans, scratching his mosquito bites, in a fouler mood than the day before. Sometimes he prayed for help, promised not to cause trouble anymore, to anyone, if only he could have his Cherokee. Eventually, however, he was forced to admit that the trail had gone cold. He quit praying and did not hide his annoyance. "Even God is against me!" he moaned. "Jesus is messing with my business!"

Then suddenly he saw It. Recognized It immediately, parked in a little town called Melcher, a glistening metallic gem with a sheen as if It had just been licked.

Garson roared into the lot of the Git 'n' Go convenience store where the Cherokee stood. He scrambled out of his car and in his haste slipped and fell down but caught himself instantly and continued into the store where an air-conditioner blasted and a pimply clerk was putting Cokes and hot dog buns in a bag for a young woman in denim shorts and a tank top. She was the only customer in the store, and Garson waited eagerly to speak to her, shivering in the cool air, unsticking his sweaty arms from the sides of his shirt and picking bits of gravel out of his palm, his eyes moving down to inspect her shorts which he immediately identified as climbers, his imagination gauging (Garson was a student of buttocks). When she turned around he looked up, pulling his hair back from his face with a clawing motion, and asked, "Stacey?"

"I don't know you," she said.

"That Cherokee for sale?"

"Why, yes. It is. You interested?"

When at last Garson pulled into his driveway in his freshly-washed, waxed and vaccuumed Cherokee with newly purchased camping gear in back, he couldn't believe his eyes. Why all the police cars?

His first instinct was to slam into reverse, spin out of there. But cops in the front yard looked right at him. So he crunched to a stop on the gravel and gently stepped out.

"You know anything about these dogs here?"

"They belong to Jerry Renfrow," Garson told them, uneasily licking his lips, hearing a weak yapping out back. The policeman whipped out a pad and began to write the name. "What's—what's happening, officer?" Garson inquired. "I've been away on vacation."

Garson peered up at Jerry and Barbara's windows. *Barbara's*, he corrected himself. Jer's gonna be in jail for a good spell now. He climbed out of the Cherokee and went into the building, up three flights.

He rang the bell. He heard steps approach the door, then there was a pause during which he knew she was looking at him through the peep-hole.

"YOU! What do YOU want?" came Barbara's voice from the other side.

"I cannot tell a lie," Garson said. "I came to apologize."

The door opened several inches, and Barbara's eyes appeared above the chain.

"What do you mean, *apologize*? Apologize, *now*? Why didn't you just tell the truth in court? To hell with you, buddy. To hell with your apology. You sent a good man to jail."

Garson brought a thumbnail to his lip and bit it. He didn't like her talking this way. He felt bad that Jer had taken the blame but it wasn't as simple as she pretended. Nothing was ever as simple as people pretended. Actually, he felt that *she* was being less than honest. The way he saw it was this: When a person's ass's in a corner and there's no choice, no escape, just the whip coming down, how can you expect a person not to dodge? Was that reasonable? Of course he could see that she had cause to be upset—hell, he felt sorry, too, and would rather someone else took the whip than old Jer—but that didn't change the original predicament, did it? She could at least have a little sympathy for *him*, too. They were all grown-ups here, after all. Hey, he hadn't come to listen to this crap.

"Let me in for a minute," he said.

Half of her face was visible in the chained opening.

"No. If you have anything to say, you can say it right where you are."

Garson shuffled his feet. There it was again, that *tone*. His impatience began to mount. Actually, he didn't want to spend much time in her apartment, he saw entering as merely a preliminary step. They could say a few easy words, break the ice and then maybe, he told himself, she'd come out for a ride with him in the Cherokee. That was the image in his mind, a glorious flag flapping in the breeze: Barbara and him in the Cherokee. He would drive, they wouldn't even have to talk. Anything could happen.

The door shut in his face.

He knocked on it and when there was no answer, he mashed the doorbell with his thumb, several times, till he hurt his nail. Still no answer. Then he knocked again, putting more weight behind it.

"Go away!" she called.

He pounded. Eventually, the door opened a chain-length and Barbara said, "I'll call the cops!"—and to his surprise, another face appeared above Barbara's head.

"Listen, buddy, you heard her," he said. "She doesn't want to talk. It's time for you to go."

The door shut again, followed by a rattling of locks.

Garson was stunned.

Who was *he*?

His mind raced, and confusion began to transform itself into outrage.

Who was *he*?

Garson paced several steps, then returned to the door, stared at its black paint.

Why, poor old Jer had barely been sent up the river, and here was Barbara with some stranger. That was damn shabby, it truly was.

He knocked again, trying to muster the concentration not to strike the door too hard, for he most definitely did not want them to call the police. He was on probation, after all. Yet, it was difficult to restrain himself as the flush rose in his neck, a burn of indignation. Goddamnit, he might have to throw that fellow out. It was the least he could do, for Jer.

The door shook on its hinges while on the other side Barbara asked, "What are we going to do? I don't trust that guy for one second! He has guns and stuff—for all I know he has one now!"

Reggie said, "No, I don't think so. He looked empty-handed to me."

"You don't know him!" The knocking grew more intense, and they began to hear curses. "Even if we call the cops, he might shoot his way in before they get here!"

Reggie gazed through the peephole. "Ugh," he said, "That *is* an unpleasant piece of work." Then he turned toward the kitchen. "There's always the fire escape, dear."

She ran to the living room, grabbed her purse and turned off the lights, then joined Reggie, who opened the window for her. Barbara scissored out onto the iron grating—"I'll call the police from the street"—and Reggie followed, the persistence of Garson's blows audible behind.

A minute later Garson leaned his back against the door, panting, rubbing his hand, then let himself slide down to the floor. He reached forward to massage his toe where he'd kicked. He was disgusted with himself for having lost his temper. Now they would never open up.

A door down the hallway squeaked—Dan Haber peered out. "You fucking want something?" barked Garson. The door closed.

Garson limped downstairs and went across the road to where his Cherokee gleamed under a streetlight. He felt miserable, ready to cry. Nothing had worked out as it was supposed to. He climbed into his front seat and peered once more at the apartment windows. They were darkened now. He let out a grunt. "What are they doin' in there? Jesus."

He rested his head on the steering wheel, fighting back tears. His hands began to tremble. He looked up again, squinted through his windshield, his mouth puckering. His legs shifted uneasily and he slowly reached over to his glove compartment and groped inside.

Under maps and papers till his fingers found . . . *there.*

A pair of satiny panties shone slickly when he lifted them in the halflight, fingering, next rubbing them on his cheek, wiping them across his lips. Moaning. He inserted them part way in his mouth.

Soon he was rocking in his Cherokee. "Barbara." His voice came out muffled. "Barbara."

TWO

What Did You See?

One

Mr Nice Guy had never seen a penitentiary before, though once he'd gone to a drive-in movie about a prison population of atypically bosomy women in a humid Southern state. An inspector, a man with notepad and pencil and thick black-framed glasses, had come to look at the conditions of the inmates, who protruded through the bars in all sorts of unexpected ways, clamored for his attention and pouted.

"This is the stupidest thing I've ever seen," said Wendy, his girlfriend at the time.

Mr Nice Guy, young and dry-lipped behind the wheel of his mother's Dodge, nodded, admitted that it was stupid, but all the while kept his eyes glued to the screen.

Now, years later, he was going to see the real thing. Not just see it, but become a part of a system about which he knew nothing, and this time it would not be a fantasy penal projection, but a relentlessly material place. He felt premonitions of its reality in the form of a sickly prickling at the base of his spine like oncoming flu.

Of course, his arrest and trial on cruelty charges had been educational. The time spent in the county jail with thieves and drunks and druggies had prepared him to a point. He was becoming used to an indoor environment of lysol and crud, stale air and canned applesauce, and now a passing cockroach on the horizon barely attracted his notice. Yet the prospect of the penitentiary (the news of his sentence spread quickly among his county jailmates and won him, for the first time, respect)—this future, scared him. There was no longer a possibility of vindication, no element of choice in his life. Everything had been decided for him, and his opinion mattered not a speck. *What will I be able to do?*

At 7:30 a.m. he was hustled from a bullet proof van under drizzle toward a shadowed gap in a cement wall, his stomach burning with nervous anticipation of his entry into the penitentiary. But then he realized he was *already* inside. The vehicle had passed through the first barrier.

There wasn't time to turn his head or look around him, just enough to catch a glimpse of two towers and, on them, blue men with guns. The ground moved under his feet—the gap in the wall loomed. Entering it, he felt the same flex-kneed queasiness he'd known as a tourist when approaching other great American precipices, the rim of the Grand Canyon, the edge of the observation deck of the Empire State Building. Only this time, he thought, I've already fallen . . . .

He had expected the clank of doors but instead there was a hermetic rubber kiss behind him, like being closed inside a giant refrigerator. Then a quick clicking walk down the most ordinary of hallways, and up a staircase to a waiting room like an optometrist's, with lots of mirrors (but no magazines). He sat gazing at the reflection of himself between his two escorts, state troopers with smokey-bear hats. He wanted to go to the bathroom, but before he could speak up one of the troopers had opened a briefcase and started asking him questions, making sure all his papers were in order. "You had your tetanus?" he inquired. "You're not epileptic, are you? Have you ever had tuberculosis?"

Mr Nice Guy nodded or shook his head as appropriate, and the trooper checked boxes with his pencil.

Eventually a man in a jaybird blue uniform like a postal worker (though Mr Nice Guy had never seen a postal worker with a leather riot baton and shoulder-strap pistol) appeared and announced: "Sorry for the delay. Processing officer is on vacation, and his assistant's sick today. This is your lucky day . . . (he paused to consult a card) . . . *Renfrow.* You're going to meet the warden himself."

He led them on a circuitous hike through numerous refrigerator doors until eventually they arrived at a carpeted office where a surprisingly young man with a cleft chin sat reading at his desk.

"Mr Renfrow," he said without looking up.

"Good morning!" replied Mr Nice Guy, stepping forward to extend his hand, a gesture which caught the troopers off guard and prompted one belatedly to grab at Mr Nice Guy's arm, which threw him off balance and sent him with a bump against the warden's desk. The warden jerked his head up, startled, and in the same instant his feet pedalled under him as he rolled back his chair on squeaky wheels: ready for a scuffle.

In a second, however, the trooper saw that Mr Nice Guy's hand was empty, so he let go. "Uh, sorry," he told the warden.

The warden crinkled his brow and pedalled back, accepted the proffered hand, then told them to sit down. He began to read aloud from the papers on his desk. It all added up to five years and eight months, he said (or maybe five years and four months, Mr Nice Guy mentally corrected, and wondered once more about going to the bathroom but didn't dare interrupt). The warden soberly ran through the list, spoke of Punishment and Debt, then eventually reasoned his way into Transitions, at which he brightened a little, next gave some statistics, grew severe again, then gave some more statistics, and brightened once more. He looked very keen when he thrust his chin into a translucent red folder and explained about the penitentiary's new and innovative rehabilitation program which offered cosmetic surgery for inmates: volunteers were sought. If, after the Counseling Workshop Mr Nice Guy decided he was interested, and could formulate a worthy self-reconstruction proposal, his application would be studied most seriously. Mr Nice Guy listened and looked around the office, noticing pictures and mementos. One photograph in particular attracted his attention: it showed the warden in evening clothes with a dove fluttering at his fingertips.

"Do you have any questions?" the warden asked.

Mr Nice Guy pointed to the photo. "You do magic?"

"Yes, I do. Why?"

"I do magic, too."

"You don't say?" the warden answered, and flipped back through his papers. "It's not mentioned in your file."

He picked up a pen, unscrewed its cap and jotted a note. Then he looked up and his lips curled back into a smile. "If you fancy yourself one of those escape artists, though, you're going to be out of your depth here. *Hunh hunh hunh.*"

Mr Nice Guy could tell the warden was fond of this joke—probably used it often—so he laughed too. "No, I don't do escapes. I have a sympathetic silks routine with a goldfish bowl climax. I used to have a wrist guillotine, too, but it broke."

The warden nodded, unimpressed, but Mr Nice Guy managed to talk shop for a few minutes, trying to establish a rapport; he exchanged notes about manipulating doves, really the only way to go with today's snug-fitting clothes since a dove curled so compactly and calmly in your inner pocket, and fluttered in such impressive panic when produced (though a good dry-cleaner was hard to find). The state troopers looked at their watches as Mr Nice Guy and his listener speculated (the warden turned out to be as nostalgic as the next conjurer for the heyday of magic live-stock) about how much fun it must have been in the old days: think of it, when clothes were baggy and a vest with waistcoat and pochettes under your jacket were standard attire, and a fellow like the great Alexander Herrmann used to walk on stage with any number of rabbits concealed on his person, ducks too, once even a small deer . . .

At this point the warden got excited and reached into a desk drawer and took out a deck of cards. While he shuffled and rippled, he explained that there was a magic club in the penitentiary, and that the library had some first-rate books, too. From the way he handled the old pasteboards, Mr Nice Guy could see that he was a serious card man.

A card was chosen and somehow it ended up in the warden's pocket.

"*Hunh hunh hunh.* You like that one?" He replaced the pack in its box. "Here, take these. I'm sure you'll run into Manny Myler. He's on your cell block, one of the best sleight of hand men alive, and that's no exaggeration. He's had plenty of years to practice in here."

Now their interview terminated, and prison guards were called to relieve the state troopers. The warden told them that Mr Renfrow would go to Solitary Block 19.

"Solitary?" asked Mr Nice Guy, surprised.

"Oh, don't worry," said the warden with a wave of his hand, "you won't be alone. That's just the name, it's not solitary anymore. There are too many of you fellows! You'll be sharing with James Davis."

Two

THE GUARDS CHANGED him into a blue chambray shirt and blue canvas pants, two sizes too big. Then he was led through iron doors, which alternated with the refrigerator-type doors, and taken down several narrow electric-lit passages and concrete staircases. Mr Nice Guy, holding up his pants at the waist, strode forth without the faintest idea which direction they were going in, or which level they were on. He was lost.

An iron hatch swung open, bringing them into a tight corridor lined with rectangles of boilerplate steel. Each bore a curiously facelike flap that the guards swatted at as they passed and sent spinning. From behind these peepholes, on the other side of the steel doors, came a formless murmur of voices, then, once, a startling burst of human laughter. This sound instantly faded, now distant, reburied, as they moved away. Mr Nice Guy's stomach clenched, his bowels burned with nervousness. The guard behind him followed so closely that he had to hop to protect his heels. He skipped down the corridor till eventually the lead guard stopped.

"Here we are, camper."

A rattling of keys, the rectangle swung open. Mr Nice Guy stepped gingerly in, then quickly forward as the door *chonked* behind him, nipped at his rear. Keys rattled once more as he was projected toward a short, stocky black man who stood with his hand outstretched. Mr Nice Guy grasped the hand and jostled the man at the same time, so that his first words were "Excuse me, hi."

He'd expected the man to step back a little, but his cellmate didn't budge.

A moment later he realized the man *couldn't* step back, for he stood next to the wall.

"James Davis," his cellmate said. "How you doing?"

"Jerry Renfrow," he replied, shifting his weight uneasily. He wanted to clutch his belly but felt too self-conscious.

James pointed to a bundle in sealed plastic on a narrow ledge at eye-level. "They brought your stuff."

The ledge was attached to the wall with shiny new bolts. This, he realized a few seconds later, was his bunk. Another shelf with neatly tucked blankets protruded beneath. James' bunk. The space between the bunks and the facing wall was too narrow for two people to pass through. James stood just beyond the foot of the bunks, beside a tiny sink and an iron toilet. Seeing this, Mr Nice Guy shifted his weight again; his nerves were too much.

"I'm sorry, I have to use the bathroom."

"The bathroom?" James smiled. "Why, all you have to do is step out of the salon and through the recreation area, and you'll find it right there."

They brushed past each other, Mr Nice Guy's shin grazed the edge of the lower bunk; he caught himself against the sink. Then in great haste he fumbled to pull down his pants, and squatted. The iron toilet had no lid. Suddenly—oh my, no going back now—he was shitting loudly, with much air, and spattering contractions.

He tried to hurry but there was more, he couldn't stop yet. So *humiliating*; for the briefest of instants he lifted his eyes from the floor and noticed that James had turned his back and picked up a thin green book, pretending to ignore him—but the man's shoulders visibly stiffened. Oh, the embarrassment! And now Mr Nice Guy realized with panic that of course there was no window in this place. *Dear God, the shame.* He hadn't been in the cell more than 40 seconds . . . and look what he was doing! When at last he'd finished and wiped himself with furious speed, then pulled up his pants and flushed, he noticed that the water circulated in only the lower third of the bowl. Above that line (I am very sorry to dwell on these details but I must, for their importance to Mr Nice Guy cannot be underestimated) the toilet was still dirty in splotches. The back of Mr Nice Guy's neck tingled.

"James, I'm sorry," he said. "I'm not doing this on purpose. I guess I'm just so nervous, more than I dreamed I was. I feel like I could cry."

"Not me, bud. I think I could throw up."

Mr Nice Guy waited a few seconds, trying to think of a pleasant way to broach his subject. Eventually he queried, "Uh, in these situations I've found a toilet brush useful . . ."

James groaned. "You ain't from charm school, are you? Take some toilet paper."

So Mr Nice Guy unrolled a wad and cleaned the toilet with his hand. Now he felt sick himself. When he finished, and flushed again, he hurriedly turned to the sink. Then he stopped. His hands began to tremble.

"Uh—can I use your soap?"

James Davis climbed onto his bunk, lay face down. After several long seconds his voice came out low, muffled.

"Yeah. You better."

Mr Nice Guy apologized again, then tried to strike up a conversation and put himself in a different light, make himself agreeable. (He was a firm believer in the importance of first impressions.) He was actually a very clean person, he reassured James, in fact when he was a boy lots of people used to call him Squeaky, not because of his voice but because of his habits, he was so—

His cellmate sat up on his bunk and opened his thin green book again, interrupting the achievements of Mr Nice Guy's hygienic youth by reading aloud,

"Whenever two or three of you are gathered together in my name, I shall be there."

Mr Nice Guy tried to joke. "Well, if you don't think it's too crowded already . . ."

James didn't laugh.

"I see it better now," he said, running his fingers down his cheek. "Why you are here. The Lord has His plan and one cannot always know the plan and one cannot think he's ever gonna understand it, but in your case I think I see: in these hours of troubles the Lord sends a man like you. You are a test for me. And I will not curse you, no, I will not strike back at he who oppresses me. Let me shake your hand again." He got up from his bunk and gave Mr Nice Guy a firm pump. "Do you keep the Word of the Father, Jerry?"

Mr Nice Guy hesitated. "Like, God, right?"

"His Lord Yahweh."

James stared so intently that Mr Nice Guy felt confused. "I—I guess I try. Mainly I believe in being upbeat. What you'd call an optimalist. That's my philosophy. Optimism is too passive."

James scowled.

"Look where that brought you, man! Behind bars! To the den of outcasts to pay retribution to a society that spits on you. Optimalist! Sounds like chickenhead talk. Look where you are!"

James' burning gaze, his fierce tone were so commanding that Mr Nice Guy obeyed his last words literally. His eyes moved around, observed the surrounding gray on all sides of the cell, at bottom and top, too. This place was like being trapped inside a styrofoam beer cooler.

Panting slightly, he tore open the plastic-wrapped bedding on his bunk and started making up his mattress which was a thin layer of horrid-smelling galvanized pink rubber. James talked of the necessity of being justified in God's eyes. Talked of the heavenly elect. Talked of the rule of paradise on earth. Of the righteous life, no blasphemous swearing, no drugs, no blood transfusions. (Here he flashed a medal he wore around his neck.)

"You're a Jehovah's Witness?" asked Mr Nice Guy, managing to slip in a word as he climbed up onto his bunk, where he noticed that if he tried to sit up straight, he would crack his head on the ceiling.

"No!" said James vehemently. "Our brothers in the Jehovah's Witnesses have been misled by the *Watchtower*, and are at this very minute tempting the Lord. I read *Menetekel*." He waved the thin green book and started explaining the theological risks at stake, citing chapter and verse.

Then he began to quiz Mr Nice Guy. How many would experience Rapture? How many years of paradise on earth before the final ascension? When Mr Nice Guy knew none of the answers but guessed anyway—"245? 572?"—in an attempt to be agreeable, James grew peeved: "But *noooo!*" James told Mr Nice Guy his future for all eternity was in the balance and frankly, his prospects did not look good.

"I'll do what I can to rescue you!" James cried. "Surely that's part of the test!"

Running his hand along the porous, skinlike gray cement of the ceiling, Mr Nice Guy glanced at his watch. He had been in his cell for twenty minutes.

Three

LUNCH CAME AS a surprise and a relief. The keys rattled, the heavy door opened with a ridiculously tiny squeak. Mr Nice Guy sat up, promptly bashed his skull on the ceiling, then lay back, moaning. The guard shouted at him to hurry so he grabbed the edge of his bunk and rolled shakily down the side, staggering toward the door. "Move your ass!" the guard berated. "Go Go Go!" Mr Nice Guy lunged forward. No way was he going to miss this opportunity to leave the cell.

"You sure must be tired," James told him as they were counted and herded down the corridor. Mr Nice Guy rubbed his head. (Earlier, to make James stop talking, he'd pretended to fall asleep; then he'd actually fallen asleep, he didn't know for how long; and when he awoke he still feigned unconsciousness while James paced from sink to door, from door to sink, mumbling. Mr Nice Guy did not twitch a muscle for fear his cellmate would start rehearsing Armageddon again.) "Today we get to go to the hall," James explained as they marched in line. "Every other day they'll bring lunch to our cell. You see it's not big enough down there to feed everybody at the same time. Going to the hall is better than room service because you get to see folks."

When they reached the dining hall there was a familiar hum of voices and click and clink of plates and utensils, and, for Mr Nice Guy, a less familiar plenitude of black men, some with big shining shaved heads which Mr Nice Guy felt an impulse to touch. But he refrained: he doubted they would like that.

"Spaghetti!" was the word that went down the line.

Mr Nice Guy planned to eat at a different table than James—surely they'd be seeing enough of each other in the cell!—but after he filled his tray James pointed and said, "Go over there, Jerry." Reluctantly, Mr Nice Guy obeyed.

At the table men nodded greetings, but no one shook his hand. And no one said anything to James when he sat down and declared, "Blessed be this day, my friends!" Instead, they twangled spaghetti on forks and went on talking. Mr Nice Guy had the impression that James was not very popular.

In fact, just as he was about to break the ice, introduce himself all around, a man played a joke. James had closed his eyes and bowed his head to pray over his lunch, his lips making little smacks, and during this time an inmate took advantage and reached over to James' tray and filched his coffee cake. He hid it under his big hand.

"All right—who took my cake?"

James looked round the table. No one said anything. Mr Nice Guy wasn't sure what to do, feeling nervous yet at the same time a thrill of excitement. Taking James' cake was a bad trick, but he didn't want to be a squealer, either. Oh, he was in the thick of it, prison life!

"Branson, was it you?" James asked the man who took it.

"What makes you think that?" Branson replied, now lifting the cake to his lips, taking a bite, smiling at James with crumbs sticking to his moustache.

"You should not mock me," said James, but he did not retaliate. He silently began to eat his spaghetti.

Hoping to improve the atmosphere, Mr Nice Guy cleared his throat and announced, "Fellas hey. I—I'm Jerry Renfrow."

"James save your soul yet?" asked a thin white man near the end. He spoke with an accent and a high, bouncy inflection, the voice of a young girl. He had yellow teeth and pale, purplish lips as if he were deprived of oxygen—not merely the only other white man at the table but also the *whitest* man Mr Nice Guy had ever seen. His complexion was like aspirin.

"Are you English?" Mr Nice Guy asked.

The very white man sighed. "Scottish," he corrected.

Another inmate, noisily in-sucking saucy strands of spaghetti, asked between breaths where Mr Nice Guy was from; the extremely white Scot asked why he was in; and when he answered these questions, they reacted immediately. The pale Scot laughed and clapped his hands, the spaghetti sucker guffawed and managed to say "Crazy fucker" between swallows. At this point Mr Nice Guy smiled and turned on his sunshine machine, sweeping the table, hoping to make friends.

"I figure that since I'm here I might as well make the best of my time, learn what I can, get to know people from different walks of life. Follow current events more closely, maybe teach myself a foreign language. Have you got a softball team?"

For a few seconds the table was silent. All eyes were on him. (Did I offend someone? wondered Mr Nice Guy, perplexed. How?)

"Hey Myler, come here!" called a shaved-head man, waving to another table, "I want you to hear this!"

A lanky black man in his forties approached from another table, an unlit cigarette protruding neatly from his lips. Prisoners were not allowed to smoke in the dining hall and many had already hurried from their tables into the yard. Though Mr Nice Guy didn't know it yet, less than twenty minutes remained before he was delivered back to his cell, with no chance to walk more than four strides in any direction till his next meal. (And he'd been hoping they would have an indoor track where he could go trotting!) "What?" the new arrival said, as others made a place for him to sit down. He didn't look at Mr Nice Guy. "Who's the new meat?"

Mr Nice Guy noticed a red carton sticking out of the man's front shirt pocket, with writing on the lid: "**Tally-Ho**."

"You're Manny Myler!" he said.

The lanky man now turned his eyes to Mr Nice Guy. "I know that. How do *you* know that?"

"The warden told me about you! Said you were the best sleight of hand man alive. Would you show me something?"

Myler eyed him, pulled the unlit cigarette out of his mouth, licked around the unfiltered end, then reinserted it between his lips. He shook his head No.

But the others at the table seconded Mr Nice Guy's request—*"Go on, Man, show us something!"* till Myler relented. When he pulled out the deck James stood up, scowling, and left the table.

"People usually hate card tricks," Myler chuckled. "They know what's good for them."

What followed was a performance unlike any Mr Nice Guy had ever seen. Myler didn't do fancy cuts and shuffles like the warden. He just rested the pack on the table, divided it, upon which weird things began to happen. Queens jumped face up to the top, or reassembled beside the deck. You didn't even have to pick a card. Watching it was both bewildering and alarming, for there was no discernible effort on Myler's part. Aside from moving his cigarette behind his ear in order to talk more easily, he made no accommodation to circumstance and this indifference enhanced, somehow, the appearance of power.

"Believe your eyes, suckers, if you can stand it."

What a disappointment for Mr Nice Guy when the guards interrupted and lined them up to return to the cells. Why, he'd never seen such wonders on the outside!

Four

BACK ON HIS bunk he pulled out the deck of cards that the warden had given him and tried to work out some of the things he'd seen in the dining hall, but of course it was impossible. Eventually, though, I might learn some of those miracles! he told himself. I'm going to have years to practice. My time in prison could turn me into a first-class magician. Maybe I'll come out of here with a career change!

Then came James' voice, tight and dry:

"Cards are tools of the devil."

"Oh please, James, this is harmless, I promise!"

"You don't know that fellow Myler. You don't know the sort of man he is. The only way he can move himself to do something is because he believes in *nothing*. He can't teach you anything worth knowing."

"What's wrong with a little entertainment? It's just a game, that's all," said Mr Nice Guy. "Listen, cards can help us pass the time. We could have some laughs together."

But James would hear nothing of games. Oh, he'd had plenty of experience with gambling, he knew the temptations of flirting with Lady Chance, whether it was Poker or Two-Handed Pitch or Knuckleball or Red Dog—these were ongoing dangers! Even solitaire was a willful distraction of the spirit . . .

Mr Nice Guy was silent for a moment, his ears detecting a wishful note. Years of experience in the Personal Service field had made him sensitive to the gamut of needy tones and by his reckoning, James' level of misery corresponded precisely to his degree of want (the famous pain and desire synchronicity, which a specialist like Mr Nice Guy knew too well, as both a primal psychic gluepot and an underestimated macroeconomic force). In James' case it registered, oh, about 7.4 on the Desperation Scale.

"James, if you want to play with my cards," he said, "you're certainly welcome. Hey, I'll give them to you."

"*NO!*" he screeched, so that Mr Nice Guy jerked up, bumped his head again. "*I don't want to play with your cards!*" This he repeated several times and resumed pacing as Mr Nice Guy reeled and rubbed, and upped his estimate to 8.2.

"*Oh yes, you are here to test me,*" repeated James, "*But I won't, I won't, I won't . . .*"

"I'm sorry, James," he said, gathering up the cards, "I'm putting them away right now, I promise."

Yet this made little difference, for after the cards were back in their carton he didn't know where to put the carton. In the cell it was impossible to hide anything except in the most obvious places, and for the rest of that afternoon and evening, James zeroed in obsessively on the subject. "Fifty-two cards, enough for a fresh ticket to Hell every week of the year. One way, my friend! Four suits, one for each season. Clubs, hearts, spades, diamonds—graven images all. Oh you're sucked in, it'll be hard to crawl back up!" And so forth. How Mr Nice Guy longed for a window, so he could pitch them out! When at last it was time to go to sleep, Mr Nice Guy was grateful for the silence, though as he thought back on his first day in the penitentiary, a tight fist of fear formed in his chest.

This had been only *one day.*

His head throbbed in the dim half-light that passed for night in this place. He wanted rest but there was no rest here. Time stretched before him. Oh, the waste, the waste! Knowing made it all the worse. So much of his life lost—before it even happened! That was the perversion. Nothingness, *planned.* Maybe I'll go crazy. With both hands he reached for the rough ceiling above his bunk, pressed hard on the grit of concrete, forcing at it from where he lay. He felt entombed.

Struggling for breath, he clapped his hands over his eyes and tried to calm himself by imagining how the sky looked at this moment. The sky, the sky —

Black . . . wonderfully rich and black. Yes, that was better. A shifting surface, raining sheets and sheets of night.

He breathed deeply, more evenly, squinching his eyes tighter. Suddenly he saw a web of constellations wheeling. Dark plates and pinheads of distant fire. All this was conjured up from within: that was the only direction to look now. Time clenched and seized up into a ball, suspended too, trapped in his person. How big I am! With longing he thought of Barbara and felt another room added to his capaciousness, love there was place for—how much more space there was still! I am immense, he thought. I contain worlds.

He opened his eyes.

The cell came back to him in a wave.

He heard James move restlessly. The deck of cards beneath his pillow, Mr Nice Guy closed his eyes again and pushed, pushed on the ceiling as James rolled over again, muttering.

Five

Dearest Barbara, (he wrote)

My address is marked above so that's where you can write to me. I promise not to move (ha ha!). There's so much to tell you that I don't know where to begin, there's so much going on inside me despite the fact that nothing happens in this place—nothing is allowed to happen. Imagine walking around all day and you can only inhale half-way, and exhale half-way. You take these little breaths all the time and you start going faster and faster because breathing only half-way you can't get enough air, and this starts making you really nervous, and you have to think of something different fast or else you strangle.

I think of you. You are my air. Sometimes I say your name just to be saying it and I feel better, or I picture you in that lace blouse with the pockets in front, you know the one from last Christmas, and it gets me through. That is how I think of you now. (Note: here Mr Nice Guy was not telling the truth, for even when writing to Barbara the professional side of him intervened, the man who'd written thousands of personal letters under various guises. He mentioned this lace blouse because he knew it would please her—in fact, referring to it in this context might make Barbara cry. He certainly hoped so. Not out of mean-spiritedness, obviously, but to help her feel most intensely whatever affection resided within. Loving was the healthiest thing for a person, he was convinced. As for himself, what he really thought of and what made him miss her terribly were other images entirely, ones that he wasn't sure she would share as important, so he kept them to himself. He pictured Barbara in a dress that was now too tight for her around the stomach but which she still sometimes wore around the house and on one occasion at his bidding she'd peeled up to expose the crescent of flesh, soft and round and smooth, and they'd held each other, rubbed, held, and rubbed their cheeks and down below ticklish and delicious till with a suddenness and intensity that caught even Mr Nice Guy off guard, with a surge less from friction than affection he streaked her belly with a hot lashing of sperm. She did not look down, perfectly aware of what was happening, but in her eyes there was still something of surprise. How he loved her. How he loved her!)

Yesterday was bad, because I learned that I'm not allowed to have visitors for seven months. That means not till after Christmas! I can't stand thinking about it so now that I've told you, let's change the subject. I have a list of things to ask you to send me:

1. A calendar. You're not going to believe this but so far I've been marking the days on my ceiling by scratching a slash, you know like in the movies? My roommate James doesn't have a calendar because he's serving life and believes the world is going to end soon anyway.

2. My radio with the <u>*headphones*</u>*, not the other one, even if it's nicer. I need headphones. (This guy I'm with talks a lot.) And a bunch of 9-volt batteries, the square ones.*

3. A print-out of my subscribers' addresses, and stamps. Maybe if I send everybody a handwritten apology there won't be as many trying to sue me. The thing to get them to understand is that this is a DELAY in Home-Made Services, not a stoppage. That's right, I'm not giving up, and you should tell people who telephone. Tell them I'll honor all subscriptions five years, eight months from now, or maybe five years, four months, depending on the appeal. Just so they understand that I'm not trying to cheat anybody.

4. A picture of you. I save the most important for last. It's weird how already I'm forgetting details. Of course I remember YOU but when I picture your face and your body to help me breathe I work on the details, the very smallest, the pores of your skin, and those are what I'm already losing. (Note: Mr Nice Guy thought to himself that it was like death, forgetting the loved one who died more every day, but he censored his morbidity and did not share this sentiment with Barbara.) *I'll breathe easier with your picture.*

Well I'm going to wrap this up here, start a letter to Mom. Could you call her, remind her to use the whirlpool for her feet? She gets lazy about it. Say yo to the sapodilla for me, and thanks in advance for all this stuff I've asked for (don't forget the usual shipment of gum, but I know I don't have to tell you). If you're short of money, sell my van. There's no point in it sitting around.

I miss you, baby, I wish you were here and I could touch your hair. I miss you I miss you I miss you.

Much love, xxxxxxxxxx

Jerry

P.S. Spearmint of course. You know my needs.

Six

At the Secreast Museum, the tunnel which connected the basement of the Colonel's quarters to the caverns was a 20th century convenience. Originally the only access was through an opening in the cavern's ceiling, a jagged hole exposing blue sky above. The hole had long since been plugged with a two-ton wad of asphalt and chicken wire, and now electric light illuminated the caverns. One of Barbara's daily tasks was to check the 256 bulbs and spots strung to the ceiling or nestled discreetly among the stalagmites on the cavern floor and to replace any that were burnt out. It never bored her, for there was the pleasure of the hunt. Lately Reggie had accompanied her on the rounds, carrying a box of high-watt accessories.

"There's one," she said, pointing up. She stepped off the pathway and crouched behind a wet, slick boulder where a winch was hidden, and began to crank the string of lights slowly down. This system was a great improvement over the old days of creaky ladders on slippery rocks; now she cranked and the loop of lights descended like so many floating stars.

"Round and round and round," she said with the rhythm, "under the ground, the lights go down . . ."

Before long Reggie offered to take a turn, and she assented, rising and rubbing her arm. "Yeah. Feels like it takes forever."

In the 19th century, before this and adjacent caverns had been discovered and explored, and the deep and surprisingly spacious mineral bowels of the place electrified, the unplugged hole in the crust of earth above was the curiosity of the county. The land surrounding it was tilled or used for grazing, the nearest town still more than a mile away. A succession of farmers had tried to fill the hole because they found it a nuisance, a hazard, but no matter how much gravel and dirt and cow dung they dumped inside, it showed no sign of becoming full.

"Those were tough frontier days," Barbara and other guides recited at precisely the same point in the tour, *"times of scorching heat and parching winds, swarms of flying pests which descended on the land in a mile-long cloud and ravaged crops, devoured tree bark and even the clothes off a farmer's back. America without the niceties!"*

The farmers shoved and poured dirt and refuse but to no avail. The hole was a mystery. People started coming from town to share picnics on the site and to pitch rocks into the gap and argue afterward whether or not they'd heard them hit bottom. The hole also became the customary place for farmers to throw dead livestock, and children threw dead or not-dead cats; a bankrupt construction supplier got rid of his stock of lime. It became a public hole available for everybody and attained a certain popularity locally, though an itinerant preacher claimed to have stood on its edge and heard the screech of devils. Hubert Keyes, an eight-year-old boy who one day went missing, was generally presumed to have fallen into the hole, or been thrown into it by his soft-minded brother Abe, just for a laugh.

"Modernity came suddenly and irrevocably: Colonel Eli Secreast, retired, bought up much of the land in the county, including the hole, and decided to build a mansion nearby. A grove of walnut trees made the location very attractive."

The town council, though flattered that the Colonel had chosen this area for his retirement, tried to discourage him against constructing so close to the hole—wasn't it rash, potentially dangerous? And besides, people might be upset about losing their place to dump trash. They'd been doing it as long as anyone could remember: it was a Pioneer Tradition. But Colonel Secreast would hear nothing of doubts: "This orifice," he was quoted in the newspaper, "is a private orifice. Gentlemen, it is mine." Then, in order to dispel further speculation about the hole (and out of a personal distaste for mysteries), he announced his intention to be lowered in a barrel into the depths: he would see once and for all what was down there.

He bought two miles of rope. Many questioned the wisdom of such an undertaking, but no one could say that Colonel Eli Secreast was a man who settled for half-measures; and certainly he was no coward. A hickory-staved barrel was secured with a double noose, the other ends looped around a draft horse. Then the Colonel, still spry at the age of 72, hopped into the barrel, lit a camphene wick and barked at his men to send him down.

What he found, and left to posterity, was the Secreast Cavern. From base to ceiling it was 217 feet high, and almost twice that width. Inspired by the spaciousness as he wandered through the depths with his lantern, he likened the cavern to an underground cathedral; in subsequent explorations, accompanied by volunteers and members of the press with dripping tallow stubs attached to their hatbrims, he noted in addition to the small trash mountain from on high (which would later, when he willed it, be moved) what he thought were remarkable similarities between the cavern's mineral formations and a church interior. As grand—no, by golly, grander!—than anything he'd seen on his travels in Europe. Right here at home, in the innermost depths of the heartland! Soaring columns, stalagmites like organ pipes, a pulpit with baptismal font—and most astonishing of all, a calcite Virgin and Child.

A sign of divine blessing on this land, said the Colonel.

" . . . and the following Spring, in a candelabra-lit cavern ceremony with over 300 guests, including Sir William Brobst, the actor Guy Snodgrass, and Alexander Herrmann, vows were exchanged and the Colonel's daughter, Sylvia Rose, was married here to F. K. Zumstein, the fabrics innovator and inventor of the football helmet."

Next stop on the tour, Barbara impressed people with the stunt of turning out the lights. A flip of the switch, and the result was an inky blackness so complete, so utter and crushing, that you could taste it on the back of your tongue. Visitors were invariably struck silent, their voices shrinking back to their tonsils while the sound of drips prevailed, a *ptip ptip ptip,* the tedious liquid passage of the last few million years. In the unaccustomed dark they were subject to strange sensations, stirrings within their minds so that, weirdly, the distinction between without and within began to blur, and it was possible to experience a totally irrational flicker that told you the sound was coming from *inside your own skull*. Extremely disturbing . . . After a few seconds visitors began to talk nervously into the sightless space and giggle for no reason, unless it was to break the regularity, to escape how big had become the inside of their heads. At this point it was better to hit the switch back on without delay, otherwise people could lose their composure—they called out in surly tones to the guides, demanded an answer, some even broke into sobs, while children had a tendency to throw up.

Light. Eyelids fluttered, capable of taking only little swallows but drinking it in, drinking it in. Experienced guides knew exactly how long to hold out before turning the switch, when to shatter the depths with a spotlight. Visitors gasped and almost fell down when the beams hit them; it was good for tips.

"How about a break?" asked Reggie, putting down his box of bulbs and sliding his arm around her waist. They'd finished with the winch and had just repositioned the light at the base of the baptismal font.

"Sure."

Surrounding the font were long stalagmites with knobby heads. "Does seeing all these while you give tours make you think more about sex?" he inquired, waving at the forest of phalluses.

Barbara, who had reached down and removed her shoe, shook out a pebble.

"Hardly. That sounds like something a man might say."

Reggie shrugged. "I was only joking."

She jiggled the shoe back onto her foot, then stepped down on it. She looked up at the cavernous ceiling. "When you're down here, do you sometimes imagine yourself inside a big, big womb?"

Reggie craned his neck. "Well—no." He laughed, looking round. "Maybe I could, though." He moved a few steps away to another part of the cave, where it was damper. "I guess this place has it all, doesn't it?" He stuck out his tongue and waited to catch a drip from the ceiling.

"It's no different down here than up above," Barbara said. "It's just that sometimes you notice things more in the dark."

She sat on a bench. She wondered what Jerry was doing now. Reggie didn't turn around, but she heard his voice distinctly. "Barbara, did you notice I'm falling in love with you?"

Her reply didn't come till several days later. Reggie gave her a ride home from work and followed her up three flights of stairs to say goodbye. She couldn't invite him in because she had to deliver bags of epsom salts to her husband's mother. Barbara didn't enjoy this task, but performing it appeased her conscience. The string of pearls that she imagined connecting herself to Jerry would have to be very long, now that he was in prison, and a fear arose within her that if it were broken, all the good things connecting them might get scattered, rolling out of reach, maybe lost; the right thing to do was not to pull and stretch but to keep adding new pearls.

Reggie volunteered to carry the bags of epsom salts down to the van, and Barbara accepted. Yes, maybe that was the way it could be with Reggie: she could enlist him in a manner that wasn't against Jerry. He hefted a bag onto each shoulder, impulsively insisting that two were not too heavy, while she took the remaining one. By the time they'd gone down the stairs and reached the van, he was bent, panting, purple in the neck.

"You really shouldn't have taken them both," she told him as the bags thudded on the asphalt parking lot, and he propped himself for a moment against the side of the van. Laughing, she came to him and rubbed his shoulders. She did this spontaneously, and only a moment later thought, as she felt his arms: Stop lying to yourself, Barbara.

Seven

WHEN SHE FELL, she wasn't in the least surprised, though it happened too fast for her to catch herself. Her head grazed a table leg on the way down before hitting the floor.

Irene Renfrow cried out once, then lay still for twenty seconds. Thirty seconds.

The floor dissolved into darkness.

Eventually it ebbed back into her vision, shimmering. She rose shakily to her knees, then realized she couldn't stand. Grimacing, she started a slow slide across the floor. Unsteady as her feet might be for walking, now she used them as clubs, kicking at the surface and gaining what friction could be found. She pushed and kicked, pushed and kicked, looking back on her gradual progress. On the way she discovered that her head was bleeding. Dear Lord.

She stopped to rest in front of the coffee table where a letter she had started to Jerry that morning was laid out beside an old wrinkled envelope closed with three paper clips. She'd intended to send this to her son but now she snatched it and brought it to her lips. "Oh Malcolm," she cried. "Malcolm, I didn't think it would be like this!"

She reached into the front of her dress where she kept a handkerchief now removing it to mop blood from her scalp. Then, rather than replacing the handkerchief between her breasts, she dropped it and inserted the wrinkled envelope instead.

Her feet beat on the floor as she resumed her voyage.

Three minutes later she was finally beneath her kitchen telephone. Steeling herself, counting: "one-two-three"—she began to push herself up, up the wall till she was propped beside the phone. She reached over and grabbed the telephone receiver, then let herself slide back down, slowly.

Weeping a little, but not losing focus on the receiver, she punched 0.

When the operator answered, Mrs Renfrow asked for an ambulance.

"This is not an emergency services number," said the operator. "Dial 911 or check with your subscriber company."

"Don't talk to me about numbers, you jackass! I might be dead by then!" She shook with anger. "If my boy was around, I wouldn't talk to you in the first place!"

Now the operator was listening. He asked for Mrs Renfrow's address and received instructions that the back door was unlocked.

"That's all I have to say." She felt faint again and released the receiver, letting it swing on its cord beside her.

Waiting for the ambulance, she began to get cold. Tears resumed, and at one point she reached for her handkerchief to blow her nose but found instead the crumpled yellow envelope. Startled for a moment, staring at it in her hand, she then remembered. Her sense of neatness was offended by the bloody brown fingerprints on the paper.

"Oh my dear my dear," she gasped.

She lifted the envelope to her mouth and with clenched lips carefully removed the paper clips. She looked down into the envelope's contents, the fibrous, nut-colored powder. "Oh my dear."

She slowly and fumblingly folded the envelope so as not to spill any, then replaced it back inside the front of her dress.

I won't give it to Jerry just yet, she thought. I'll hang on to it awhile longer.

Eight

"You gotta watch yourself, Jerry. You're asking for trouble."

Mr Nice Guy looked down from his bunk at James pacing from the sink to the door, from the door to the sink. We are human pendulums, he thought. We exist to mark time. In three minutes (or 90 round trips from cell horizon to cell horizon) James would hop aside and it would be Mr Nice Guy's turn. Each turn lasted ten minutes. (He averaged only 20 trips per minute: less wound-up than James, he was inclined to saunter.) He did not answer James' remark for he feared another lecture about becoming one of the 144,000 heavenly elect, about being pulled up in the Rapture instead of following his present trajectory which was plummeting down, down to hell.

"In the time of the Rapture, my friend, some of us shall just disappear—iron bars and walls and guardtowers will count for nothing! One shall turn, and the other shall be gone! Which shall you be? Which?"

No, Mr Nice Guy didn't want to hear it again. He was weary of James' relentless talk, hour after hour in these cramped conditions, and wished he could trade his place to be with someone else, anyone else, didn't matter who, as long as he could have a change! Give him any of the men he met in the cafeteria, the assorted troublemakers and screw-ups behind bars for larceny or drug charges or worse.

Give him—start with the top of the list—a fellow like Marty Harris, who was amiable, always had something friendly to say, and wasn't even a criminal, really, just a man with a weakness for exotic pets, recently busted on manslaughter charges after his python had crawled into his baby's crib. Or there was B. T. Jefferson, an older, wizened man who was probably as innocent as he claimed, whose burglary charges were trumped up: the only reason he was entering so many houses on the sly was to get rid of surplus zucchini from his garden. "There was no other way!" he insisted. Or give him Donald Otte, a premeditating vengeance murderer, it was true, but also a possessor of good manners, in every respect a model of civility. A former assistant to the State Comptroller, a man with no previous criminal record (Rotary Club member, father of three), Donald had researched, stalked, then strangled the designing engineer of those little ventilation jets on airplanes that no matter how you turn or try to twist them out of the way, they blow on your neck and give you a sore throat. Donald Otte had had one sore throat too many.

Marty or B. T. or Donald—each a prince, compared to James! And make no mistake, Mr Nice Guy did not presume to be choosy. He would've branched out to someone like Chinny Weaver, who kept a navel lint collection in a beer mug, or Chinny's cellmate, who was said to be an eccentric; he would've even considered a gangster like Giles Galamenel, widely reputed to control several politicians and journalists and to have the ear of a top bureau police chief (his ultimate downfall, when agents with a warrant found it in his dresser drawer). In his most desperate moments Mr Nice Guy would've consented, even, to move in with the notorious Sambo, probably the most unpopular man on the cellblock and someone as argumentative as James but with whom, Mr Nice Guy reasoned—rashly, no doubt—the message would at least *change.* Finally, he could listen to a different tune!

Sambo was James' declared enemy. His uncompromising rival. An agitator who fancied himself a political prisoner, his animosity toward religion was one of his pet causes; in his mind, he was categorically against all systems, and had taken the trouble to print F*U*C*K A*M*E*R*I*C*A bumper stickers, plaster them on his car, his mailbox and front porch stoop. He started wearing an embroidered ballcap with the same message. Was this clear? he wanted to know.

After his house was bombed and his car smashed, he'd been charged with inciting a riot. Refusing a lawyer, he'd defended himself on the grounds of free speech. Lost. Now in prison he was framing his appeal and at the same time trying to legally change his name. He insisted that the others call him Sambo. Most people did because that was the only way to get him to shut up, for a moment at least. A white man from Mequon, Wisconsin, he'd been born Marvin Jansen.

Yes, Mr Nice Guy could even entertain the idea of living with *him*. In fact, he began to wonder if some of Sambo's contrariness was rubbing off. Yesterday, in the middle of one of James' harangues, Mr Nice Guy had suddenly snapped back, "Give it a rest, man! I got Holy Rapture comin' out the ying-yang!"

James froze in his tracks.

Mr Nice Guy immediately collected himself; he could scarcely believe his outburst—where did *that* come from? He apologized profusely. James, however, was not going to let the confrontation pass.

"Jerry, there is no rest for the Lord. No alternative to Rapture . . ."

James' hands waved excitedly, but in truth Mr Nice Guy's words pleased him. Though Mr Nice Guy didn't realize it, his usual conciliatory attitude and politeness irritated James, frustrated him to distraction. Give him a good head-to-head battle any day! James ached for a challenge, he was at the top of his form when the tone intensified. Yet previously, in response to crushing eschatological questions, Mr Nice Guy had merely nodded non-committally, shrugged or, on occasion, let out a low whistle. (What did that mean? What? James wondered, and paced faster . . .) Even worse from his point of view were Mr Nice Guy's answers, when finally prodded into theological discussion, his diffident *Gee-I-don't-know* and *Well-it's-hard-to-say* and especially, his devastating, perky, *Could-be!* Such replies unnerved him and threatened his ability to continue. They made him want to scream. In fact one day he did cry out and slap himself on the side of the head when Mr Nice Guy answered a battery of straight textual prophecies about eternal damnation with a little shrug and the words (which still echoed in James' mind, the horror): *"Okey-dokey."*

"Say something more!" James shouted at him. "That won't cut it, fella! You think the devil gives a hoot about your wishy-washy? Yes or no? Choose!"

"I respect your sincerity," Mr Nice Guy replied, "it takes all kinds of beliefs to make a world."

James wobbled, caught himself on the sink, and burst into tears.

But now, taking advantage of the slight leverage acquired after a real challenge had occurred, James advised him:

"If you don't watch yourself, Jerry, there's fellows in here going to hurt you. You do things and they read you wrong. Would've happened already if I wasn't keeping an eye on you."

Mr Nice Guy ran his fingers along the wool blanket on his bunk, down its flossy raspberry stripe, and tried not to listen. He wondered for maybe the 3000th time if this part of the blanket might be of a different fiber than the rest. (In the cell you had to find whatever entertainment you could.)

"I can't watch after you forever," James said.

Mr Nice Guy had no idea what he was talking about but was sure of one thing: he was fed up with James following him around during his precious time away from the cell.

"Nobody's asking you to watch after me. Why would anybody hurt me? I haven't done a thing. Nobody's even said a bad word to me."

"You have too done things! From the very first day, Jerry. Look at your clothes, how big and baggy they are."

Mr Nice Guy didn't need to look at his clothes. He'd studied them down to the number of stitches in the toes of his socks. "That's not my fault, James. These are the ones they gave me."

"But if you'd complained and insisted on having clothes your own size, then people would know that you won't be pushed around. You *accepted* those clothes, Jerry. It's a tip-off, everybody in here knows that they *always* test a new guy by trying to give him a fat man's outfit. Don't you realize the guards have been laughing at you ever since? And with guys in here it's like a sign around your neck, says you can be pushed around. It's dangerous, you better believe it. It marks you."

"Nobody's mentioned anything like that to me. Not once."

James stopped pacing and gazed up with astonishment. For the first time Mr Nice Guy felt uneasy. James' nostrils flared.

"You think they're gonna *tell* you, man? Make an announcement? Look: the other day in the yard, you let Willard move out of your way. Oh my dear Lord, I said to myself, you took his place! Scared me to death, too, when Catlin offered you a cigarette. I was sweating that you might not refuse."

"I don't smoke."

James groaned, threw up his hands, and resumed pacing, very fast now, back and forth. This was his shift into pinball mode, reserved for highly stressful occasions.

Mr Nice Guy said, "What's the big deal? Somebody steps aside. Somebody offers a cigarette. What's wrong with a little kindness in this place?"

"Somebody? That wasn't just somebody!" James exclaimed. "You don't *know* those guys, you're not part of their gang. There is no kindness for *you!* You accept something from them, even what seems almost nothing and the next thing you know it translates into something big, you listen to me now, Jerry, *big*—either you have to pay back with interest or you're marked open game and then you're going to get yourself beat up, I'm telling you the truth, you're going to get yourself dicked, dicked bad, it'll happen so fast you won't know what hit you. You hear me? Four guys at once and just in case you're the sort of fellow who might like that sort of thing, they'll stamp on your hands, and kick your sides in too, to make sure you won't like it. You'll know what it means for the first time in your life to wish you were dead."

Mr Nice Guy jumped down from the bunk, stopping James in his tracks.

"I—I had no idea. What should I do?"

"Just watch yourself! Stop walking that dangerous line. Don't take kindness from nobody unless you KNOW you can trust them, and right now the only person you can trust in here is me. Don't get friendly enough to look weak. I see you going over to speak to Myler in the library or you watch him perform—you're just asking for it, Jerry, just asking for it. You see that stuff, and your guard goes down." With the heel of his hand, James shoved Mr Nice Guy hard on the shoulder, almost a punch. "Listen, man, do you *have* a guard?"

"Sure I do," he said, and stepping back up to James, added, "Would Myler really harm me?"

For the first time since his arrival, Mr Nice Guy felt the stirrings of physical fear—a special tightness in his shoulders, a throb in the back of his head. His thumbs twitched at his sides. Myler was a transfer inmate who, previous to coming to Solitary, had been in The Pit, as the Death Row facility was called. Only the persistent efforts of anti-death penalty activists had gotten him sent up. And now, the rumor went, the political pendulum was swinging the other way and the State prosecutor might succeed in sending him back down. Apparently Myler frustrated both camps for he refused to take a side on the issue. A faithful patron of the penitentiary library, he told everyone he was still studying the question.

"Myler might not touch you *personally,* with his own hands, but that's just because he wants to protect his hands. It's his friends, some of the meanest, cruelest suckers in this place. Myler will associate with anybody or anything not because he likes them but because deep down *they don't matter to him.*"

"He's never been unpleasant to me."

"Of course not! Caring about nobody truly allows him to be nice. It's one of the most extreme forms of selfishness there is. You know it was his friends who messed up Little Rodney? You think the boy was always like that?"

Little Rodney was one of the sorriest figures on the cell-block, a slight, hunched young man with a twisted, clawlike hand that he clutched to his groin at all times. He rarely spoke and when he did, he was almost unintelligible and had a marked tendency to slobber.

James recalled, "When he first came here he wasn't like that at all. Just the opposite. He thought he was scrappy and talked big. It was the guards who busted his hand but the rest was done by Myler's friends in the showers. Labor Day weekend. They forced him to suck and when they did they broke his teeth. He's almost completely deaf now, too. They ruptured his eardrums. You can do that with the flat of your palm if somebody's holding a guy's head steady and you haul back, come down with all your might and trap the air."

"Jesus," said Mr Nice Guy, closing his eyes.

"Rodney's signed up for the cosmetic program so for all we know he'll come back one of these days looking like a movie star but you wouldn't want to go through what he did, would you now, Jerry?"

Mr Nice Guy shook his head slowly and climbed back onto his bunk, feeling almost sick. He took care, as he crawled onto his mattress, to duck for the ceiling. Bumping his skull had been his only physical worry until now. He probably remembered 99 times out of 100. Of course, there was always that one time, that one moment he'd forget or sit up in surprise and *wango!*—he cried out, for usually he cracked his head on the same place at the same angle, on a tender spot which was not quite healed from the previous forgetting, and golly, it hurt like the dickens!—but still, this was a private little accident, nothing like the brutality James described. Mr Nice Guy could exert some control over it, seriously hope to master it. A small but unmistakable stain on the ceiling above his pillow served as a reminder of his limits (and also as another of the cell's sources of entertainment, for, lying in his bunk, he stared for hours at the ceiling, like the firmament of his universe, with its one pathetic star, his own blood). Today, though, after what James had told him, the occupation of whacking the sore spot on his head seemed like a lost innocence, the good old days. Already he missed it . . .

Now his cellmate accused: "Yet you go out of your way to talk to Myler. You seek him out. It's like you want something. Why?"

Mr Nice Guy fingered the lump on his skull and lied: "Oh, I don't know why you think that. You must be mistaken."

James grunted and thumped the bedframe from below with considerable force. "I smell it. The floor is yours, fool."

So Mr Nice Guy slithered down yet again and took his turn pacing from wall to wall. This round he moved faster than usual, tried to escape in his mind by thinking of the wonderful trots he used to take through the Woland Gardens. Birds birds birds!

He resented James' words, the fact that his cellmate, with his severe intuition, had sensed the truth. He *had* sought out Myler, choosing him precisely for the quality that James condemned. Myler's zero expectations of the next fellow seemed to Mr Nice Guy an unwillingness to impose, a forbearance. Occasional abrasiveness was just the local manner. Myler's attention to detail, his sleight of hand with the smallest ordinary objects in the service of the extraordinary, available personally to *anyone* to see and wonder at—you didn't even have to speak his language, fellows like Jorge Peña exclaimed with as much amazement as anybody—were to Mr Nice Guy nothing less than beautiful. An intimation of the Optimal. With nervous eagerness he'd approached Myler at one of the study tables in the penitentiary library where he was a regular fixture.

Mr Nice Guy sat down and whispered, "Hi. How're ya?"

Myler nodded slightly but continued reading, sober, gold glasses on his nose and as silent as gravity itself.

Only when Mr Nice Guy touched his arm did the gold-rimmed eyes look up. They fixed on him, hard. "What're you reading?" asked Mr Nice Guy.

Myler looked up at the clock on the wall, and cleared his throat.

"Hangings."

"Hangings?"

Another nod. A paper with scrawled numbers lay before them. "You counting them or something?" Mr Nice Guy inquired.

"No, that's a conversion table."

"Conversion?"

Myler blinked, lay his book open on the table.

"Yeah, all this information is in meters and kilos. I'm putting it in the English system. You're so curious, how much do you weigh?"

"A hundred and fifty."

Myler looked down at the numbers, then scribbled a few more. "About Five foot Ten?" Mr Nice Guy nodded. A moment later Myler announced, "Then you'd need a rope about six feet six inches. That would be for a correct use of the long drop, break your neck, none of this strangulation bullshit. But you got to figure precisely because if there's too much slack in the rope your head'll come right off."

"My head?" said Mr Nice Guy. "Off?"

"It happens. There's no surplus of professionalism." Myler sighed. "What do you expect? People around here can't really be counted on to get it right, can they? Or do you think so?"

Mr Nice Guy found himself shaking his head. No.

"No point in fooling ourselves," Myler declared. "Sure, plenty of them would be happy to see a nigger swing, but they don't really know how to assume it. Are you aware that in this state they still put the knot under the right ear? Americans are still, to this very day, knotting under the right ear. If you can believe it. Small wonder they get maximum stretch and uncertain results."

"I—I never thought of that."

"Well, there you go. But we can do better, can't we? We can always do better. For a start we could learn from the past. We need to be *coherent.*" He reached forward and tapped the book in front of him with a graceful finger. "France back in the 1400s, say—they had competent hanging for the men, and the women they buried alive, for reasons of decency. Now you could be for it or against it but at least it was *coherent.* Yet not frozen in place, either: they were able to allow for the individual. There's a chapter right here on how one Madame Bajard petitioned at her trial for a hanging and in the end she won. They hanged her with her skirts tied tight around her knees. They adapted to the situation. Sure, nowadays we smile, but are we really so smart, are we going to get it together at least that much, I mean *structurally*? Talk all you want about modern changes—all that fuss about hiring a female hangperson in Kentucky—what I'm saying is that rules are all fuzzed, the point of departure is not clear. Everybody settles for less."

"Shhhhh!" hissed Sambo from another table, amid thick law volumes. "I can hardly hear myself think."

Myler blinked, picked up his book and resumed reading. Mr Nice Guy remained at his side, uneasy about bothering him with personal matters when obviously he was busy cogitating on bigger questions but on the other hand eager for his advice, now that he'd finally gotten his attention. He nudged Myler's arm again and confided in careful whispers about his claustrophobia with James, that even when out of the cell, he could feel James' eyes on him. "It's like having a special guard of my own who concentrates on me every minute," he complained. "It's driving me nuts. How can I get away?"

Myler eyed him, running his hand round his chin; he still had traces of acne despite his age, somewhere in the forties. Eventually he said in a thoughtful tone, "You could always kill yourself."

Mr Nice Guy gasped. Searched his face for a trace of irony, but found none. "I couldn't do that!" he exclaimed.

Myler pushed his glasses back up on his nose. "Suit yourself. But of course men in here do it all the time. We had two last year. Another the year before. They get forgotten and replaced by guys like you. Have you considered it?"

"No. No, I wouldn't."

"Well. Don't be hasty. Think it over."

Back in his cell with James, when he thought of this conversation he knew he couldn't repeat a word of it. James would just get upset. While he paced from wall to wall he replayed words silently in his head as James read aloud from the book of Numbers. They were becoming like an old married couple who knew each other's every move; but the longer they spent together the more impenetrable became the other's heart.

James was a convicted murderer. Mr Nice Guy found it hard to believe. Even though James shared the details (he made a point of confessing his sins), even though he made no attempt to spare himself, Mr Nice Guy listened to the man beside him with a sense of mystery. When James told of his crime his voice suddenly changed, grew so deep that he seemed to be talking from his stomach. There was no air in the utterance, just clenched pain. A baker by trade, he'd been in debt, he said, having fallen into a prison of smoke, consuming $150 worth of crack per day. One night, short on cash and starved for more smoke, he'd stuck up a Handy-O store. After dumping the register drawer's contents into a plastic trash bag, he'd opened fire with a .32 pistol, shooting the Handy-O employee and a woman customer who was standing by the milk coolers. On his way out he shot a peanut-buttered cracker display, too. "Totally out of my head, Jerry. I can't explain it. I had the money but I started shooting anyway."

The employee, fired on at short range, died on the spot.

When James revealed this story his eyes glowed and he nervously fingered the medal around his neck, but he did not weep. He told Mr Nice Guy that he thought of his victims every day. He'd entered jail an unbeliever but after serving eleven months and twelve days, he'd picked up a copy of *Menetekel*, an event which transformed his life. It was this experience, he declared, this encounter with the Word of Yahweh, not the earthly judge of the State, nor its jury, nor imprisonment, that had shown him the necessity of confession and atonement. He'd written to the Handy-O employee's family and to the woman he'd wounded, and had asked their forgiveness.

He'd sinned against Yahweh and sinned against his people, too, he said.

"Did they ever answer your letters?" Mr Nice Guy asked.

"Yeah. They don't forgive me. They hate my guts."

It seemed incredible: James, a *killer*.

Mr Nice Guy touched the iron door with his fingertips, spun on the balls of his feet, then paced back towards the sink. He reflected on his cellmate's concern for his safety and wondered: what does *he* do? He's hardly the most popular man on the block. "What's your method?" he inquired, turning around once more. "How do you get people to leave you alone?"

"I'm not afraid to die."

Nine

"PACK YOUR SUNTAN lotion?" Reggie asked.

Barbara nodded.

"Just wait till you feel that warm water!"

They were at the airport gate, standing in line to board their flight to Mexico City. From there they would take a bus to the coast, then a ferry to the island of Quiertolan where they would spend Christmas. Barbara clutched her carry-on bag of toiletries and her airplane reading, already regretting the weight of *The Memoirs of Eli Secreast* and deciding to concentrate on the thin volume of *Hablamos español.* As the line moved forward, she felt that this vacation island was merely an abstraction. The place was not real yet, would not be till she had set foot . . . and even then, it would take some time to register. In fact, Barbara suspected that she wouldn't truly experience Quiertolan till after she'd returned and gone back to work at the museum. The tropical sun would not be real till she resumed traipsing through dark, dank caves.

At first she'd balked at the idea of this trip. A tropical island with Reggie—it was so sudden, so irresponsible! Rash. But Reggie had persisted. "Sure we could do it! It won't cost as much as you think. Wait till you see the way the sun shivers off the waves, those big white rocks. Like ice bergs in the sun! Wait till you eat the lobo fish. I want to share all that with you. You *have* to be there, Barbara!"

It occurred to her, even in her initial refusal, that she could afford a ticket, if she sold the van . . .

The ferry chugged past a broken line of what looked like enormous human molars interrupting the waves, toward a coppery mountain rising out of the blue-black sea. The breeze loosening her hair, Barbara gazed up with fascination at the brilliant white washed houses with tiled rooftops which dotted the slope. She imagined the people underneath the roofs, families bent over kitchen tables, couples listening to music or making love on messed-up beds, children laughing and looking out the window at the reflecting sky or down into the bay where a ferry crawled in and a woman, a hand shading her eyes, gazed up.

Barbara had reached her husband by telephone the weekend before her departure. He'd sounded well, pleased with the headphones and De Jong gum she'd sent him. (One of the better gums commercially available, De Jong gum was a Dutch product which used Indonesian materials and eschewed synthetic resins like mannitol or sorbitol.) It was only toward the end of their conversation when their allotted time had expired and short beeps rained on their connection that she experienced both guilt and panic as she yelled into the receiver that she would call again on Christmas. According to penitentiary spousal quota, that was their next allotted opportunity.

"It will be our first Christmas apart in six years," he shouted through the closing interference. "In my heart I'll be up there at the Billy Hare Lodge with you."

"I know—"

They were cut off.

When they checked into their room on the bluff above the sea, in a hotel which clung to the side of the mountain like a barnacle, she was alarmed to see that there was no telephone.

"Isn't it terrific?" Reggie asked, waving his arm at the open blue window, the airy space beyond. "Look at that, will you? Doesn't it make you want to jump out?"

He spoke in a rush, consumed with plans for their adventure, even if on his trainee salary he had little means to pay for it. (Reggie was prone to impulses; he'd lost his job previous to coming to the Secreast because one day, with no prior warning, he'd taken an umbrella and cracked a senior colleague across the knees with it. The colleague had cried out, amazed. Later, he couldn't really explain himself. It was just something he knew needed doing.) For this trip, Reggie was substituting money with enthusiasm and plastic. This, he believed, was a matter of principle. He was in love, and knew he was in love, so wasn't it incumbent upon Barbara and him to make the most of it? Atmosphere counted! Wouldn't it be absurd to let something as impersonal as money lay claims upon their most personal emotion? Actually, it would be *wrong!* Yes, he had a moral obligation to cultivate, as best he could, their love. Toward that end, money should *serve.* The night before in the restaurant, smiling at her over the menu, ordering the wine—Mmm, why not that one? Bet it's tasty—then later waving her off with his credit card when she offered to pay her part, he'd told himself: There, that'll show *it*! Money had to know its place.

"It's beautiful," she said, moving toward the window for air, since suddenly she found it hard to breathe. When he came up behind her, slid his hands around her waist and began to kiss her neck, she turned and blurted, "I promised to call Jerry but I don't see any guest telephones. There wasn't one in the lobby, either. He's expecting me to telephone on Christmas Day."

Reggie dropped his hands, his face slack. "Hey. Well, you can call from the desk. Don't get excited. I'm sure you can use it."

Barbara instantly regretted her words; they had jumped out before she could catch them. Throughout the voyage to Quiertolan, each stage of the way, she hadn't once mentioned her husband. She'd tried to be protective of both him and Reggie, telling herself: if there's a problem, it's my responsibility.

She felt tenderness, yet curiously a portion of her consideration for Reggie, even the warmth of her kisses was also an expression of her intimacy with her husband, a ghost ever at her elbow, in the manner of a couple who've lived and breathed together long enough to start resembling each other. She had, in truth, been behaving like Mrs Nice Guy!

But now it was Barbara Oliver who reached out and touched his lips with her fingertips.

"I'm with *you*, Reggie. That's the here and now."

Reggie kissed her fingers. "We'll figure out the time zones," he murmured consolingly, "we'll call him right after his Christmas dinner."

She blinked. Through the window, tumbling in with the sunlight, came the sound of the breathing ocean, the snort of surf. He added, "Let's get you in the water."

The beach was impressive but tricky. Barbara stood working her toes into a shelf of sand and watched the waves roll toward the island, smash into the molars and keep on coming, faster, spuming and rising through the channels, so that her toes let go and instinctively she stepped back. The water finally reached her vantage point (safely, respectfully four inches deep), skating warmly around her ankles. Her lips parted with pleasure.

"It's like a big bath!"

When the water receded she pursued it, laughing, bouncing with short splashy strides. Already a convert, she ignored the swirling smash-up ahead and paid no heed to the hill of water surging toward her. She bent over and scooped handfuls onto her sun-pinkened arms. Reggie ran past her with his arms pumping, his hair waving behind him. The incoming swell crested and loomed above his head and the instant before it dropped and crushed him, he leapt straight into the wall of water, his long body piercing it like a spear. He disappeared.

A few seconds later he reappeared on the other side of the wave, laughing and flipping his hair back. Then Barbara saw nothing because the water hit her, knocked her off her feet. She closed her eyes and enjoyed the salt warmth engulfing her, rushing around her limbs, so relaxing, the motion. Eventually her head found the surface again and she inhaled and rediscovered air with a click of pleasure in her throat; now she began to swim and moved away from the beach with strong, spaced strokes, staying on top of the swells while birds creaked overhead.

Before long she swam back to shore to put on more cream. Barbara was wary of the sun. She was also a little nervous about Reggie, for she noticed that he wasn't a particularly capable swimmer, and that he underestimated the power of the water. She wanted him to stay out of the currents. She reached in her beach bag and pulled out a tube whose contents she applied to her skin with liberal splats. In the past, less than an hour on a cloudy day beside a northern lake had left her as pink as a shrimp.

A teenage boy came and squatted nearby, smiling as she smeared the cream thickly, especially on her face and shoulders. He was sandaled and brownskinned, the only local in sight.

"Buenos dias," said Barbara.

The boy replied in kind, then shook his head and laughed.

Her face was now a slick, milky white. The boy was staring at her legs, her breasts. "Adios," she said and got up.

From then on she enjoyed the waves while alternating the sidestroke, the backstroke, and to her relief Reggie left the water and began playing frisbee on the beach with some other tourists. Judging by their shouts, they were German. (So Quiertolan's not far off the tourist map after all, Barbara thought.) Reggie called for her to join them but she refused to leave the water, not only because of the burning sun but because she wouldn't like the way she looked running after a frisbee. Two of the players were long-limbed girls who chased self-consciously in their sling-shot bikinis, their high bottoms, it seemed, somewhere up near their shoulder blades. They walked like storks.

Barbara watched Reggie prance and show off, but could see it wasn't serious flirting. Mainly he loped and clowned with his catches. With some remove, looking at them impersonally, Barbara found the scene very pretty, the green disc soaring in the light, their bodies moving after it, interrupting the sun and the wind off the water.

Back at the hotel room that evening, before she showered and washed the seawater out of her hair, Barbara took a green cotton summer dress out of her suitcase, draped it over a chair, and looked at Reggie standing in front of the window with its view of sea and rocks. He spoke to her about dinner, but she saw him more than heard him. When he turned she noticed how much his back was browned, and observed the little ropy muscles there, the rising lines of his flanks, the small round of his buttocks.

She stepped up behind him, reaching round to feel his chest, his hard and smooth little breasts and nipples. She began to kiss his back and tasted salt there. He stopped talking. Her hands quickened their movements, now ran around the flattened drum of his stomach. Then up to his chest. She kissed his back again, and again.

Ten

"It's going to be a real wing-ding. Are you sure you don't want to join us?" Mr Nice Guy asked. "You got to break your routine, James! We'll both go nuts in here if you don't."

"Jerry, you know I can't participate when they'll have that music. And there's going to be a Christmas tree, what can I say? It's impossible."

James did not believe in celebrating Christmas. In fact Keepers of the Word were supposed to discourage anyone from observing this misguided rite. It distracted from a truly faithful allegiance to Yahweh's will.

On this matter, however, Mr Nice Guy would not budge an inch. He adored Christmas! He wanted to hum or sing along with those carols he listened to on his headphones. For Mr Nice Guy, Christmas contained the savor of all the happiest things on the outside, the color and fun of everything denied him in prison. How wonderful, those festivities! Religion was only a part of it—there were so many other sensations and emotions, too. How could James deny himself such joys?

"*Chestnuts roastin' on an open fire—*" he sang softly.

"Stop!" cried James, pointing at him, "stop!"

"But James, chestnuts aren't religious. You can roast them any old winter day. Can't I sing *that*?"

"You know very well it's mighty Christmasy. Don't fool with me, Jerry," he warned.

And Mr Nice Guy had to admit to himself that he would never want to sing about chestnuts, it was true, unless Christmas were attached. His foot began to tap (*Jack Frost nippin' at your nose . . .*). He clapped his hands on his knee to still the motion. It was hard to control himself.

And Barbara. Beautiful, beautiful Barbara. She and Christmas were indissociable. One seasonal memory repeated itself in his mind, of a time before there were any obstacles, before the troubles of the present were even conceivable. Lying in his prison bunk after brushing his teeth, smiling and rubbing a front tooth with his fingertip, feeling himself grow excited down low, he turned the memory over and over, like a gift so touching and precious that you can't bring yourself to put it down. A wintry afternoon before they were married. Their first stay at the Billy Hare Lodge, which was a series of train cabooses converted into cabins, parked round a frozen lake of polished black ice. Originally a rich man's folly, it had been intended as a fun hide away where his children and grandchildren could come visit him. They never came. Since then a pair of Dutch brothers had farmed the outlying lands and rented the occasional caboose to anyone who could find the place. Mr Nice Guy had found it, a perfect romantic spot complete with frozen waterwall. He saved it entirely for himself, undivulged even to the most love-adventuring Home-Made Services clients. That afternoon he and Barbara planned to go on cross-country skis to see the waterfall. He'd described how it was frozen, hanging crystalline in the air with a ferocious hush, each vein refracting the winter sun. They paused on the steps of their caboose to lace up their boots. They removed mittens, each of their breaths a vaporous toot, looking out on the snowy hills whose curves were interrupted by dark bursts of huddled pines. Barbara's hair was longer then, over her shoulders, her cheeks and forehead pink from the frosty air; she breathed with her mouth partly open, showing her teeth.

Sure, he reassured her, his cracked bones had healed enough to go skiing. As they talked, occasionally in the middle of a phrase she would flip her hair out of her face to look at him, and he told himself, seeing anew and more intensely her cheeks and the soft mound of her lips: My, how beautiful she is.

Lying on his prison bunk years later, he couldn't recollect what else they'd said—inconsequentialities, in any case—but he basked in the sensation of that distant wintry moment, for *then,* precisely *then* in his life, something had shifted. New territory had opened. Sitting on the edge of the caboose he did not want the conversation to end, did not want to lose this glorious anticipation; he wished his life could stick in that moment—Right There—in a sort of timelessness. He desired nothing finer than being with her like this. The snow's white bled a bluish tint, recent rabbit tracks went round the corner of the caboose. Yes, to stop: like the waterfall. And suddenly, with the vast winter emptiness his only witness, it occurred to him that she, too, was purposely prolonging this moment. She made no move to get up. With an amazing and stunning certainty he realized that *she felt the same way*. This was too much, his throat ached with happiness and overwhelming gratitude that he didn't know where to put.

Tears came to Mr Nice Guy's eyes at this memory. He pictured again how they'd leaned into each other on the steps, holding one another, their skis propped beside them, unused. Unnecessary.

"She's going to call me on Christmas Eve!" he told James, for maybe the twentieth time, then he caught himself (he'd used the C-word): "I mean the 24th of December, she's going to call me the 24th of December. I've put through a contact authorization for then."

"Good for you," James replied wearily.

For the Christmas Eve dinner he sat in the section reserved for his block. He shared a table with Sambo and Phillip Covay and Doc, the translucently pale Scot who always seemed ready to make conversation with Mr Nice Guy—because he was white, according to James, though Mr Nice Guy didn't believe that was the reason.

Doc was a real physician, in jail on malpractice charges related to a weight loss method he'd marketed. He was the closest thing to a celebrity on the cellblock. His product had enjoyed a brief craze for it required no exercise or change in diet. Rather, it depended on cutting a person's sleep to four hours a night and wearing few clothes in a regulated chilly environment to maximize the body's calorie burn-off.

"It really worked, the results are documented," Doc insisted, his hands becoming excited when Mr Nice Guy had asked him about it. "The only reason I'm here is the money drain, I couldn't properly defend myself because people kept suing me for side-effects. There are so many whiners in this country! It's a quarter of a million dollars for one case of bronchitis, half a million for pneumonia! And throw in the mental anguish of sore throats—I couldn't begin to pay it all off!"

At the Christmas Eve dinner, Doc offered Mr Nice Guy part of his turkey loaf and gave his cranberry ring to Phillip Covay after Sambo refused. As could be expected the holiday offended Sambo, but for other reasons, of course, than it troubled James; tactically, too, Sambo differed, and would not settle for a mere boycott. He saw it as his political duty in consciousness-raising to attend the scheduled festivities and, if possible, to keep anyone from enjoying himself. Tonight his mission encountered an unexpected difficulty in Phillip Covay's presence at the table—not because of anything Phillip said or did but because Phillip, a weightlifter with a pony tail, was also a full-blooded Chickasaw. This fact intimidated Sambo, unstrung him more than he could admit. (He was susceptible to genocide-envy.) For his part Phillip ignored Sambo. His interest in politics did not include Christmas. He worried mainly about his own criminal conviction and its seemingly endless process of appeals; he was another of the inmates who claimed his presence in prison was an accident. "All I did was buy a used refrigerator. How was I supposed to know there was a kid inside?"

At dessert, Doc offered his cellophane-wrapped popcorn ball to the table, and Mr Nice Guy took it gladly.

"You don't eat much, do you?" he told Doc. "I like these. My Grandpa used to hand them out on Christmas." Mr Nice Guy's eyes glistened at the memory. "He grew the stuff. So did his father before him. Popcorn farming is what my people took up when they came to the New World."

"Enjoy it then," said Doc, twisting sugar into his coffee. "Jesus."

"Why don't you stick that goddamn motherfucking popcorn ball up your shitbrained idiot ass?" suggested Sambo.

Mr Nice Guy looked at him, blinking. Slowly shook his head.

Then a guard blew a whistle for their attention.

It was show time! Entertainment was provided by the Good News Songstrels, a church group with acoustic guitars. On their portable stage stood a tree with blinking lights and foiled icicles and overhead a green garland festooned the concrete firmament—it was a good thing, Mr Nice Guy told himself, James wasn't here to see this! There was a flurry among prisoners when a box containing pine sprigs was passed around, which they laughed at, pretending it was stupid, but the lucky few who got a sprig held it to their nose and sniffed greedily.

Mr Nice Guy did not push hard enough to get one, so he went back and helped himself to a glass of non-alcoholic punch and sat on a folding chair near Phillip and Doc. The songs were beginning! The church group invited everyone to join in, so Mr Nice Guy sang along heartily, enjoying the chance to vent his pent-up cheer. After the second carol, Doc turned to compliment him on his tenor. Many of the prisoners, however, refused to sing and during this time looked around awkwardly, except for a man in the second row who squeezed his face in his hands and wept.

"Have a holly jolly Christmas
It's the best time of the year!"

"All together now!" called Melissa. Her hands left her guitar and she clapped above her head. She was the boss Songstrel. Mr Nice Guy clapped along, and like most of the inmates, whether singing, clapping, or crying, he gazed at Melissa's attractive plump blue-hosed legs.

Guards stood on the ready, scowls on their faces—it was no fun working Christmas Eve, Mr Nice Guy sympathized, noticing several with whom he'd struck up an acquaintance, which was possible when no one else, prisoner or guard, was listening. They wouldn't acknowledge him now but there was Pitcher, a farm boy with wire-rimmed glasses who bred prize-winning rabbits, and Luke, who'd been a college composition teacher before getting into the correctional system because that's where all the work was now. Mr Nice Guy would've liked to tell them, too, "Merry Christmas, guys!" But this wasn't possible in public. They hovered by the stage, guaranteeing the mandated 18 feet between the singer and the prisoners. Melissa had as much protection as a pop star.

"That was great, fellas!" She smiled at her audience. "Let's try another one!" A companion Songstrel, a young man in a white shirt and blue tie ("Hi, I'm Bruce! Bruce Gibbons!") started shaking maracas:

"Feliz Navidad!
Feliz Navidad!"

Mr Nice Guy's gaze returned to Melissa's blue legs, and he tapped on his breast pocket, feeling the phone authorization slip there. He looked at his watch. Soon he would gather up his popcorn balls and go talk to Barbara! He could hardly wait.

One hour and twenty minutes later Mr Nice Guy hurtled into his cell, propelled by the shove and curses of the guard behind him who whisked his hands for several seconds, muttering, then shut the door with a bang.

"Oh sure!" Mr Nice Guy yelled as he struggled to his feet. Keys rattled, then footsteps continued down the corridor. "Merry Christmas to you, too!"

James sat on the edge of his bunk, alarmed. "I can't believe my eyes. What in the world? What happened?"

Mr Nice Guy didn't answer but limped around the cell, his kneecaps throbbing. He wondered if he'd cracked them. He hadn't been able to break his fall because in each hand he grasped a popcorn ball, and his first reflex had been to protect them.

He tossed one to James. "Here, friend. I brought this for you."

The red cellophane crackled when James turned it over in his palms. "What's going on, Jerry?"

"I don't want to talk about it. That's what's going on. Let's drop it. Tell me about your December the 24th."

James' face, till now registering only surprise, suddenly shifted violently—his face was like a plate breaking—and his eyes began to run. "Well, to tell the truth it's been tough, Jerry. I just can't pretend: I miss Christmas Eve. I'm struggling with it. I think of my son Walter and how he and his mom are surely celebrating tonight—she refuses to hear about the Word—I think of Walter there without me beside him. And . . . I might as well admit it." James slumped on the edge of his bunk, tears streaming down his cheeks. "I want to give him a present. I can't help myself."

Mr Nice Guy, touched by his cellmate's pain, forgot his own for a moment.

"Oh, I'm sorry, James," he said. "I really am."

James shook his head, sniffling, and brought the reflecting red popcorn ball up between his knees. With a weary flip he tossed it back.

"Here. I can't eat this. It would be like eating one of your chestnuts. Or a candy cane. Oh Lord."

He lay back in his bunk, knuckles to his forehead, his chest heaving. Mr Nice Guy had never seen him in such a state. He hobbled over and pulled himself jerkily onto the top bunk, where he massaged his knees, then reached up and pressed the ceiling above him, feeling the grit of cement with the heels of his palms. Oh Lord indeed. What a night. What a pair we are.

Eventually James' voice, calmer now, drifted up, "You have a fight with your woman on the telephone?"

"She didn't call!" Mr Nice Guy blurted, rubbing his knees faster, "she didn't call! I don't believe it, James. I got my authorization, waited by the Incoming Line, and she didn't call. On Christmas Eve! And they hardly let me stay five minutes beyond my allotted time, those . . . *bastards!* On Christmas Eve!" A sob escaped him, then his tone became panicky. "What's happened to her? Maybe she's in trouble! *On Christmas Eve!* What's happened to her, James?"

He rolled on his side, grunting and groping under his pillow while James said slowly, "Maybe this is a lesson for us both. Think a second, Jerry. How would we be if we didn't pretend there was something special about today? Why, neither of us would be hurting. That's the source of our problem: treating this day as special. Lord Yahweh knows what's best for us."

But Mr Nice Guy didn't want to hear it. Already he'd broken into the rest of his supply of De Jong gum, which until today he had been rationing preciously: now he was unwrapping the remaining pieces and sticking them one after another in his mouth. His jaws worked mightily as the wad grew and grew, a quantity no casual consumer could have dared or tolerated. He chewed and chewed while James witnessed to him in the name of Keeping the Word, chewed till his jaw no longer obeyed and an entire side of his face quivered and the rest of his body seemed entirely detached; he lay back helplessly in the bunk with his mouth open, his hands and feet spasming, a numbness spreading in the lower back of his scalp. His eyelids fluttered, spittle trickled out of one corner of his mouth. Never had he chewed so much De Jong gum before! His awareness faded for a time.

Existence no longer pressed on him.

Eventually, images of Barbara began to flit before his eyes again, and he moaned when they faded to make way for the sound of James' voice droning on about the Rapture. He became aware that he could move his limbs and operate his fingers, so he reached up to his mouth, where he extracted the fist-sized gob of putty. He surveyed it for a moment with a hallucinatory sense of having somehow removed one of his organs. This was all that existed inside him. Oh, he couldn't throw it away! In this waking nightmare he unwrapped the cellophane of a popcorn ball and safely enclosed the gum-gob inside. Now the liberated popcorn ball loomed snowily before his eyes. The only thing to do, it seemed, was to eat it. He broke off pieces with his shaking thumbs. While James spoke of the New Tabernacle, he unwrapped and ate the second popcorn ball, too. Then he gripped his mattress, panting. He couldn't breathe. Sliding down his bunk, he staggered to the sink and stuck his mouth under the faucet, gulping water. Then he climbed back up on his bed and closed his eyes. As the popcorn began to swell in his stomach, Mr Nice Guy clutched his gut with an appalling sensation that he was going to give birth. He cried out in pain.

"Call Doc," he gasped, but James would do nothing of the kind. Instead, he stretched out his hands over Mr Nice Guy's belly, lifted his gaze heavenward, and began to pray.

The following day, Christmas (though neither of them uttered the word), his digestion was better. Now, however, as though their crises came in shifts, James' depression about his son Walter crashed to new depths. He bit his finger till a bubble of red appeared and stained his chin. He was eerily silent and refused to leave his bunk at lunchtime. Mr Nice Guy didn't think James should be abandoned in such a state so he cajoled permission for their lunches to be brought back to the cell.

Later, to his dismay, he discovered that sharing lunch with James meant they'd have to stay in all afternoon and miss the activities arranged by the warden for the holiday, including the all-inmate magic show. Myler had promised to perform Down's Eureka Pass and the one-handed Coin Star. Marvels he'd only read about! He banged on the door but no guard came to answer.

So he swung himself up on his bunk and tried to pass Christmas Day without thinking of Barbara. It wasn't easy. He unwrapped and threw the gumwad, hard as a stone now, into the trash pail where, from such a height, it landed with a resounding *jonk*. James jerked up on his mattress, "What? Who?" Then he groaned, let himself fall back down. Mr Nice Guy took the remaining red cellophane wrapper, then the green one, and for the next nine hours attempted to amuse himself by holding them up to the electric light.

Eleven

"WHERE IS HE?" Barbara exclaimed, fighting back tears. "Why isn't he there? Something must be the matter."

Reggie paused. "I don't think there's any doubt about *where* he is."

"But the prison switchboard said his name wasn't marked for today. And I insisted, I made a fuss, so they put me through to the telephone bank. They ran a request for him. But he wasn't at the call waiting room. *Not there*. It's not like he could forget, Reggie. It's Christmas!"

Another pause.

"I'm sorry, Barbara," he said, "I don't know what's going on. But it's pretty obvious that with a man in his situation, your relationship is going to have, well, limits."

He said no more, treading gently with his allusion to the future—*their* future. And though she often thought of this subject herself, she couldn't bring herself to speak about it now. It must be a choice, she told herself, it must come naturally. Not forced by circumstances. Again, in her mind she could hear Jerry's voice,

> *If I ain't so smart,*
> *There's always heaven above . . .*

That morning had been perfect. They'd eaten papayas on the rock bluff above the sea. They'd bought each other straw hats as Christmas presents to protect their faces from the sun. She stabbed a papaya with a pocket knife, and as the waves rolled in, Reggie bent over and licked the juice off her wrist.

"Merry Christmas, my love," he said.

"Merry Christmas, Reggie." She reached out and pushed back his hair with a spontaneity of affection.

"There is no reason that this should end," he said, smiling up at her.

Twelve

"GARSON, YOU'LL BABYSIT, won't you?"

Grumbling, he ignored his sister and went over to the refrigerator and plunged his hand into the freezer compartment, pulling out a carton of ice cream. He took it to the table and with a wooden spoon began to slap neapolitan into a bowl. There were people who ate ice cream only in summer, but Garson ate it in all seasons, a bowl every night, big frosty scoops: Christmas Eve was no exception. He needed his ice cream. So he sighed to see that his mother hadn't thought to stock up in anticipation of his arrival. The refrigerator was overflowing, yet ice cream had been neglected: there was barely enough for one serving. Tomorrow stores would be closed, and then what would they do? That was one of the things that pissed him off about Christmas: everything was closed, you couldn't do anything.

Connie stared at him across the table. Her usual beg and wheedle: Do Me A Favor. She'd painted her fingernails plum purple, and her hands shook as she lit a cigarette.

"Who you seeing?" he asked, though he already had an inkling.

"Larry," she replied straight out, and Garson looked over the spoon he was licking with surprise. Such honesty from his sister was unexpected. Instead of trying to cook up an excuse (she was an accomplished liar, the best in the family, everyone agreed), this time she included him in her plan. A new technique? Larry was her meth-gobbling ex-husband who by court order wasn't allowed to see the kids, though Connie herself still met him in secret.

"Will you?" she asked. "It's getting late. What time is it?"

Garson slowly lifted his wrist, then studied his watch. "Half past the monkey's ass."

"Cut it out. You always say that."

"All right, I'll babysit. You two goin' to midnight mass?" he asked, then snorted.

"That's right, you got it. Front row."

As Garson watched his sister put on her coat, something in the confident way she hitched her shoulders told him he was wrong to assume that she and Larry were going out to a bar where a juke-box played Christmas songs and they could get drunk and talk sloppy and sentimental about old times. No. They weren't stepping out at all. They were meeting someplace private to fuck.

"Bring me back some ice cream," he told her.

Her kids, Brandy and Travis, had been allowed to rip open a few presents in advance so that they would have toys to play with in her absence. Garson's mother wouldn't arrive before 2 a.m., when her shift at the hospital ended. He grumbled when Connie repeated her instructions about thawing the turkey. He didn't want to hear that. That was another thing that pissed him off about Christmas: when he came home people were always asking him to do things and if he said yes they took advantage and asked him to do something else.

In fact, he'd planned to be out West by now, maybe in a cabin high in the mountains, just him and the occasional caribou. But a judge had nailed his tail to the floor. He was on probation for the unregistered weapons charges he'd got saddled with when the police had busted Jerry and he couldn't legally change residence to another state for six months. Many a morning he'd wondered if he should just hit the highway and flee, but so far he'd reasoned with himself, stuck it out. He was determined not to start his new life looking over his shoulder. He needed to save up more cash, too. Say, another 2000 volts. That wasn't easy, though he had plenty of ideas, fantasies—such as finding somebody comfortably wealthy, not rich and famous or anything but just comfortably *wealthy*, and sending that person a few anonymous death threats. Then shortly afterward he would appear at that person's door to propose his services as a bodyguard. Why, he'd get snapped right up! He could look the part. His experience with Jerry had taught him a few things about meeting human needs. He would be willing to wear a suit for this sort of job: he could see himself driving the boss's golf cart, eating ribs in fancy restaurants, sucking a cocktail straw poolside with a shoulder-slung pistol under his jacket. Cool. He'd keep the death threats coming, and once he'd learned personal details of his employer's life, would be able to choose ways to make them especially unnerving, really fucking scary. Then he could ask for a raise. Actually, if he could break into a situation like that he would be willing to postpone going West for a while.

Luck wasn't on his side though; Jerry's incarceration had been a blow, had stopped his regular paycheck. For the time being, his connections with the comfortably wealthy were, he had to admit, non-existent. He tried working for a roofing contractor for a couple of days but hated it—who could *like* carrying tar roof shingles up a ladder? Forty pounds each trip, and since your arms were full you couldn't hang on, you had to balance every step, rung by rung. Or else fall and break a bone. He quickly decided to punt that bullshit. Then he'd gotten hired at the airport. Initially he'd fantasized a position on a ground crew, picturing himself astraddle an airstrip with flares in each hand, dispatching screaming jets all over the world. Inside a 767, a young woman pressed her face against the glass oval, watching him, her little waist twisting, straining against its belt. She turned back to the aisle, calling out, "Stop the plane!"

Instead they'd assigned him to the Duty Free Shoppe, selling booze and cartons of smoke and useless crap. Seemed easy enough. But before the holiday rush he got fired. He didn't know why.

Garson settled in front of the TV with his bowl of ice cream, but it was impossible to enjoy himself because the kids were making too much noise with their new toys. Sometimes they cut in front of the screen.

"MOVE IT!" he boomed.

Brandy started playing with her little brother's Robo-Man, so he cried; she held it above his reach while he jumped up and down like an excited little dog, becoming more and more frantic, actually convulsive. Garson watched them for a minute, then changed channels. That was another thing about Christmas Eve TV always sucked.

By midnight the kids had exhausted themselves and fallen asleep on the rug. Garson had gone out to the Cherokee and retrieved a bottle of vodka, switched off all the lights in the house and turned down the volume of the TV, so that the only illumination came from the screen's flickering and the Christmas tree's blinking. All was quiet. Sipping the fine burn of vodka out of a jelly jar he'd found in the cupboard, he became reflective. His mood improved.

Garson remembered Christmases past, mornings when his father, a baker, was not at work making cakes for other people but at home in the kitchen, making sticky buns for him and Connie. He recalled presents from his childhood such as a cap with earflaps which fastened under his chin and which he pretended was a football helmet as he ran headlong through snowdrifts; he remembered a new bicycle and how when the ice finally melted his sister had perched on the handlebars and they'd gone into town. He pictured how her big butt would never fit between a pair of handlebars now. He felt a twinge of melancholy at the thought of Connie's present situation, driving into town to meet a loser like Larry for a Christmas Eve fuck.

"On the other hand she isn't alone," he said softly, the bottleneck clinking against the jelly glass.

But he wasn't sad for himself. He slumped deeper in his chair and observed the colored twinklings from the Christmas tree on the heads of the unconscious children, and he began to hum. For the moment, he was happy.

Thirteen

ALTHOUGH IT WAS not a conscious choice, Mr Nice Guy felt himself hardening after Christmas. Barbara's telegrams from Quiertolan left him unsatisfied. Even after their misunderstanding about which day to call was explained, an annoyance remained about the fact that the rest of the world did not pay enough attention to detail. The world was wrong, he thought, with a peevishness he hadn't felt before.

A more particular resentment grew, too, in the form of a question: why, when others were playing volleyball on the beach (in truth Barbara had gone nowhere near a net, but that's how he pictured her, with her friend Meg from work, frolicsome)—why was *he* holed up in a windowless cage? While sand toasted the feet of the free, why were people like him trapped under cold electric lights in a vault of poured concrete? Mr Nice Guy acquired the concentration and singular focus of a convict. Questions of crime and punishment, guilt and innocence receded into the background, and the issue became: who got to run around in a wet bathing suit in the sunshine? Who did not?

His new prison job afforded little satisfaction. After reviewing the results of his psychological profile, the warden had devised a special assignment for him in the penitentiary's license plate division: screening requests for customized plates. Effective January 1, he was supposed to weed out the ones that might be construed as obscene. People were always trying to sneak something lascivious out onto the road. He was still waiting for a reply to his own proposition to organize a chorale, with barbershop quartet spin-offs, though his heart was no longer in it.

During this melancholy period he found himself once again seeking instruction from Myler in the library, who was busy with his own research. Mr Nice Guy's conversation was largely ignored, but at Myler's table he saw things he'd never troubled himself with before—photos of Cuban garrotes, a color layout of a very modern Californian gas chamber (a double-seater), and reproduced engravings of a Hanoverian breaking wheel and of a bare-breasted 18th century Turkish woman condemned for adultery being sewn into a sack with live cats in preparation for being thrown into a river. Mr Nice Guy lingered wistfully over this last image, for a moment recovering his former self, some of his old tenderness. One soldier held the sack agape while another grasped a cat by the scruff of the neck. Woman and cat looked at each other, mouths open. Mr Nice Guy wanted to reach out, touch the braid of her hair. He turned the page with sadness.

Myler explained to him in an even, scholarly tone that vises designed to crush the head, very popular in medieval northern Germany, were most likely an importation via the Holy Land and the Crusaders (taking into account centuries and technological development) of a practice originating in India, whereby the crushing was accomplished with the foot of a trained elephant.

"Golly. How would you feel about going that way?" asked Mr Nice Guy.

"You must be kidding. That's too circusy for me."

"Yet they do give the guys in The Pit a say-so," persisted Mr Nice Guy. "That's what I heard. What method would you prefer, if they send you down?"

Mr Nice Guy was referring to the Liberty of Choice principle that the new legislature had enacted for the penitentiary's death row, according to which the condemned prisoner, not a state bureaucrat, determined whether hanging or electrocution would prevail.

"That's the big question, all right. I'm still studying on it," Myler said. He brought his fingertips together, those fingertips that Mr Nice Guy had seen do the impossible, now in a position most humble. "There's no obvious answer. It's a fact you can't trust hanging. My lawyers managed to get me photos of the last job they did, they bungled it. And they still, after all these years, haven't got the bugs worked out of electrocution, either. That's maybe even worse. Strange, too, when you think how it happens at home, some guy plugs in his refrigerator—zap! short circuit—and he's dead in seconds. Makes it look so easy. But then they put some other guy in the chair, and there are cases where it takes ten tries, twelve tries, up to 20 minutes stopping and starting, restarting, till the job is finally done. Embarrassing, the motherfucker just won't die. And afterward everybody feels sick because his brain smells like burnt cake. That's why it's such a delicate business. How can you get enough, but not too much? The idea is to kill you, not mutilate your body—the people in charge are still uneasy about that. Because of course if instead of the usual 1800 volts they jacked it up to 3000, and why not 20, 30 amps, then it would all be over with in a second, no doubts or fooling around. All that would be left of you is a cinder, though, and that's the catch, they'd rather keep you presentable; it's very important to them that *even dead you still look like they do*. No, those people still haven't figured it out, no more than a good safe hanging."

Mr Nice Guy found his discussions with Myler edifying, for in addition to his growing numbness to horror, there was a practical side. He understood for the first time, after Myler's account of Edison and Westinghouse and their experiments of running high voltage through sheepdogs, the difference between AC and DC.

There were mornings, though, when he awoke and looked around him with alarm at the realization that his numbness also corrupted his relations with others, and as the day proceeded he sought to prove otherwise, only to catch himself trying to awaken emotions not with caressive deeds but by chafing, by being purposely abrasive. He would pick a fight with James. Once his cellmate squashed a cockroach running up the waterpipe, and Mr Nice Guy reproached him (not believing his words for a second but simply to antagonize the man), arguing that a cockroach shouldn't be treated that way, for it was a living thing, too, and had a soul.

"Get off it, Jerry," said James. "You can't mean that."

Mr Nice Guy shook his head piously. "Pity the creature."

This foray onto James' turf naturally could not go unanswered, and his cellmate cited prophets, chapter and verse, and waved *Menetekel* booklets in the air, in response to which his listener feigned incomprehension and defended the hereafter of the cockroach, and even began advancing wildly imprecise biblical exegesis about the case of the locust till James grew so agitated that his pacing became punctuated by little jumps. As he listened to his own voice, Mr (Acting Like An Asshole) Guy asked himself: Why am I doing this? Is this really me? What am I becoming?

Feeling ashamed, he suddenly broke off, exclaiming: "Yeah, actually I see what you mean, James. Sorry! Never mind the cockroach. You're right. Absolutely."

But this unexpected turnabout made James suspicious, so he continued. What Mr Nice Guy had uttered required at least 90 minutes of refutation before James could wind down. As a penance for his hardening, Mr Nice Guy listened without protest, and when James finally finished and retreated to his bunk and his books to find more examples, Mr Nice Guy took out his pad and pen and Home-Made Services subscribers' list and started another handwritten apology. Only 372 to go.

Fourteen

MASK OVER HER face, she counted backwards till she forgot to count, forgot to tense her knees. Then—at last!—they didn't hurt anymore and she thought of Jerry, so small that he fit between the bars of the tiger cage. Malcolm waving his arms. "*My God, how did he get through*?" The tiger approaching, tail rising and jerking, stripes rippling. The jaws opened, exposing pink. "*Oh my God*!"

The tongue licked round little Jerry's ice-cream-stained chin, then around the side of his neck and on his elbow when he lifted his arm for protection. He looked back over his shoulder, giggling. "Gee, it's sandpapery."

Barbara was thinking of Mrs Renfrow at the hospital as she held Reggie in her arms and made a mental note to send her flowers in the morning, probably gladiolus if she could find some, for she knew that Mrs Renfrow was fond of gladiolus. Then she could tell Jerry what she'd done.

Reggie was so close she could feel his breathing, the slow marking of seconds. She pulled him tighter still. Chin on his shoulder, she was glad he couldn't see her eyes. She didn't believe, in her heart, that it was necessarily wrong to love two people. Such things happened. But she also suspected that she wasn't a person who could do it well, that at the end of the day she was someone whose love wanted and needed focus. That's the way I am. Suddenly she let out a choking cry, for she could not hold it in and when he tried to pull back, asking, "What's the matter? What is it?" she resisted, struggling to hold on tight, refusing to let him see her face. What's going to happen to Jerry? she thought. She was a practical person. She told herself: My heart does not have room for two.

When Irene awoke, the white sheets, white walls drifted first closer, then away; then closer again. Eventually she remembered where she was. She did not hurt but she felt vaguely ill. Not herself. Eventually her vision focused better till she could see the room was flooded with daylight. Suddenly she could think of tomorrow.

She dreaded talking with Jerry and Barbara. She wanted to protect them. Why must they know? Why?

No longer was it a question of sheltering them from the world. All kinds of bad things might befall them, and some already had. But with her own age, and weakness, and sickness—it was above all age—the desire to shelter them had taken on another form.

She threw her head back hard on her pillow, tossing left, then right; she began to weep. Her hand beat at the blanket at her side. She wanted to protect them from seeing what the world was doing to her.

Fifteen

SEEN FROM A distance, the planet lurches with seasonal insouciance towards the sun. Trust me.

Sixteen

THE NEW YEAR brought with it reforms, part of the Back-to-Basics Crime Policy popular in the capital. No more television was allowed in the penitentiary, though James and Mr Nice Guy were unaffected by this measure since in Solitary there were no televisions in the first place. They did, however, get to attend the film projections brought in as a substitute. The first one was about an otter. Another reform was Mr Nice Guy's new job as license plate censor, and yet another involved a change in the prisoners' uniforms. The inmates shed their chambrays and were given traditional stripes. Chain gang units were being constituted, too (that was James' assignment), for shoveling snow and for replacing gravediggers who were at the time on strike.

When he was issued his new stripes, Mr Nice Guy noticed that both top and bottom were at least two sizes too big. And he remembered what James had told him.

"I can't wear *these*," he said, tossing them back on the counter. "Give me something that fits."

And to his satisfaction another, smaller, pair of stripes was pushed his way. As he turned to leave, a guard at the supply corps entrance nodded slightly. Pleased, Mr Nice Guy nodded back, and also at the guards he knew personally, Pitcher and Luke, who stood nearby. Then the guard at the entrance stepped over, clubbed him with all his strength across the knees.

Mr Nice Guy stumbled, cried out. The guard came at him again, and this time found his ribs. Two blows and he went down. "Move, asshole, get goin'! Get up! Get up!" Mr Nice Guy curled on the floor, gasping, and tried to gather his strewn clothes. The guard started kicking, and Mr Nice Guy rose as far as his knees, scrabbling through the entrance, dragging his striped top with him. The guard scooped up the bottom and threw it over his head in front of him. "*Move! Move! Move!*"

"Pitcher, help!" he called, "Luke!" and this was a terrible mistake, for up to now they had hung back, and not touched him. But when he said their names they came forward and pursued him on a stumbling, zig-zag course down the narrow corridor, punches raining down all the way.

At last he reached his iron door. (Never had it looked so good to him!) He stepped back, made room for them to unlock—and the guard gripped his shoulder, took aim, screamed, and clubbed him with all his might in the groin.

Mr Nice Guy didn't remember hitting the floor. Or even the door opening. There was very little aside from the pain, deep, deep within, no longer even physical, all the way to his soul. It *replaced* his soul, now.

Eventually, he woke up at the sound of someone crying. A few moments later he realized it was himself.

"Don't try to sit up, Jerry," James was saying, gently. "Stay put now." He noticed that he was in James' bunk, which confused him, until he understood that his cellmate hadn't been able to lift him to the top.

He tried to get up, then immediately lay down again.

"It's okay, man. Sleep. Sleep."

When he awoke again he didn't want to talk even after he remembered. He lay quietly gazing at the texture of the wall, the little pores there, the prison skin. James didn't know he was conscious till he gathered himself up and hobbled out of the bunk toward the metal toilet.

"You doing better, Jerry?"

"Uuh," he said.

He needed to go badly. He directed his penis, gave the push-relax to open his bladder, felt the buzzlike relief of the warm current leaving him.

Then he watched with horror as the stream turned from yellow to red. A choked cry escaped him and he stepped back, his flow now missing the toilet. The walls wavered, the corners of his vision shimmied. He fell in a faint on the floor.

"What are we gonna do with you?" asked James, holding a wet undershirt that he applied like a rag to Mr Nice Guy's scalp as he blinked. "You cut your head, Jerry. You hit the edge of the sink."

It was several seconds before Mr Nice Guy could respond. He didn't care about a cut on his head. "James, I'm pissing blood." He felt he wanted to sob but couldn't find the tears. He was too busy worrying. "Oh God I'm messed up."

"Now settle down. It's gonna be okay."

"I'm pissing blood! They got me, James, they really got me!" He bent at the waist, took the wet undershirt from James and pressed it to his face, wiping. Then he struggled to his feet, noticing that his pants were still undone, down around his knees; how humiliating. He pulled his pants up but didn't close them, and crawled painfully onto the top bunk.

"James, please, get me a doctor."

A silence. Then James replied, "I can't, Jerry."

"What do you mean you can't?" Mr Nice Guy moaned.

"Not at this hour. You don't know what time it is, Jerry. I'm sorry but it's really not as bad as you think. I've seen guys get it a lot worse. Run your finger in your mouth, check your teeth.

Mr Nice Guy obeyed.

"All there?"

"Yahhh."

"Good! I thought so. I tried to check earlier when I was making sure you wouldn't choke on your tongue but you didn't know it was me and kept struggling, got all turtle-snappy. Your face don't have a mark, Jerry, except for what you just did on the sink. And you *can* walk, so your insides can't be too jumbled. Listen, I've seen guys can't talk afterward, or even reach their knees. Think of Little Rodney."

"Just get me a doctor. I don't care."

James held firm. "Absolutely not. If we interrupt the guards on their rounds now they might serve you up another dose, finish the job. It's still your turn, you know. And frankly, Jerry, I don't think you can take it."

"But I'm pissing blood, James, blood!"

Now James grew impatient. "It's all cleaned up now, no thanks to you, you're not gonna have to look at it. Just hang on for one day, that's all I'm saying. See how you feel tomorrow, okay? If you go to the infirmary though, remember to watch what you say, don't tell them it was guards or they'll find out and then you'll really be asking for trouble. Just let on it was an inmate and they won't ask too many questions. Say it was me. At lunchtime we can get Doc's opinion about you, if you want. He likes you enough not to lie."

Mr Nice Guy had turned on his side and faced the wall, slid his hand down in his pants to cradle his bruised genitals. A few minutes later as James paced below, Mr Nice Guy, holding himself, got an erection. At least that still works, he thought gratefully, suddenly tearful, moved at the doglike faithfulness of his body.

"I remember when I first came here," James continued, "this was before I became a Keeper of the Word, back when I was getting into trouble a lot. The prison psychiatrists put me on Mellaril, which is weird stuff. When I would masturbate, there was no sperm. Of course they didn't *tell* you that Mellaril did that, that it shut down your testicles. I didn't know the reason. I thought I'd become, like, a ghost. Scared me to death, I'm telling you. Actually, it made me crazier, I got into all kinds of bad scenes after that! I mean, *nothing* came out. It really messed with my head."

Mr Nice Guy sobbed, his penis big in his hand, and asked in a muffled voice through his pillow that James be quiet. Now his imagination conjured horrible images of what might or might not come from him. He released his grip and wished the swelling would go down. Oh, this place ruined even the most personal things! Mr Nice Guy began biting his hand hard, for a supplement of new pain in a new locale. Eventually, that made his swelling go down.

The next morning the prison doctor examined him and said that the problem would pass. "No ski holiday for you though," he chuckled, scribbling out a work-release form and a prescription for Mr Nice Guy to pick up at the dispensary.

At lunch Doc looked at the prescription bottle, listened to a description of the symptoms, and shrugged. "You'll have to wait and see."

When this answer didn't satisfy Mr Nice Guy, Doc sighed and said maybe it wasn't too late for him to get into the experimental rehabilitation program featuring cosmetic surgery. Volunteers were now being screened.

"I don't need that, do I? What has that got to do with me?"

"Hey, it's potentially for *everybody*," said Doc. "According to statistics, recipients feel better self-esteem afterwards and, upon release, show a significantly lower rate of recidivism. They might do something interesting for you." He got up from the table, began to move away. "I wonder if I put in to have my breasts enlarged . . ?"

For the next three days Mr Nice Guy carefully took his medicine and endured the side-effects. His hands trembled; his head shook violently, and he experienced an alarming sensation that it had become partially loosened from his neck and could be stilled only when he wedged it in a tight, firm place such as by lying prostrate and clamping his pillow on top or standing and squeezing his skull in a corner of the cell. He found an unmildewed spot and pressed his face there for long stretches. This, though, was a pretty demoralizing way to spend an afternoon. James doubted the drug was only for his physical complaint and suspected it was intended to unwind him psychologically, too. After all, Mr Nice Guy had never experienced such bouts of weeping before. One moment he felt a clouding, the next he took a breath and tears suddenly covered his face. Another breath, more tears. He knew they came from inside him but how did they get out? There was something strangely mechanical about it. Another breath —

His only gladness was that it happened in James' company, that Barbara couldn't see him this way. The first day his urine cleared, he stopped taking the medicine. And shortly thereafter the trembling stopped. James encouraged him in this decision. "Drugs sure can mess up the creation. Even for a white fella like you."

"Of course," said Mr Nice Guy, touching his chin. Confirming, with satisfaction, that it no longer shook. "A drug doesn't care about the color of the skin of the body it's in."

James' eyes narrowed. "Still, it's different if you're white." He went to the sink and ran himself a glass of water, then looked down into it.

"I don't see why," said Mr Nice Guy.

"You wouldn't." He lifted the glass, drank, and Mr Nice Guy watched his Adam's apple skate up and down. He thought James was trying to ignore him, but eventually he continued, "A white boy does drugs, he abuses creation, the temple of the body. That's a sin against Yahweh. But a black user's more complicated. A black user sins against creation, against Yahweh, *and* against his brothers and sisters because to be an addict is to become a slave again, to give in to those wishes of white folks. It's the body failing the spirit *and* the people." Now he looked Mr Nice Guy in the eye. "That shows you how much I owe Yahweh, Jerry. Yahweh not only saved my soul but made me a free man on this earth."

"I don't want you to be a slave," said Mr Nice Guy. "You can't say that just because I'm white I want you to be a slave."

Silence.

"But I don't, James. I'm your friend. You can trust me."

James brought his palm to his forehead, and pressed. "Don't get righteous on me, okay? It's not only you involved, I'm not saying that. Listen, I used to buy the stuff from my own people, right? And I sold some, too, and that was just like in slave times in Africa you know, when the big traders had the help of the locals selling their neighbors. I even killed for the trade—both the man and the woman I shot were of my people. You have nothing to tell me about trust, my friend. Till the day I die I'll regret things I've done, and I'm not blaming anybody else for my acts. I assume them. You hear? But on top of the trade, Jerry, the ones running the big wheel, they're not from Africa, and you know it. You might not be one of *them*, but they are your people and I've never heard of you doing anything to stop them. What have you done to stop them? When are you gonna take responsibility for your people?"

"Hold it there! Just 'cause they're white doesn't mean they're *mine*."

"That's mighty easy, isn't it? You're no troublemaker, are you? You're even proud of it. But you know that suits them just fine? Lets them do exactly as they please? Mighty nice of you, Jerry. *Nice*, yeah—it's a sin of both pride and sloth."

"It is not. Don't talk like that!"

James glared, put down his glass on the sink ledge with a sharp rap.

"I'll talk how I please because I *am* a troublemaker, see? I make no excuses to anybody, white or black. That won't make me nice, that won't guarantee me a lot of friends but that is not my problem. When I tell brothers in here that they've sold their own flesh and blood, when I tell the gangs, you think that makes me popular? I don't give a DAMN about popular! When I tell white guys like you you're enslaving us, you start puffing. But what am I supposed to do, apologize for the truth?" He waved his arms at the cell. "My only bitterness is that I find my freedom *here*. It is not yet complete. It awaits the Rapture."

Such words caught Mr Nice Guy off balance. After all this time in the cell, after all they'd shared and been through together, James saw him in this light! The very idea stung.

"James, James. What about others? What about your son Walter?"

James had begun pacing, but now stopped in his tracks. His mouth twisted, his voice suddenly pitched lower. "Well, what about him?"

"Doesn't he have a future in this world before the Rapture? I think he does. I think he should! I know you're concerned about Walter. So am I."

Judging by James' glare, Mr Nice Guy knew he had touched a nerve. Quickly he continued, "You know the way I see it? When you get down to it, we're in the American family, I mean literally. You know how people in Africa are darker than you are, they're darker than most black people over here. There's been mixing. That old genealogical tree has many a twig! If you go back a ways, not that far really, we might actually share a common ancestor. Or at least an overlap by marriage and all the permutations before and after. Now I know that most of the mixing was done by rape, I'm not making excuses for the way it happened, but the fact that it DID happen is where we are today, and there's no going back on it. We might as well come out and say it: we're relatives, James!"

Mr Nice Guy hopped down from his bunk and approached him, held out his arms for an embrace. "Come 'ere, Cousin."

"Do you think," said James, standing stiffly, not lifting his arms from his sides, "that's supposed to make me warm to you?"

"I hear you, Cousin J!" said Mr Nice Guy, hugging, patting him on the back. "I know! It's something we got to work on, something that will improve. The way I see it, we have to rEenergize the mix, and do it the right way this time. There are so many hard feelings now because people feel no connection, no reason to bother. But your relatives you got to put up with. Thicker than water, you know! So I say let's go all out. Let's strengthen the family ties. We need black guys and white girls, black girls and white guys, hitching up: having kiddos! That's the ticket. Make us all even closer relatives!"

James freed himself from Mr Nice Guy's grasp. His voice came out a croak; it was as if his soul had coughed. "What makes you so sure black folks want white folks horning in? This is a time our people need more unity, not less."

"Why does that mean less unity?" asked Mr Nice Guy. "You know how most of the children will look—they won't be considered 'white.' This'll make your community *bigger. Stronger.* And by the time you throw in all the cousins and in-laws, James, we're talking a new unified America! Why, if Barbara dumps me while I'm in here (*Mr Nice Guy felt a stab at his words, the first time he'd allowed himself to admit this fear aloud*), who knows, maybe one day I'll be asking you to recommend me to some friends of yours. Hey, I'm not bad-looking, I'm reliable, my business was doing well before they threw me in jail. I wouldn't be such a bad match, would I?"

"You're nutso, though," said James.

"What about your sister Lucy?" said Mr Nice Guy. "You told me she was divorced. Is she pretty?"

"Cut it out, Jerry."

"Imagine if (*oh Barbara!*) I become a bachelor again when I get out of here, and me and your sister hit it off. And you know, one thing leads to another. We get married, and we drive up here together to see you on visiting days. Your son Walter and his Mom come over to our place for Sunday dinner, to visit Aunt Lucy and Uncle Jerry, and we'd write you letters about it. Pretty soon, you know, one thing leads to another and since my testicles will be healed by then, your sister and I have a bundle of joy! And in honor of the man we'll never forget, who made it all possible, we call him little Jimmy! What do you think of that?"

James sat down abruptly on the edge of his bunk, pressing his fingertips to his temple. His lips moved silently. Eventually he said,

"Maybe you are a troublemaker after all."

Seventeen

GARSON WASHED THE last of the shaving foam down the sink, toweling his face till it tingled pink, then reached over to the witch hazel balanced on the radiator, shook some out on his palm and commenced to slap his cheeks. *Smack . . . Smack . . . Smack.* This was a family tradition. As a boy he'd watched his father do the same every morning before going to bed after a night at the bakery. "Gets the circulation going, keeps a man handsome," he explained as young Garson looked up with his hand down the front of his pajamas where it invariably wandered till somebody reminded him: "Stop it!" (His nickname in the family was The Inspector.) His father, talking into the mirror, said: "You hit yourself (*Smack*) as sweet as you can stand." Other oft-repeated wisdom from his father was "The early bird gets the worm" (which young Garson had misunderstood, supposing it had something to do with his hands in his pajamas) and "You eat yeast, you shit slick."

Now the grown-up Garson contemplated his reflection with a feeling approaching serenity. Another new morning meant he was one day closer to freedom. One day closer to breaking the shackles of the State and going West. He would escape the past and start anew. He felt stronger and more confident every day. *Smack . . . Smack . . . Smack.*

Garson smiled jaggedly into the glass. People like Jerry and Barbara assumed his chipped front tooth was the result of a fight but that wasn't true. It came from being a lover. Maybe when he was out West he'd find himself a woman, too, someone better than the women around here. What he needed, Garson thought, was a nice girl but not too fussy. Was that asking so much? He didn't think so but Christalmighty sometimes it seemed like the tallest order in the world. The last woman he'd gone out with, for instance. Lindsey. Her parting words: "Listen, buddy, go take a flying fuck at a rolling donut."

Was that nice? He hadn't even yelled back, but just sat there and took it, too drunk to get out of his chair.

When he was out West, though, he'd find somebody nice. (But not too fussy.) Maybe he'd find someone good-looking, too. Even really good-looking—maybe the women out there weren't the same bunch of horsefaced skags he found out here, with butts as broad as barn doors. Maybe out West he'd find himself some sort of sex kitten. It might be possible, out there. You never knew. Actually, starting a new life, that's what he'd shoot for: a sex kitten. Why shouldn't he? America owed him one! The idea was exciting just to think about. And along the way, till he found her, he'd keep the door open for someone nice but not too fussy, someone who'd be understanding, and join in the fun when he brought home the sex kitten.

The last nice girl he'd gone out with was Donna McKinney. After she'd consented to share dinner with him, he'd lifted his eyes to the ceiling and thanked God, that old sly Dude, who maybe wasn't against him after all. Getting ready that night, he'd cradled empty space in his arms, holding Donna in his imagination. Pure joy! He'd stepped into the shower, rubbed his scalp with gusto to a furious flower of suds, lifted his face to the spray and begun to sing,

"Donna Donna Donna
I wanna wanna wanna

At that moment the showerhead fell off its mount and hit him squarely on the mouth.

"*Ahhhh*!" he screamed, jamming his hands to his lips, reeling and dancing under the rain, then looking to his feet in time to see a drop of white enamel go round once, twice, then down the drain.

He left the shower with soap still in his hair, and toweled off his body while tears rolled down his cheeks. Oh, it hurt: it *hurt*. He leaned over the sink and checked himself in the mirror, saw a new gap in his top front row.

"Oh no. Jesus, no."

She was expecting him in half an hour. He fumbled in the medicine cabinet for a bottle of aspirin, twisted at the top which merely went round and round—"Jesus fuck!" he cried, bearing down—then with a mighty crack the neck came off in his hand. This he threw in the sink, then shook out onto his trembling palm eight, nine, ten tablets, which he leveled into his mouth and sucked on grainily while he got dressed, struggling into a new white shirt bought for the occasion, sweat beading on his face.

Why now, of all nights? Oh God help me.

The evening was not a success. It pained him to talk so he uttered few words, all the while keeping his upper lip drawn down to mask his tooth.

"Why, you've hardly eaten a thing," Donna said several times. "Don't you like your steak? Aren't you hungry?" And later, "Are you mad about something?" She repeated this when the evening was over and she was getting out of the car.

"I'm not mad," he said desperately, leaning across the seat toward her as she shut the door.

In the museum rotunda Eli Secreast's memorabilia was displayed in glass cases, his scrimshaw collection and a diamond-shaped coal scuttle of his own design which he'd attempted to patent, his souvenir femur of Chief Black Hawk as well as valuables that the Colonel had purchased in Europe with the profits of his successful land dealings, including a Le Lanadou sundial and a medieval prayer book printed on the skin of unborn animals. Today Barbara and Reggie greeted Boy Scouts who filed through the museum doors—the third group already this morning!—boys with muddy boots whose winter campout had been ruined by rain and who came for lack of other distractions to kill time in front of Colonel Secreast's spoils. They sniggled, their breaths fogging the glass. In the close confines of the staircase descending to the caverns, the Scouts smelled like a pack of wet dogs.

Underground, they were even worse. They started experimenting with echoes, trying out wolf howls, with the exception of one quiet, concentrated boy, who was poised to fart. Barbara and Reggie endured and tried to hustle them through the tour as quickly as possible. They functioned on automatic pilot, rattling off information mindlessly. At one point when Reggie's group came up behind Barbara's, he was surprised to hear her announce:

"And here (her inflection rose as it had for these words at least a thousand times before) we have our famous Swooning Swan, an intriguing example of Nature's handiwork that astonished Eli Secreast the first time he spied it with his candle and which can still astonish us today. It took millions and millions of years—"

Then she noticed Reggie's discreet wave. The shake of his head. Turning partly, she suddenly realized that she wasn't in front of the swan formation at all, she stood before the wedding arch. She'd skipped part of the tour! She paused, coughed into her fist, and the Scouts looked back. Sensing something was up, they were for the first time fully attentive.

"Millions of years," she pressed on, "so you can hardly imagine the scope of its creation. See the swan's neck, the cut of its wings . . ."

And they seemed to follow her. She made them see. As Reggie watched her, he felt more strongly than ever: Yes, she's the one. I already believe.

Eighteen

My Dear Jerry,

I'm writing this before they put me under anaesthesia. I hadn't mentioned this operation in my earlier letters my poor boy because I'd hoped it wouldn't be necessary, I didn't want to worry you. But now the doctors say I have no choice but another operation because this diabetes keeps coming and won't turn around. It's hard to know how to say it.

They're going to cut off my legs, Jerry. I am not afraid of not waking up, I can accept that, I am ready to die now, if that is what the Lord wants. But I'm concerned about what will become of you. What place is there in this world for my boy? Have you learned? I pray to Jesus for the miracle of seeing you again before I go.

Now I've told you. I'm sending your father's envelope with this letter. It's yours now. I must finish. They will come to get me soon. I send you all my love my dear boy,

Mom

Upon reading this letter, Mr Nice Guy folded it up and put it in the front shirt pocket of his uniform, then immediately unfolded and read it again. It was too much for him to contain by himself. He read it a third time, aloud, to James who was doing push-ups on the floor, trying to keep warm, for the cell was indifferently heated. As he read, James stopped at the top of a push, angling his chin to look at Mr Nice Guy atop his bunk. He didn't reach the end of the letter.

James hopped to his feet.

"Oh my oh. Man, I'm mighty sorry, Jerry."

Mr Nice Guy lay back and pushed his hands on the ceiling, his muscles tense, as tight as stretched bands. "I should be there. With her. Not here, not here . . . "

James began to pace, then suddenly threw out his arms, tilted his gaze upward and prayed aloud for Mrs Renfrow. Mr Nice Guy heard the words and instinctively felt attracted to their import, yes, Yahweh, *Be with her. Please.* Though he remained silent, hearing the prayer somehow helped. James went on for over an hour—a strong man—and for the first time Mr Nice Guy was grateful for this Keeper of the Word.

Then they went for lunch, where Mr Nice Guy was unable to take his usual pleasure in the outing. He had little appetite and glumly cut his fish sticks while James took charge of the conversation, alluding to trials from heaven and eventually explaining to Ruben Benitez why the Pope wasn't *really* a Catholic. (Ruben disagreed.) James announced that the prisoners were suckers, almost to a man. Mr Nice Guy found such talk impossible, so he got up and moved away. He spotted Myler, and went to him.

"I need to talk. Come with me."

Myler's mouth moved down, his eyes grew smoky. "So you're giving orders now. *You?*"

"Hear me out," Mr Nice Guy said.

With a sigh, Myler got up and he and Mr Nice Guy joined the line to the canisters of coffee. (Kept tepid so that if thrown, it could not serve as a weapon.) This line offered the closest approximation to privacy. Mr Nice Guy searched for his words. "I got a letter."

Myler said, "You got a letter, and why should I give a jack jersey fuck? Why do you keep coming after me, man? What do you want? You're not good enough at manipulation that even if I wanted to teach you, which I don't, you could learn. You don't have the touch, or the drift, see? You're the sort of person who's still trying to pull a rabbit out of a hat. For real. Actually, it sort of blows my mind. I don't believe in magic."

Mr Nice Guy repeated, "I got a letter."

Myler drew himself up, and for an instant Mr Nice Guy thought the man would hit him. But he didn't; he merely helped himself to a paper cup and sighed, "All right all right all right. Let me guess. It's from your girlfriend."

"No, that's not it."

"That's not it. Okay. Spill. I'm tired of guessing. Speak."

"It's terrible. My mother—she just got her legs cut off."

The line moved forward; Myler glanced back at his table. Men were beckoning toward him. They wanted him to perform.

"Is that what you want to tell me?"

"Yes. And—I don't know, I was just hoping—don't you have something you can say?"

Myler pulled at the spigot. "Right. Right." When his cup was full, he turned to Mr Nice Guy, put his hand on his shoulder, and looked him in the eye. "Okay. Let's see. Someday, my friend, you'll look back on this day and laugh."

Then he walked away, chuckling.

Mr Nice Guy teetered, just as he had in court (it seemed a lifetime ago) when the judge had pronounced his penalty. Where are my friends? he wondered. Oh, where?

He stumbled back toward James. Though the man annoyed him continually, he was the only one he could count on. "Hey. Where are you, James?" he called through the milling crowd. There was a commotion around the table.

"Watch out, fuckhead!" called Sambo. "They're at him!"

He did not understand. Men pushed and scattered, going in opposite directions. A guard yelled and there was a line-up whistle.

Then he saw him. On all fours, curled up behind an upended chair. Panting.

Mr Nice Guy hurried over, knelt beside him.

"What is it, James? What happened?"

The whistle sounded again, insistent. The crowd had disappeared and they were alone. James did not answer; there was just the raspy sound of his breathing. Then he fell to his side.

"Oh, Cousin J! Dear God!"

This side of James' shirt was soaked dark, and the stain seeped broader, wetter, before Mr Nice Guy's eyes. James' lips formed words but he made no sound.

"Help!" Mr Nice Guy called, turning round. "Help!"

A guard shouted for him to get in line. A pool was beginning to form by the chair leg. Mr Nice Guy curled his fingers under the chain at James' collar and gave a quick jerk, breaking it, gathering it up in his hand as he stood, shouting back, "Get somebody! Fast!"

Nineteen

NIGHTS HE COULDN'T sleep. Alone, he spoke to himself—and answered. This was solitary.

Perversely, he began to be haunted by worrisome fantasies about Barbara. Was she thinking of leaving him? She'd given him no sign of this in her letters, and her visitation rights would soon begin—be thankful for that! he told himself—but doubts nagged him. His mother's situation remained desperate, though Barbara reassured him she was in the hands of a top specialist, and a few days later a short note from Irene herself arrived, declaring the amputations a success. "The job's done now," she wrote, as if in reference to a bit of handiwork around the house. And soon, she added, her doctor would treat her with an experimental technique involving zooplasty.

Mr Nice Guy wasn't sure what that meant, but the sound of the word alarmed him. He anxiously awaited the next day, when he would have a chance to look it up at the prison library. His poor mother, zooplastered . . .

That night he prayed for her, and at 4 a.m., still unable to sleep, feeling helpless (somehow it didn't soothe the way it had the time James was in charge) he picked up a copy of *Menetekel* off his cellmate's bunk. He found the same words that he'd heard James use. He was hungry for company, and in his mind he heard the voice. He tried by force of imagination to recapture its intensity.

He attempted one of the prayers in the magazine. Spoke to Yahweh about his mother and asked for help for James, too, who according to rumor had been helicoptered out of prison to a university hospital for treatment of his punctured lungs. "I have to do whatever I can," Mr Nice Guy reminded himself. Next he prayed to Jesus and Allah for good measure, for he knew that his mother was partial to Jesus and that James debated about Allah with other inmates, and he felt determined to leave no base untouched.

At the prison library the following morning, he hurried past Myler and Sambo reading at their usual tables, and went to the far end of the encyclopedia shelf, extracting the last volume. With a sharp intake of air he found an entry on zooplasty and focused his attention. The procedure involved, he learned, the transfer of animal tissue to a human being. His stinging, sleepless eyes grew rounder and he looked up from the page, blinking, for a horrible moment picturing his mother with grafted monkey's feet.

Oh no no no. He shook his head with sudden violence, forcing the image away.

His eyes returned to the text, reading it a second time. Surely the doctors knew what they were doing, he told himself. He sped through the article a third time, longing to squeeze more information out of it. Then, on the facing page, he noticed the entry on Zoroaster.

He plunged into the description of ancient Persia, of Zoroaster's precepts of Good and Evil. Oh, his mother needed a dose of Good now! He found himself breathing a prayer to Ormazd, as the article said Zoroaster used to counsel. Maybe Ormazd could give Jesus, Yahweh and Allah a hand. He would do whatever he could.

Throughout the following week, the news he received about his mother was not disastrous: her condition remained stable. He also learned that James had been transferred back to the prison infirmary. A good sign! He got permission to pay a call, and one afternoon approached James' bedside.

"Hey, cousin," he said.

James' eyes fluttered open. Since he'd been sleeping, it took him several seconds, his chin bobbing a little, to screw on his gaze.

"Oh—Jerry. It's you."

"How're you feeling?"

"Not too bad. They'll have me back in our cell in a few days."

James' voice was raspy, his face thinner. His hands looked strangely small grasping the edge of his sheet.

"That's terrific news!" said Mr Nice Guy. "I was really scared for you. You must be making a great recovery. Wow, huh? Home sweet home, eh?"

James nodded slightly. "Yeh."

"And I want you to know—I've been praying to Yahweh about you. That you'll be back soon."

"You have? You really have?" James struggled to sit up, wincing but smiling at the same time, balancing on his elbow. He faced Mr Nice Guy eagerly. "You mean that? You're telling the truth?"

"I wouldn't lie to you, James. You see, I picked up one of your *Menetekels*. Got the idea out of there."

"Oh—it is true! My ears! My joyous ears! A convert at last! So all this tribulation has been worth it. You've found the golden path."

"I'm doing what I can. After what happened to you and Mom, I started thinking more about these things. I was so alone."

James beamed. "Oh, praises be! It's wonderful!" He tried to lift himself further but then fell back on his pillow, gasping, "Praises be! Jerry, my friend. I have to admit that I had a lot of doubts about you but I was wrong to feel that way, I see now it was Yahweh's plan. Praises! You're the first person I've ever brought to the path. Do you know that? The first! This is one happy day!"

His head rocked back and forth, and his eyes glistened.

They chatted for a while, and James told him they'd proposed cosmetic surgery while he was in the hospital, they wanted to give him a nose job, but he'd refused. James also inquired about Mr Nice Guy's mother, and learned about the zooplasty. His face wrinkled on hearing this news. "Never heard of that stuff. But Yahweh's teaching is clear about not meddling with creation. Prayer is the only real answer, Jerry."

"Oh, I've been praying my buns off," said Mr Nice Guy. "I have doubts too. I've asked Yahweh and Jesus and Allah and Zoroaster, you name it. I've tried my hardest."

James started.

"Huh? What do you mean you've been praying to Jesus and Allah? And Zorro?"

"Zoroaster! With Ormazd, too." Mr Nice Guy explained his technique, how it made sense to him to get them all in on the act, pitching in, to make the world a better place.

"But you can't do that!" James croaked, struggling up on an elbow again. "We're talking Faith here, you're not in a shopping mall, man! You've got to stick to your faith, and I mean the true one, a keeper of the Word of Yahweh!"

Mr Nice Guy clasped his hand, tried to reassure him. "I'm not doing any harm. This is the optimal approach, this is for doing the maximum of good—"

"No, no! That ain't the way it works!" Now he fell back once more, this time clenching his fists to his cheeks, and began to pray aloud, his eyes open to the ceiling. "I said I'd forgive him, but it is hard, harder all the time. Help me!"

Alarmed at a sudden trembling in James' face, Mr Nice Guy wondered if he should call a nurse. A guard stood several beds away but didn't seem interested. James calmed, though, and closed his eyes. His lips still moved, silently. Mr Nice Guy squeezed his hand.

"James?"

He did not answer: only a long expellation of air, the profoundest of sighs.

"Maybe you should just accept me," said Mr Nice Guy. "You don't have to forgive me."

"After what you did that day?"

Mr Nice Guy did not understand. He leaned closer.

"What day, James?"

"You know very well what day! The day I was stabbed. When I was lying there."

"All I did was call for help. I got you help. I saved your life, James."

"You stripped me of my medal. That's what you did."

"That was for you, James. For you!"

"You gave yourself that power. They pumped me full of unknown blood to bring me back here. A sin, and on top of a sin, a mockery of me. If you hadn't done that, I wouldn't be talking to you now, continuing this pain and sorrow. When I was going, you know, I was so close to going—I felt myself leaving my body. Everything down here was so small. So small! I thought it was the Rapture. If you hadn't done that, I wouldn't be *here,* period. Jerry, I'd be home free."

Then he turned his head to the side and refused to speak any more.

Twenty

HER VISIT WAS scheduled for 9:00 a.m., and at five past, her purse freshly searched, she was escorted into a conjugal visit trailer. It was a little two-wheeled tin box such as senior citizen tourists pulled on the back of their cars to national parks. This one, however, had come to rest on a gravel strip in the heart of the walled prison complex. The only wide-open space was the sky above.

The interior was clean, the sheet over the thin mattress neatly folded; a NO SMOKING sign stared down from every wall. Yet the air inside the trailer was stale, and chill enough for Barbara to see her breath. Their visit was the first scheduled for that day and the bottle-gas heater had just been turned on. She did not remove her coat.

She sat on the edge of the bed and looked at her watch. Conjugal visits were allotted fifty minutes, of which seven had already slipped away.

A crunch of footsteps outside. The door squeaked on its hinges. Bent over, ducking for the aluminum lintel, he entered.

Barbara stood and they embraced—"Oh my poor dear," "Hi Raba"—then there was silence and they sat side by side on the edge of the bed.

"This is hardly our caboose by the lake, is it?" he said.

"No."

"Maybe you'd be more comfortable here? The mattress is less sloping where I'm sitting."

"No, I'm fine."

"Really? It would just take a second."

"This is good, believe me."

"But Barbara—"

"*No*, Jerry. Stop it."

There was another silence.

"I've waited so long for this that now it doesn't seem real," he said, looking at her, both laughing and sniffling a little.

"It is though, dear."

Her first impression of him after six months apart was to find him pale and unusually severe in appearance, probably due to his short haircut, and on second glance he seemed softer around the cheeks than she'd remembered him, definitely older, despite his striped uniform which, though surprising to see, looked simply childish.

"Those are quite the pajamas," she told him, tugging on one of his sleeves.

Mr Nice Guy rubbed his knees, and sneezed. "I know. Nobody here likes them. On some of the larger fellows they're especially unflattering."

"Don't get me wrong," she lied, "You're looking great, honey. Great. Honestly."

He clasped his hands in front of him for a moment, then slid an arm around her, pulled closer.

"It *is* cold in here, isn't it?" she said, trying to laugh.

Now sitting very close, they spoke softly. They remarked on the interior of the trailer, the framed reproduction above the headboard of a small deer in a sylvan setting drinking out of a stream. They discussed the condition of Mrs Renfrow, whom Barbara had recently visited. "She sends her love," Barbara told him. Mr Nice Guy nodded slowly.

"Barbara"—he threw both arms around her—"I brought mine." When he started kissing her, she began to cry.

"Oh don't, don't," said Mr Nice Guy. "Please."

They soon discovered that there were no tissues in the trailer, so they pulled apart and Barbara dug in her purse and eventually found one which they shared. After they regained their composure, they spoke more easily. She told him that it was now official, Home-Made Services had been declared bankrupt, so that ought to simplify some of their legal problems.

"I've almost finished the letters of apology," Mr Nice Guy told her. "Only 16 to go."

During their time in the conjugal visit trailer they did not move much. They just sat clinging to each other closely, occasionally kissing, often rubbing their cheeks together. This they did during pauses in the conversation, an altogether satisfactory substitute for words. "We'll get there," he murmured, "we're going to have our day at the Billy Hare."

"Of course," she said, not sure if he really believed it.

Suddenly there was a bang on the tin wall, and they jumped.

"Five minutes," a voice called.

Softly they repeated to each other several times that they loved each other, still clinging tight, till there was another bang on the wall. A guard poked his head in.

"Mrs Renfrow first," he said.

They embraced one last time, both thinking: the next visit will be in three months.

"Be strong," she whispered.

"You too," he said.

When she followed the guard, they met another guard waiting beside the trailer with a change of sheets in his arms. She lowered her gaze, eager to get away from this place.

Twenty-One

THAT NIGHT IN his cell Mr Nice Guy masturbated to thoughts of Barbara but the freshness of her image, the coconut scent of her hair, actually brought him sadness. He drifted off into a nervous sleep, uncomfortable bursts of sunshine in his brain making him toss and moan. His machine was backfiring. This image receded only to be replaced by the appearance of his mother. "Rub my feet, dear," she said. "Rub my feet."

"But I can't. I can't. You know I can't." A horrible sense of helplessness taunted him.

Yet she insisted, even as he fell to his knees and protested, reminding her, "Mom, you don't have any legs."

"I know that, silly. But these phantom feet are killing me."

So, dutifully, he grasped at space in front of her, and began to polish the air.

"Oooh," she said, "oooh."

He began to weep, his fingers gripping round the untouchable heels and ankles.

With a cry and a jerk, Mr Nice Guy kicked down his covers, rolled to one side. His eyes fluttered open, then closed again, and he thought: What a *horrible* dream.

There was the sound of footsteps pounding down the metal stairs. Muffled cries, growing louder. He rolled over onto his other side, his nostrils flaring. Cries and pounding. Then a BANG! in his cell as the door swung open.

"What?" he cried, sitting up, promptly cracking his head on the ceiling, lying down again, rubbing his skull, moaning. Oh, these dreams! He'd never had such dreams!

"Get up, asshole!" a voice yelled. Mr Nice Guy opened his eyes, blinking. "Get up!" A hand jabbed at him through his blanket. "Get up! This is our chance. Run, man!"

When he turned, the invader was already leaving. Light spilled in from the hallway. Yes, his door was open.

Amazed, he told himself: This Is Not A Dream. He slid down from his bunk, his bare feet on the cold concrete, and tiptoed in his underwear toward the opening. He heard shouts and curses in the stairwell, and several men ran past his door. Men in stripes—prisoners. He smelled smoke, too.

Smoke!

He poked his head into the corridor. To the left hung a haze, churning toward him. A prisoner emerged from the cloud and ran past with a yell as emergency buzzers began to whelp.

Mr Nice Guy hesitated at the threshold, thinking: Oh my, the guards are going to come down on us big time, once they get control again. But the haze approached his door, the fumes grew stronger and stronger, and he knew he couldn't stay there long. So he went back, hurried into his stripes, his boots, and before leaving, reached into his personal affairs to retrieve his father's moustache.

Reggie huffed and puffed, Barbara closed her eyes and ran her hands over her breasts, remembering Jerry's touch. It was like *that.*

Whope! Whope! Whope! went the buzzer as Mr Nice Guy climbed down the metal staircase. He heard a gunshot and immediately crouched lower. The smoke was thicker now. He lifted up the front of his shirt, pressed it to his face to relieve the burning in his sinuses. Presently he saw someone lying in his path—an arm thrown back, the twist of the torso—and knew the man was dead. He would've preferred to go in another direction but with the smoke behind him there was nothing to do but step over the body. Soon he caught up with several other men in stripes and followed them, though they didn't seem to know where they were going either, for they bickered in confusion and swore at each other. As the fumes grew denser they stayed close, each following the heels of the man in front of him. No one dared go off alone. The main thing was to keep moving.

But now smoke was coming at them from the other direction, too. Tears in their eyes, groping at the walls as they went, they stumbled on, while the temperature rose and heat rolled in waves. For several panicky seconds they stopped to deliberate about whether they should turn back, but the man in front declared that they couldn't, that this was their only way. So they continued, following him, and reached another set of stairs leading down, which they followed to another level, treading on several bodies in the process, whose softness underfoot made Mr Nice Guy shudder.

Oh, of all the pickles he'd been in, and by now he'd seen a few, this was certainly the worst! He pressed forward, wondering if James had been able to escape the infirmary. What about Doc and Myler's section? By now their numbers had grown: there were prisoners behind following *him* through the smoke. As if he knew where he was going! When the fellows in front paused, the line bunched and each man bumped into the man in front of him, hacking and coughing. The head of the line started pulling and prying on a hatch in the floor. Were they going *further* down?

No: as soon as the hatch opened, men began to emerge, crawling out like a stream of ants. The line cheered and coughed, prisoners clapped and hollered. "We got The Pit! We got The Pit!" Then they continued, shirts pressed to their faces, the smoke so thick now that it was a blind trek.

Dear God, he thought. Deliver me from this hell.

A nice feeling gathered in her, both high and low, and at the same time there was a constriction in her throat, an anticipation. Tears seeped quickly out of the corners of her eyes, running down each side of her face. Another slow spasm, and her chin trembled uncontrollably. She tossed her head from side to side, and sobbed.

"What is it?" asked Reggie, looking down. His hair hung over her.

Her mouth crumpled. She tried to pull herself free, for she knew what she had to say to him.

When they stumbled into the breech, passing through a sort of concrete rupture, eyes still weeping with smoke, the night air cut into Mr Nice Guy's lungs so wonderfully that he felt drunk. Gunshots went *pip pop pip* and seemed toylike, almost gnatty, insignificant, but all the while he kept low and greedily drank in the fresh air. Oh, it was wonderful! A helicopter reverberating overhead suddenly emitted a blinding beam of light: a voice horned from above.

In a few seconds, though, the P.A. system cut out with a squawk and the helicopter rose wildly to the left, for one of the prisoners in front of Mr Nice Guy had lifted a long barrel and started firing: tongues of orange spat into the darkness. Only then he realized that some of his companions were armed. There was a terrible sputter and screech as the helicopter tilted straight up, and in its haste to maneuver away, got caught up in electrical suspension wires. Now it pulled like a trapped insect till the wires suddenly broke and the helicopter swung violently in the other direction, careening straight into the prison wall with a scrape of sparks, then a cracking explosion—a blaze Mr Nice Guy felt on his cheek, a gargantuan firefly self-immolating.

Men raised their arms to the sky and cheered as flames rained down. They ran through the arch, Mr Nice Guy with them in the pack. On the other side there were cars waiting and Mr Nice Guy piled in with the rest, eight men on top of each other in a confusion of elbows and knees, doors flapping as they roared off into the night.

THREE

What Will You Do Now?

One

THEY GOT OTHER cars easily enough. The first town they came to, the first block of houses, two prisoners jumped out. The rest of them drove on and Mr Nice Guy, feeling less cramped than before, straightened his shoulders, unbent his popping knees, and settled in the back seat to get comfortable. Yeah, that was better. Drive on, pals! A few seconds later, though, the man beside him started punching and hauling. "You too, Jack, move it! Go with them. You're not coming with us!" The car stopped and they threw him headfirst onto a front lawn, sending him sprawling into tulips. "Adios!"

Tires screeching, they sped away.

Mr Nice Guy picked himself up and brushed himself off, stooping once to try and put aright a tulip he'd knocked over but it was no good; he'd broken the stem. The bloom drooped. It wasn't the sort of thing you could fix. In the streetlight dimness he could discern at least four he'd damaged that way, so with a guilty look in either direction he left the scene, walking fast.

He followed the sidewalk toward the two prisoners who'd jumped out of the car before him. They moved in the murky distance, darting from poles to bushes, running bent low across open yard spaces. They stopped at the front door of a ranch-style house encircled by shrubs and a moment later, Mr Nice Guy heard an ethereal tinkle of broken glass. One man cradled a gun in his arms while the other crouched beside him, reaching in and around a pane, groping. In a wink the front door was open and they pushed into the house, the man with the gun in the lead. The door closed. Everything was silent. The house appeared as before, offering no sign of what it had swallowed.

Mr Nice Guy grabbed the leaves of a bush in a neighbor's yard where he stood, and hesitated.

Gee, this could get bad.

He looked around, feeling exposed and conspicuous despite the shadow afforded by the bush.

Suddenly, offering an impression stronger than anything he'd witnessed this crazy night, a fragrance wafted to him on the breeze. Oh, what was that? He turned his head one way, then another. Then he shook the bush. Yes, right here. *Lilacs.* Oh my my my! He shook it again, and breathed deeply. It was fabulous. He took another long draught. Presently, he detected also the underlying odor of fresh dirt on his clothes, a delicious pungency from when he'd fallen on earth. It had marked him. This too he inhaled eagerly and let seep into his brain. His nose, after a stark prison diet of ammonia and human stenches, became an excited organ. It was Spring!

He felt as though he were waking up, though already perfectly conscious. Here he was on the outside, and with what timing! The darkness was full of blessing! How about that grass? He moved his head with the darting manner of a bird, to pick out its powerful presence, which was all around him.

Soon, though, the onslaught on his system was such that Mr Nice Guy felt as if his joints were coming unmoored. He reeled with a chlorophyll rush. Unsteady on his feet, he clutched a branch tighter for balance and lifted his other hand to cover his nose, calm his snifter. Lordy. So much sensation so fast was, despite its goodness, intense to the point of becoming uncomfortable. He let go of the branch. Across the street an empty lawn chair in a front yard yawned at him temptingly, and the idea of sitting in that chair was appealing indeed, in the velvet of the night, but something told him that if he did, if he sat down in his present state among the shapes of surrounding shrubs so voluptuous, he would not be equal to their beauty or his joy, and he might never get out of that chair again. Weaving up the sidewalk, almost sick with pleasure, he headed for the house the other escapees had entered.

The vestibule was unlit but the glow from several lamps in the inner reaches was visible as he slipped inside, silent as a moth. He passed through the darkness toward the living room and found several people there, awake. A copper-haired woman in a nightshirt and two children in pajamas huddled on a couch while one of the prisoners held them at gunpoint. The prisoner spoke in a low, threatening mutter, saying something about gasoline. Suddenly he whirled and leveled his weapon at Mr Nice Guy, who stood blinking at the light and squeezing his nose against the smell of new carpet. "Hey, no—wait!" Mr Nice Guy shrank but an instant later the other remarked, noticing his prison stripes, "Oh, it's you. You almost bought it! Next time, baby, why doncha knock?" He laughed, turned back to the family, now lifting the lip of the barrel just under the mother's chin. "Where are your car keys?" he demanded.

The woman answered in a whisper that they were in the kitchen, next to the telephone. "Go get them," the man growled over his shoulder at Mr Nice Guy.

But Mr Nice Guy did not move, for the sound of this voice froze him. Sobered him instantly. Could it be? In this place?

He *knew* this voice.

"What are you waiting for? Move, goddamnit."

Stiffly, he turned and walked off in search of the kitchen. His head pounded, his fingers twitched lightly at his sides as he recollected a time not so very long ago which seemed, nonetheless, like the piece of a lost life.

"It has to be," he whispered.

It was The Angel.

When he found the keys by the telephone, just as the copper-haired woman had said, he paused to collect his thoughts. The Angel! So much had happened since he'd last seen him, since those days of trial and confusion. And now he had returned. Mr Nice Guy swallowed. *They* had returned.

But why should I feel surprised? he wondered, dabbing his finger in the frosting of a half-eaten cake that sat on the counter. He noticed the family's ink-scrawled calendar on the kitchen wall with its eventful spatter of dates and appointments. Certainly the world hadn't changed, regardless of his presence or absence. It pursued its own ends, was still busy scratching itself. Even the advertising of the calendar's photo called out to him with meaning, for there was something affecting in its goofy crusade to persuade, with a kind of purposefulness alien to anything he'd experienced in prison. The photo showed a wicker basket overflowing with puppies, their open yappy mouths crying out in advertisement: *"99 PIZZA TOPPINGS!"* and *"FREE DELIVERY"* and *"I LUV IT!"*

He dabbed his finger in the frosting again (butterscotch), and his trained eye instinctively moved past the photo's shiny black dog noses to the handwritten notes on the calendar below, indications like "Abbie's birthday" and "Kim's dinner?" and "C-scope," sometimes with a squiggly arrow indicating a change of date, or another arrow branching off from the first, and introducing other corrections. The calendar was a *mess*, no doubt about it, and rekindled in Mr Nice Guy some of his old excitement for his vocation, the prospect of someone who could benefit from a few Home-Made Services. Yes, This World, unlike the place he'd just left, was an existence where people and commitments and rendezvous mattered; This World required choices, many choices, and you created yourself in your handling of even the smallest details—oh, how delightful—sometimes especially then!

Mr Nice Guy had to force himself to turn away from the calendar, for it fired his brain as intensely as the lilacs had excited his nose. (He'd already spotted a possible scheduling conflict for the 21st: immediately, he felt more alive.) He smoothed the butterscotch ridge along the border of the cake so it would look less disturbed then abandoned the kitchen, remembering an obligation of his own: a person oughtn't leave others alone with the armed Angel for too long.

I've got my own rendezvous, he told himself.

When Mr Nice Guy reentered the living room, another prisoner came tromping down the stairs at the same time and dropped an armload of clothes in a heap on the floor. "This should do it," he told The Angel. "Take your pick."

Hastily they shed their prison stripes and began trying on pants and shirts. Neither asked Mr Nice Guy to take a turn holding the gun while the other undressed. They did so right in front of the family, and it was not a pretty sight. The Angel's pale skin, the cream-cheesy flab of his flesh contrasted starkly with the eyebrows of black hair above his nipples and the thick patch around the navel of his wobbly gut. The other man was coffee-colored, with bristly hair on his chest, and his fat was more evenly distributed. Even so, he was able to laugh in agreement when The Angel remarked to the woman, about the looseness of the confiscated pants, "Your hubby must be one fat fuck. Isn't he? ISN'T HE?" The copper-haired woman drew her younger child closer to her, closed her eyes and nodded. The other convict threw Mr Nice Guy a baseball shirt, number 10, which he pulled over his head. The pants they gave him were blue wool, with a darker strip of cloth running down the side. A postman's pants. (He turned his back to the others when he put them on, trying, as much as the circumstance of holding a family at gunpoint allowed, to be discreet.) He gathered up the waist and looked down at his exposed ankles. Not only was the woman's husband stout, he was also short. Should he insist on better-fitting clothes?

"What'd you do with those keys, meathead? Hand them over," The Angel ordered, and Mr Nice Guy obeyed, judging from his tone that it would not be a good idea to complain about the situation, or what he'd been allotted. Even on the outside, it might get him into trouble. He twisted the excess waistline into a knot. Girding his loins.

"Sit closer together now, face this way, everybody," the other prisoner instructed, positioning the mother and children, as though arranging a pose for a family photograph. With a cut telephone line and an electrical extension cord he began to tie them up. He worked swiftly. "Closer, folks!" Then he applied duct tape over their mouths. "Steady—yes—there we are. Perfect!" He stepped back to admire his work.

"Thank you for your hospitality," called The Angel, moving toward the front door.

Mr Nice Guy hesitated, searching for a way to give the mother a sign, some visible hint that as soon as he got a chance, he would see to it that they received help. He might even have risked dialing 911 a few minutes ago if only that calendar of theirs hadn't cried out and distracted him . . .

"Let's roll!"

The other prisoner shoved him forward so that Mr Nice Guy was half out the door before he called over his shoulder, "All is well, believe me—"

Two

BARBARA HEARD THE news on the radio while sipping her morning coffee. Reggie had left in the middle of the night and she hadn't tried to stop him. One moment she was gazing vacantly into her cup, contemplating stirring in more milk, the next she sprang up, almost knocking over her chair in her haste to turn up the volume. The report spoke of a shoot-out, sniper victims, men at large. Barbara paced circles around the kitchen table, pensively slapping a teaspoon on her palm. Goodness gracious. This was serious. You never knew what the radio might sneeze out!

She did not want to give herself time to panic: she reached for the telephone and called the only prison number she had, but it did not answer. She let it ring and ring as she played with her hair with the teaspoon handle, whispering "Come on, come on." Yet she didn't really expect them to pick it up, either. Not during a prison riot.

"Be calm," she told herself. "He wouldn't go looking for trouble. Not my Jerry."

Next she called the police, who told her that dealing with inmates' families was not their role. So she tried calling the state correctional agency, and was passed to several services till amazingly, she got through to the state correctional officer himself—who, when they were first connected, seemed to be under the mistaken impression that she had called to *give* him more information about the situation at the penitentiary, not ask for it. When he realized his error, and that she was merely an inmate's wife, he excused himself immediately, and after a buzzing and a slow bleed of beeps, Barbara found herself stuck in a sort of telephone void, not disconnected exactly but not connected either, floating in a limbo of fruity organ music. It was still oomphing and poomphing after she hung up and lifted the phone again. She was unable to redial.

"What the—"

She dropped the receiver and left it lying on its side, pulsing like an exposed nerve.

Now she paced in a circle extending beyond the kitchen table, going as far as the sapodilla, to which she reached out, running her hand along the pointed tips of its waxy leaves. Jerry had always asked her to speak to it, for the sake of its health, which was a task she'd never felt comfortable with—honestly, what on earth could she say to a plant? What thoughts to share? Yet this time words came of their own accord: "He's got to come back to us. He's got to. Won't he?"

Barbara squeezed a leaf, clinging to it, but a moment later moved on. She couldn't keep still. Checking the phone again, she still heard the roller-skating music, so she hung it up and went to the living room, turned on the television, and zapped through the channels. But at this hour there were only soap operas, game shows, and the news channel's asinine bragging about its weather satellite. Please . . . She snapped off the control and kept moving, though purposely avoiding their bedroom and the temptation to do the obvious things a person might indulge in in such a situation (she'd already tried them anyway, these last few months)—she would *not* look at his photograph or reread one of his letters—no, she refused to dwell on past conversations or imagine new ones. None of that, except . . . Barbara crossed her arms in front of her, and determined that she would do the one obvious thing she had not yet attempted. The only one that remained. She would pray.

For this, she went to the guest room.

Barbara felt that she needed a different setting to talk to God. This was because, to tell the truth, she and God weren't on regular speaking terms. Not that there had been a particular argument or falling out, but over the years she had gone her own way, and God hadn't seemed to follow. God hadn't budged. Maybe that was her main source of uneasiness about praying, when you got down to it. Now when there was a big problem and her husband was in danger it wasn't easy to try to speak to God again, actually sort of embarrassing, to be making an overture when it was so obviously to ask a favor. Still, she had to do it, for Jerry.

She sat on a straight-backed chair, searching for a way to begin, for words that might capture the feelings that flooded her. Surrounded by the guest room's assorted bric-a-brac, the heirlooms her husband had saved, she screwed her fists against her knees as she waited for inspiration. She disliked the room, for here were stored all the inedible, unasked-for presents they'd received over the years: movie posters and vomity wall-hangings, a blown glass dog and bamboo lamps, the couch pillow shaped like South Dakota—all saved and catalogued in Jerry's mind in readiness of a visit by their giver, on which occasion the gift would be brought out before that person arrived and displayed in a place of honor. Barbara had reservations about how much space keeping this junk required (sometimes she referred to it as the Museum of Futility), and would've thrown it all out but for his insistence. Surprise visits by donors were especially stressful (she hated stalling people in the hallway while her husband rehung pictures). Yet she was impressed by his speed and ability to pull out the right heirloom every time, under everyone's nose. Now she closed her eyes to her surroundings.

"God, where is he?"

The doorbell rang. She started, opened her eyes. Oh my, how could . . . so fast? Her hope soared—this was amazing! An instant later she doubted, and as she hurried to the door she regretted her doubt, concluding as a matter of course that it only compromised her happiness. If not for this doubt, she fretted, her happiness would have come true. He would've been there. Oh, why do I doubt?

She opened the door to blue-suited men.

"Mrs Renfrow?"

"Who wants to know?"

Reaching into their jackets, they produced identifying police badges. They didn't flip them or flash them the way she'd seen detectives do on TV. They leaned toward her and held them out like boarding passes.

"Well?" she said. "What do you want?"

She felt a pulsing in the side of her neck, a churning anxiety at the prospect of what their news might be.

"You *are* Mrs Renfrow?"

"Yes, yes, I am."

"May we come in?"

She stepped back from the door and led them to the living room, where they accepted her invitation to sit on the sofa. Barbara, however, remained standing, looking down at them. "Tell me then. What is it? Has he been hurt?"

But it turned out that they had brought no information of their own but were rather interested in what she could tell *them*. They began to pepper the air with questions.

"No," she insisted, "my husband has not contacted me. I have no idea where he is. Don't you?"

"Mrs Renfrow, you do realize that anything you tell us may be used against you?" asked one of the men in a gentle voice. Hands neatly folded on one knee, he tilted his head slightly and appeared embarrassed by his own words, as if she might reproach him for uttering a cliché; Barbara noticed, glistening on the cuff of his pants and flashing on the sole of his shoe, flakes of mauve, blue, and green, evidence of where they'd snooped before visiting her. Oh dear. The cops had been in the confetti again.

"Am I under arrest?" she asked. "Is that what you're saying?"

"No. You are not. But I'm just warning you anyway."

His partner, younger, sideburned yet balding, inquired if she would give them permission to visit the rooms of the apartment. "Just one walk-through."

"Do you have a warrant?" she inquired, though more in observance of a sort of procedural etiquette—wasn't that what a person in her situation was supposed to say?—than out of the belief that she could really stop them.

"No, we don't," said the older officer. "We are not pretending with you, Mrs Renfrow. We will not overstep our role. We ask your permission. In the interest of simplicity, really, because in the long run it could be easier for all of us to get it over with now. I promise you that in less than three minutes we'll be gone."

Barbara hesitated, then decided to let them. If she didn't say yes, she reasoned, she would have to put up with a future visit. "Okay, but please make it as quick as you said. I don't want to be late for work."

The man cleared his throat, reached inside his jacket and produced a paper for her to sign, which he smoothed on the coffee table. He clicked a pen, held it out. "Oral permission is problematic. This simply formalizes what you just told us."

Barbara was already beginning to regret her decision, but she accepted the pen and went ahead and signed. The sooner to get rid of them. And true to their word, the men did not dawdle but moved at a steady and purposeful pace through the rooms, opening closet doors, checking in the kitchen and peering in the bathroom behind the shower curtain. They ran their fingers along the window ledges. The apartment was not large so the procedure was swift. As they prepared to leave she even experienced a brief sense of satisfaction at having invited them to look, for now she felt vindicated. Then the older man asked, "You had a guest last night?"

Barbara stared back at them. She hadn't even thought—and the bed was made, how could they know?—and the longer she paused, the more awkward it became. Even though there was nothing to say but the truth.

"Yes."

"Was this guest Mr Renfrow? Please remember that you are not obliged to answer, though questions are allowed according to the permission release that you have signed. If you choose not to answer, we shall adopt a more formal procedure, and you will have to accompany us."

"You mean I'll be under arrest?"

"You understand correctly."

The floor seemed to tilt at an angle under her feet. She didn't want to believe that this conversation was taking place. It was as if someone in a bad dream had reached out and shaken her, and suddenly she had awakened, opened her eyes: and that bad dream person was standing over her.

She looked into their smooth faces. “No,” she said, “it was not Mr Renfrow.”

A smile crept onto the older man’s lips. She wanted to lift her hand to his face and pinch that smile off. “Let us hope not,” he said, his grin widening. As he and his companion moved into the hallway he added, “We shall have to see you again. Soon, I’m afraid. Goodbye, Mrs Renfrow.”

Three

THE NAME OF the place was BB's. A rectangular cinderblock building along a two-lane highway, the only interruption on the prairie. Two gas pumps, and on the edge of the parking lot a towering pole with a sign, visible for more than a mile, proclaiming GAS**FOOD**DIESEL. Otherwise, rolling farmland stretched in all directions.

"It's not open," said The Angel.

"I see a light," said Royce.

"The sign says the place is open," Mr Nice Guy put in from the back seat. "Don't you see it in the window?"

He was right. They'd driven all night, mainly down gravel roads and, since they'd found no maps in the glove compartment, by navigating with the moon and stars. This part Mr Nice Guy liked very much. Each time The Angel shut off the engine and killed the lights, the three of them climbed out of the car to gaze at the sky, check their bearings. Everything was still, the only thing you felt moving was the earth itself. The Angel formed a quadrant with his thumbs and index fingers to observe the path of the moon and the slow arc of the Big Dipper. He spoke of going southwest.

"Were you a Boy Scout?" Mr Nice Guy inquired.

The Angel nodded. "You too?"

"For sure. God yes."

Mr Nice Guy thrust his hands in his pockets and tilted his head back. He had lied, though there was no good reason. Somehow it had just popped out. He *wished* he knew that Boy Scout stuff—as a kid he'd wanted to join—but there were also his sleight-of-hand lessons. It was a long story.

Now, in any case, nothing prevented him from enjoying the stellar beauty, its sensual glittering. In prison, oh, how he'd missed this! How much he'd needed it! Stars on the outside tugged and teased the ones inside him. Made him feel whole.

Staring at that deep, deep dark ink, he wanted to throw himself headlong—

"Get back in the car, fuckhead! We're not gonna stay out here all night!"

Reluctantly, Mr Nice Guy turned around. The car's headlights pierced the darkness; the engine coughed once, then shook to life. He got in the back seat. No point in contradicting The Angel nor revealing that he knew who he was, at least not yet. The safest and best strategy in this tricky situation was to hang back, win his confidence. The Angel had a plan, according to the other escapee in the car, a man who'd introduced himself with a laugh—was it a joke?—as Royce.

"What we're gonna do," Royce explained, twisting to stare at him as The Angel's eyes darted to the rear-view mirror and met Mr Nice Guy's, and the fingers of one hand released their grip on the steering wheel and rose to his mouth where he sucked a scraped knuckle, "is cross *back toward the pen,* then continue down from there. You see, the first thing they'll assume is that we're trying to get as far away as fast as possible from where we took the car. But that's not our modus fuck-you-Jack."

By dawn their chosen route had brought them to this shoebox cafe. With rumbling empty bellies, they pushed through the door and the bell jingled. The Angel was in the lead, striding purposefully toward a booth and sitting down. Watching him, Mr Nice Guy could see that he did not want to call attention to himself or his awkward-fitting clothes, yet his determination produced exactly the opposite effect, for The Angel's gait, a certain stiffness, invited suspicion. Mr Nice Guy had been incarcerated long enough to recognize this special type of prisoner and realized, as he and Royce followed and slid into the booth behind him, that The Angel was not a criminal in the professional sense. He was simply a murderer.

In any event, no one saw them enter. The place was wide open; the front of the cafe, stools, counter, and even cash register were abandoned. Only the overhead lights and the drippety orange juice machine and the radio, tuned to country music, assured them that someone was here.

"Close your eyes, darlin', darlin', dream yourself away . . ."

A tightening in The Angel's cheeks, lines at the corners of his mouth, wordlessly expressed his disapproval of the radio, for news broadcasts they'd heard in the car were full of reports of last night's riot and breakout. Many of the escapees had already been caught, the news said. The death toll was supposedly five prisoners and three guards, though they did not believe such a small figure. Surely it was worse. Mr Nice Guy worried about his friends but didn't speak his thoughts aloud. Had James escaped the fire? Were Myler and Doc all right? What about Little Rodney and Sambo? How had they fared?

When at last an employee emerged from the swinging kitchen door, Mr Nice Guy saw that they needn't worry about calling attention to themselves with their dress. This fellow wore a spattered T-shirt (at such an early hour, no doubt yesterday's grease) and gravy-stained pants, out of which hung a yellow handrag, vaguely obscene. A crisp new paper cook's hat was his one concession to appearance, balanced atop his head, as immaculate as spun sugar. He was a soft, flabby man. His pink face, his arms, his hands, his fingers, his visible breasts, his stomach, his thighs, were fat. His rear resembled a pair of bowling balls.

"What can I get you guys?" the man wheezed.

"Open, darling, I'm here, here to stay . . ."

They ordered pancakes. And eggs with sausages, and bacon, toast, and hash browns. The Angel also requested a waffle, while Royce put in for a Monster Cinnamon Roll. The cook asked if he wanted it microwaved nice and hot, and Royce told him You bet. A few minutes later the cook brought out a cinnamon roll as big as a frisbee, with pats of butter melting into golden puddles on its white glazed frosting. Royce exclaimed, “Sweet Jesus save me!”

“Your buckwheat groats are coming right up sir,” the cook told Mr Nice Guy.

The coffee was vastly superior to prison coffee, and the men could not get enough of it. Beside the expanse of heaped plates at the booth a second pot was brought over. As the meal progressed the cook stood beside them, filling and refilling, not bothering to move anywhere because it was easier than going back and forth. His waitress, he complained, hadn’t shown up that morning so he was stuck with double duty.

“Isn’t that just typical?” said Royce. “People think they can get away with anything in this country, don’t they?”

“I’m afraid so. She said she’d be here but she’s not.”

“Well she was just tickling your rump then, wasn’t she?”

The cook grinned, and Royce went on, “I gotta tell you, though. This is damn good coffee. Top of the line.”

“I’m glad you like it,” said the cook.

“No, I don’t just *like* it. I think it’s damn good. Damn good! Isn’t it, fellas?” Mr Nice Guy and The Angel nodded, and Royce continued, “I mean you could think it was espresso or something. It’s that good. This is one terrific cup of coffee.”

“Well enjoy it.”

“I certainly will.” He finished his cup, held it out for the man to refill, took another sip, then resumed sawing a stack of pancakes with his fork. “I’ve seen cups of coffee but that little baby right there (he pointed with his chin), that one, Mister, it blows them all away. Believe me.”

“I get it from a guy in Cinamarron Springs,” the fat man confided.

“No shit! Well that must be the place. It’s killer, it really is.”

The man lifted the pot, and scratched under his arm. “Yeah, we’re probably in the top ten in the country.” He nodded at Mr Nice Guy. “Warm you up?”

"Mmmmm," he nodded back. His mouth was full of toast.

"How's that waffle, sir?"

"Very good. Just like Mom used to make," The Angel replied.

The door jingled, some other customers entered and the cook put down his pot, lumbered off to greet them. In the booth, Mr Nice Guy's companions hunched lower over their plates, acting busy with their food, though the new arrivals paid no particular attention to them beyond a general "Good morning" tossed in their direction. This The Angel and Royce acknowledged mumblingly.

The new customers sat at the counter and offered their backs as they scanned menus.

"Don't stare right at them," The Angel hissed at Mr Nice Guy. "You think they can't see you in the mirror? And why do you talk so much?" The Angel asked Royce. "Can't you shut up for two minutes? We're not here to chit-chat to death. Let's finish up and get out before someone else comes in."

"Aw, there's time for a cigarette," said Royce, leaning back with a sigh, wiping his mouth with a paper napkin and tossing it on the table, now patting his stomach, "there's time for a cigarette. Those people have already seen us and nobody's paying any attention to us anyhow. Let's have a good smoke."

The Angel shook his head. "No hanging around. We have to gas up and get back on the road. We're not taking extra chances." He began easing out of the booth. "There's time to go to the bathroom—that's all."

He hurried away, his hand on his abdomen. At first Mr Nice Guy thought this was because The Angel's need to go was urgent. Then suddenly, he realized there was another reason for those jerky steps: one leg of his baggy pants contained a shotgun.

"Gorgeous, huh?" said Royce, lighting up, blowing smoke toward the window. Mr Nice Guy nodded, looking out the cafe across the road to a pasture with willow trees whose narrow, lime-colored leaves shimmered in the morning light. Royce waved a hand, parting the cloudy air in front of them. "Don't this feel great? I mean, don't this feel great? I can tell that I'm getting over my post-natal depression. Right this very hour."

Mr Nice Guy smiled. "Not sure I follow you there. That's for women. I doubt you've given birth, Royce."

"No, but I was *born,* man. And now I'm getting out of it, free as one of those breezes moving what's beautiful out there. I can feel that, I can feel . . . *me.*"

Mr Nice Guy nodded again, gazing at the green field, as satisfying as anything he could've imagined last night when he was sniffing blindly in the dark. Reality as sweet as the imagination! His full stomach gurgled with contentment. When the cook came over, offering more coffee, he replied "Sure," for it was, indeed, damn good. Royce was right about a number of things. Why, breakfast here, with this view, with sunbeams filtering through the glass, caressing his face and curling up on his lap—you didn't have to look any further; a person could feel blessed. He lifted his cup, took another swallow. His cup had writing around the brim, *DrinkMe DrinkMe DrinkMe* except in one spot where the letters were worn, where right-handed sippers naturally placed their lips, which now showed only *Dr Me.* With an originality due to squeamishness, Mr Nice Guy reversed his grip, brought his mouth near the end on an unscarred *ink.*

"Maybe I'll stay right here," said Royce with a laugh, running his fingers down his cheek, blinking slowly at the window; he turned, called to the cook: "What do you say, chef? I could be your waitress. I'm cute enough for you, ain't I?"

The cook let out a high, whinnying laugh, then moved away without answering. Mr Nice Guy looked again at the willows in the field, musing in a similar vein to Royce. Yes, more than scenery, this place was nice enough for a person to want to linger. Become a part of it.

A new dream took shape in his mind. Never mind trying to launch World Services JR, he told himself. Never mind all that hustle and the unpleasant dissembling it would entail, for whatever he did next, Mr Nice Guy realized, if he wanted to stay free of the authorities' grasp, he and Barbara would have to pass themselves off under different names. But that could be fine: never mind all that striving to be someone big. It was only vanity. At this time of newly acquired freedom he believed that he saw more clearly and could think more lucidly than he had in years. A person need look no further than the world at this window.

Maybe, he told himself—excitement rippling so he could hardly sit still in the booth—it would be better to cultivate a new line of Down-Home Services in the countryside. Yes, leave the city behind. The place of the future for pursuit of the Optimal, at least for a criminal at large such as himself, was not in the old cities with their predictable pecking orders, but in settings of space, of potential freedom. You had to be able to stretch out your anklebones. And then, you had to be canny enough to stay stretched, make something of your freedom. Not just let it wash over you like a wave, but know how to climb up on it, and surf. Perhaps, given the chance, he would be able to figure out a harvest procedure to bring the price of dew down. His jaw trembled as he pictured a long hothouse teeming with sapodillas. He would enlist through his own devices the power of the sun and wind. He and Barbara would even farm a little popcorn on the side, as his grandfather and great-grandfather had done before him. And wouldn't this be the time and place to start having children?

It all seemed possible. The essential thing was to *believe*. The Future, he saw clearly, was an age of belief.

By then The Angel had slid back into the booth. In his reverie, Mr Nice Guy abstractedly stroked his front tooth and below the table began to swell, while a scheme formed in his head. A way to run! All his plans depended on it. If somehow he could shake The Angel and Royce, steal a car of his own (he would pay it back eventually and in the meantime, in lieu of restitution, leave a Thank You note)—if he could get wheels, he could find his own way of escape.

Yes, he knew where to go: straight North. Up to the Billy Hare Lodge, to a caboose by the lake. Barbara and no one else would know how to find him there. And when she had slipped away, joined him, they could make plans for their next life. Yes. Yes!

This train of thought was interrupted when he was tapped on the arm. The Angel was staring at him. Mr Nice Guy removed his hand from his mouth, crossed his legs. The Angel inquired, "Say, don't I know you from someplace?"

Mr Nice Guy averted his eyes. "No. No, I wouldn't say that. There's more coffee here if you want some. It's damn good, too. Go ahead, I've had enough. You take a little moo juice in your java?"

"Hmmm." The Angel ignored the offers. "Seems like I know you." He cleared his throat. "I'm sure I've seen you before. What line of work were you in?"

"Personal services." Mr Nice Guy picked up the check, leaned toward the edge of the booth. "This one's on me, guys."

Royce stopped him. "You got money?"

Mr Nice Guy blinked, slapped his hands on the pockets of his borrowed pants. Of course he didn't have any money. Funny how old reflexes reasserted themselves. "Uh—I guess you're right. No, I don't."

The Angel pulled out a roll of bills and peeled off several, pushing them across to Royce. "You pay. We don't want any trouble here. We'll be in the car."

No doubt the money was stolen from the mother and her children, Mr Nice Guy surmised. At this moment they were probably still bound with electric cord and gagged with duct tape, having spent all night that way, unable to move except maybe roll down to the floor. He imagined the little ones crying, kicking their feet at the ceiling. Did they ache to go potty? It was something to think about. Yet on the way to the door this image evaporated in an instant. He stopped, despite The Angel's beckoning him to follow him into the parking lot, and watched Royce pay at the cash register.

Sweat broke out on his forehead. He asked in a tight voice, "Hey, please, could you lend me a quarter?"

Royce collected his change. "Sure." He flipped a coin through the air.

Mr Nice Guy caught it and hurried to a gumball machine near the entrance (proceeds for the Kiwanis' Eye Bank, he noted with approval) and with shaking fingers fed the coin into the slot, watching with elation as a big green gumball rolled impressively into sight, then fell coolly on his outstretched palm. His bones shuddered, a cloud of happiness rose in his brain. He popped the gumball in his mouth and followed Royce to the door as the fat man called to them, "You fellows come back now. You'll have to try my lunch special. I got a patty melt's out of this world!"

Mr Nice Guy couldn't reply, for his jaws were flexing eagerly. He experienced the pleasant sensation that he was biting into the cloud in his head, dispersing it throughout his being, and he gave himself entirely to the task. Royce called over his shoulder to the cook, "Catch you next time, old sport!"

They stepped out under the morning sky's blue dome. The car's engine raced, The Angel rolled down the window. "What's with you clowns? C'mon! We're losing time." Mr Nice Guy sensed danger as he moved toward the vehicle with a sensation of new lightness, the voice pulling him as if by a string, the rhythm of his jaws and the pleasure flooding through his muscles causing him momentarily to trip, though he managed to regain his balance with a little skip. He caught the car door handle. Despite the danger, he thrilled with the morning air. It was going to be a beautiful day.

Four

IRENE PUSHED DOWN the blanket and rolled onto her side, her mouth opening as her cheek pressed into the pillow. The hospital bed sheets dampened around her; a new bubble coursed through the IV tubing. At her window, morning light shone brightly. Inside her head, the moment grew more romantic. Malcolm sat across the table and smiled at her. Lifted the bottle. "More wine?" he asked.

"Oh, I don't know if I should."

"Well sweetheart I climbed a mountain and visited a cave and consulted with a little wise man with a long yellow beard sitting on a stone and he cogitated and arrived at the opinion that yes, most definitely—in fact he insisted on it—you should!"

She laughed and they gazed at each other, light flickering off their faces from the candles. They were both fond of candles, so they burnt many, choosing various lengths and scents but ever for the same celebration: being together. Recently she'd brought him a pure beeswax taper the color of her honey hair and it had pleased him tremendously.

They brought their glasses together. *Chink.*

"Maybe we should put on the Blue Tunas."

"You think so?" She laughed again. He was wearing a silver-striped tie with the new stick pin she had bought him. She was in her emerald strapless, held together tentatively at the front with a brooch in the shape of a tulip blossom.

"Why not? You look gorgeous when you dance with your hair over one shoulder. You know what I mean. Irene, I want to see you dance with your hair over one shoulder." He swayed his head left, then right, before bringing his glass to his lips. In response she did the same, and after her sip, flipped her hair forward, stroked it into place on one side. Twisted it into a glossy rope. Looking directly into his eyes. Then, just as they were putting down their glasses and getting ready to rise, there was a powerful *thud* underneath the table. The bottle and candles rocked, and they reached quickly to steady them. A cry arose.

Malcolm sighed and pushed back his chair, lifting the tablecloth and peering beneath.

"Darn it, I've told you a hundred times not to play down there. You just hurt yourself."

A young Nice Boy emerged, rubbing the top of his head, eyes pinkening in pain. His mother grabbed him by the elbow and pulled him aside, began rubbing her palm on his scalp, too. His thin fish lips puckered.

"My Lord," she said. "You would've flattened your head by now if it weren't for the bumps. How do you do it?" She counted: "One, two, three . . ."

"I didn't mean to."

"Son, you can't stay down there," his father said. "You see what happens. I swear, little buddy, you're not gonna be able to think straight."

Under their gentle remonstrance, he was sent upstairs to his bedroom where he brooded, contemplating his exile. He was supposed to stay in his bed and go to sleep but this wasn't possible, for restlessness seized his entire being; in his muscles and in every joint he was like popcorn popping; the blankets fell off. Downstairs, Irene and Malcolm had put on their favorite record and begun to dance. He could hear the music, and climbed out of bed, tiptoeing across his threshold. He moved silently to the top of the stairs. From this vantage point he watched them slowly turning to the rhythm. His father's hand slid along her waist, her hand ran through the hair at the back of his head. They whispered to each other, her lips forming inaudible words—what were they saying?

In her hospital bed, Irene drifted out of her dream, out of its sweetness, and woke to the clean, terrifying white of her pillowcase.

Five

"HOLY SHIT!" EXCLAIMED Royce.

A wall of red cows in the windshield. The Angel swerved, the car fishtailed left, then right across the road with a sound like a giant rag tearing. The Angel yelled out, jerking the wheel back again to regain control. For a moment the front of the car seemed to straighten—cows behind them now—then a mighty force whipped and they plunged into a ditch.

The car suddenly seemed light, yet was as unguidable as a sled in the air. One bump, they tilted crazily up; another bump and they were rolling. The windshield flashed green blue, green blue, how many times?—till a bone-crunching jolt brought everything to a halt. Only the windshield continued the sense of their momentum. With a sound like static the glass buckled and veined into spiderwebs, quivered and cracked: then that stopped, too. The glass did not fall out, but there was nothing to see.

In that nothing, time shrank to a dot—and disappeared.

No one moved.

The engine whirred, and when Mr Nice Guy collected his wits and saw his surroundings again, even the sunlight seemed bent inside the car. He reached forward, pushed down one knee, then another, shakily unfastened his seatbelt, and leaned in from the back seat to turn off the ignition. "Hey, you fellows all right?" he asked, nudging their backs. "Hey, guys?"

Slowly The Angel pulled away from the steering wheel, moaning, clutching his chest, blood streaming from his nose and down his chin, while Royce didn't move at all. His face was in the dashboard radio. "Hey! Hey!" Mr Nice Guy poked him. During the confusion, the futile attempts to open the crumpled car doors and to rouse Royce (blood seeped around one ear and now pattered audibly on the floor mat), Mr Nice Guy's mind was clear about one thing—they should get out of the car promptly, in the event of a fire. He told them so.

"Whuhhh . . . "

Gasping, his lips bobbing out of the red pool of his face, The Angel looked back at him in the rear-view mirror like a fish choking in gore, trying to reply. He still hugged his chest where the steering wheel had branded him.

"This way!" shouted Mr Nice Guy. Lifting a leg, he kicked out the rest of his passenger window. The jagged glass chinkled away. "We can get out through here!"

The Angel groaned in pain; it was soon obvious that he could not bend or twist around into the back seat, so Mr Nice Guy helped him by rearing as high as he could, taking aim with his heel, and kicking out the cracked window next to The Angel. A minute later, after Mr Nice Guy had crawled out his window, he managed to pull and lever The Angel out of the car. "That's it, that's it! C'mon, baby, push, push! You can do it!" Once they were able to coordinate their efforts, it made all the difference. He slid out into the waiting light. "Atta boy! Yes! Yes! Yes!" Now The Angel sat upright in the weeds. His head turned slowly, taking in the trees and sky, purple swelling bloating his face. He let out a bleat. Mr Nice Guy found his footing and trotted excitedly along the ditch, unhurt, shaking broken glass out of his hair. "I'm so sorry, I really should've insisted that you and Royce use your seatbelts. For God's sake! Even if you didn't want to hear it, I should've insisted. Isn't that the way?" He bent over and squinted into the wreck.

"Auhhhhh," said The Angel.

"How we gonna do it? What do you think? We have to figure out a way to pull him free."

"Noo, oh." With two grunts The Angel stumbled out of the ditch, arms flapping at his sides. Kicking up dust before him, he began limping down the gravel road.

"Wait!" called Mr Nice Guy.

"Motherfucking cows!" cried The Angel. He coughed once and spat ferociously, and with this action seemed to recover his speech. Blood on his face and shirt, he paused to pick up a rock and chuck it at a fat red cow grazing at the edge. The rock fell short in the grass, and the cow slowly raised its head, looking first at The Angel and then at the smashed wreck of the car, chewing. "We get out and make it all this way and now look what stops us—*cows*! I can't believe it! Get off the road!" The Angel screamed. "Get back in your fences!" He seized a handful of rocks and threw them, spraying the cow and two of its sisters close by. Rocks rained on their backs and flanks, which sent them huffing down the ditch, crashing through the weeds.

"We have to pry him loose!" called Mr Nice Guy, pulling with all his strength on Royce's door handle, but to no avail. The crumpled car body made opening the door impossible. "Hey, come on, give me a hand!"

The Angel didn't answer, continuing on foot down the center of the road, cursing. For over a minute Mr Nice Guy tried to force the door by himself but it wouldn't budge. Though the window glass on this side of the car was shattered, it would've required a Hercules to extract Royce at this upward angle without the help of another person, especially since Royce couldn't cooperate, either. No matter how much he called to him or pounded on the metal to rouse his attention, Royce didn't stir.

"I'll be back. Just hang on, okay?"

Mr Nice Guy climbed out of the ditch and hurried after The Angel, repeating to himself: Mustn't panic. Mustn't panic. There's got to be a way. The first farmhouse we come to, we'll go right in and call an ambulance.

One hundred yards down the road he caught up with The Angel just as a glint appeared on top of a hill—a car approaching in the distance.

"Get down!" The Angel commanded, heading for the ditch weeds.

"But they could help us. We should stop them and get some assistance. For you, too. Look at you!"

"Get down!" Then The Angel stiffened, lifted a hand in the air, let it drop. He stared as if struck again. He had wiped off the blood on his face but wide smudges remained, which had begun to brown and dry, while around the edges of his nostrils fresh red still trickled and gathered on his upper lip. "I forgot the gun! Can you believe that? It's still under the car seat!" He stamped in a circle, little clouds rising around him. "All because of those cows, those fucking cows!" A new energy seized him, and his arms worked wildly. He strummed the air and punched the side of his head several times, hard. "Can you believe that? Oh Gawd. Get down, asshole!"

Mr Nice Guy protested but The Angel didn't wait to listen. He charged Mr Nice Guy and grabbed him under the armpits, pulling him toward the ditch. When Mr Nice Guy resisted The Angel kicked savagely at his shins to break his balance, and wrestled him down into the weeds. There The Angel pinned him to the ground, with one hand on his throat while the other went higher, hovering above the bridge of his nose.

"You open your big mouth, I'll kill you right here with my own hands, you little troublemaker, I swear, I'll stick these fingers into your eyes and dig into your sockets all the way into your brain till it *kills* you." Bringing his face closer, he hissed, "You're going to do as I say." He breathed heavily. A red bubble formed at the end of one nostril, grew—then popped. Mr Nice Guy, weeds poking into his back and his shins singing, didn't dare move. He barely inhaled, for there was no doubting the man's sincerity. The balls of The Angel's brown-stained fingers, their nails, were less than an inch away. The Angel made a digging motion with his nails, bringing them closer still, menacing; his breath came in rasping shudders. A short time later a car rattled past on the road above them.

Then, releasing Mr Nice Guy's head from his grip with a dismissive shove, The Angel sat back on his haunches in the weeds. Talking aloud to himself, he began to fret. Should he run back to the car and get the gun? Would they be able to extract it from the wreckage? And what about the lost time? No doubt the passing car would've spotted the wreck in the ditch—those cows on the loose would've forced the people to slow down. Once more, The Angel cursed those beasts, those stupid, useless goddamn animals, those four-legged cunts! While he ranted Mr Nice Guy sat up and massaged his shinbones, then reached under his shirt, checking. The Angel saw him and demanded, "What you got there? A knife?"

He leaned toward Mr Nice Guy. Not threatening, but hopeful.

"No," said Mr Nice Guy.

"What is it? What?" Without waiting for an answer he seized the front of Mr Nice Guy's shirt and thrust his hand into it. Mr Nice Guy shouted out, not with pain, but from horror because The Angel moved so fast and with such sudden violence that Mr Nice Guy experienced an unnerving sensation that The Angel were capable, if he desired, of reaching in and ripping out something from *inside* him—his very heart. The Angel would take anything he wanted.

"Stop wiggling, for God's sake!" The Angel said. "What is this? Dope?" he inquired as he slipped the paperclips off the envelope and tried to peer inside.

"No, it's my father's —" said Mr Nice Guy, leaning forward, hands and face tensing, concerned that The Angel might spill it.

But The Angel merely handed it back, uninterested. Mr Nice Guy gathered up the paperclips and before resealing the envelope, bent back the top flap to take one last look for himself. At that moment a breeze moved through the ditch and blew the contents away.

"Oh no! No!" cried Mr Nice Guy. His head jerked right, then left in dismay. He reached out with twitching fingers, trying to grasp the vanished powder in the air. But too late.

Oh, *where?*

Lost.

The Angel watched him with swollen eyes. A bruise formed a puffy purple line around the front of his head. "You sure we haven't met before?" he asked, gingerly touching the line. "Ahh—ouch! Holy fuck. This is bad." He felt his way around the circle. "It's like I've seen you somewhere."

Mr Nice Guy didn't answer; he was contemplating the scattered dust of his inheritance.

"What's your name?" The Angel suddenly demanded. "You haven't said your name."

Mr Nice Guy replaced the crumpled envelope in his shirt and told The Angel the truth.

The Angel pondered. "Renfrow? No, that name doesn't mean anything to me. Still, it seems . . . you sure you weren't ever on Death Row?"

Mr Nice Guy shook his head again but did not volunteer the rest of the truth, that he'd sat in the jury box. He was in no mood for small talk.

"Well, you must remind me of somebody out of the Pit."

He shrugged, and the conversation was interrupted when another car crested the hill, windshield flashing in the sun. Once more they ducked in the undergrowth, lying flat as it rumbled past. This time Mr Nice Guy did not have to be told to lie still.

"The road's too dangerous," said The Angel when he peeked out of the ditch again, moving crablike through the weeds. "We can't wander around in broad daylight like a couple of turkeys. That's just asking for it. Our car's been spotted so the cops will be here before too long." He craned his neck the other way and pointed across a field. "See that farmhouse over there, those buildings? Let's give that a try. We can cut cross country. We ought to find what we're looking for in all that clutter."

He made Mr Nice Guy climb the fence before him, and quickly they shambled across an open pasture toward a clump of trees, where they would be out of sight from the road. Mr Nice Guy returned to himself and took stock of the situation. Though sore and shaken and mighty leery of The Angel, he was still determined to call an ambulance for Royce as soon as he could reach a telephone. Maybe he could try it from the farmhouse. And he still wanted to do something for the family they'd tied up and gagged the previous night. He hadn't forgotten them, oh no. Things sure had a way of accumulating, when you were free!

Not to mention the tricky matter of keeping an eye on The Angel at the same time, making sure he didn't dig his fingers into somebody's eyeballs, or worse. Out here you had to think of the future, too. And to top it off, he would have to find a way to give everyone the slip and run for the Billy Hare—soon.

Really, there was so much at once, now that he could choose.

"Come on," The Angel said. "What are you waiting for?"

Six

"WHAT IS IT?" Reggie asked. "Who are they? Barbara, what's happening?"

She turned to him. They stood at the base of the spiral staircase in the main cavern, watching the Special Services police test the batteries of their high-intensity search lights and clip-on walkie-talkies. One man wrapped a coil of yellow rope around his shoulder. On the other shoulder was strapped a gun. Over by the three-million-year old stalagmite organ pipes where Sylvia Rose Secreast had said her wedding vows, an unhappy police dog crouched, nervous, tail down, while officers unzipped canvas cases, and pulled out bullhorns. "*Test . . . test one-two-three,*" they hacked, setting off echoes in the caves' intestinal darkness. The dog moaned.

"Barbara, speak to me."

Reggie's gaze was fixed, a determined jut-jawed expression like that of someone ready to take a punch. She wished he wouldn't do that. She had no desire to argue. And she realized that despite their time together, she had in some respects underestimated him. She reached out, touching his arm lightly, then let her hand fall. She knew that he was asking not only about the scene unfurling in the caves but also about last night. But what was she supposed to say? He had understood then, hadn't he? After all, he was the one who'd gotten up and left. There was no point in pretending that it hadn't happened.

"What do you want me to tell you?"

"The truth. You haven't been very good at that."

She nodded slowly, for he had a point, but she also had other, more pressing thoughts, in which Reggie had no place. Was it possible, she speculated, that Jerry knew of a planned break-out when they saw each other at the conjugal visit? After all, he was listed as one of the escapees, whereas many prisoners didn't get past the walls. Most didn't, in fact. Was her Jerry involved in such a scheme?

The idea seemed amazing but maybe she'd underestimated him, too. She remembered his altered state. And in her mind she replayed their last conversation together, on the edge of the bed where they could see their own breath. Had he been trying to tell her something? *"We're going to have our day at the Billy Hare,"* he'd said. Did Jerry's attention to detail go so far? The notion was almost spooky.

And in its way, impressive. Barbara wondered: Has he done this for *me?*

She knew he was capable. Actually, why should she be surprised? Maybe it's true, she mused. She pressed her lips together. The past contained the future, and this, once you became aware of it, put demands on the present. It was her move now.

Reggie chose precisely this moment to slide a hand around her waist, kiss her on the side of her mouth. She pulled away, a shiver running through her, and faced him.

"It's finished," she said. "Please. I don't want to be mean to you. But surely you know."

He let these words hang in the air. For a moment she feared he would persist, perhaps put both arms around her, launch into a confession and try to kiss her in one last desperate attempt to win her over, right here where they'd started, in the caverns. But instead he wrinkled his face: "Finished for you maybe," he said, his voice raspy, "but I can't stop what I feel. And it wasn't long ago that you felt the same. Are you sure you're not lying to yourself?"

She nodded. She didn't want to pursue this. It would only get in the way. Instead she rubbed her forearms against the chill and stuck to a truth. One important truth, which pushed aside the others. "I used to think I knew better, Reggie, that that was my edge. But now—" She paused, searching, till she heard, like a remnant of a melody inside her, the words she wanted. "I ain't so smart. See? And I'm going to do something about it."

Reggie gave a bitter laugh. Yet he didn't move away, and together they watched the lights play off the mineral walls, their beams scattering in the darkness. Barbara tried to change the subject. “They’re looking for my husband. They got it in their heads that he might be hiding down here. They think that this place is part of a plan. For all I know they’re following me.”

As they stood there in silence an officer approached, flipped open a spiral notebook and held it out to Reggie.

“Do you know this man?”

A photograph was pasted on the page, a grinning face.

“I know who he is.”

“When was the last time you saw him? Has he been on these premises?”

“Actually I’ve never met him. I’m afraid I can’t help you.”

“But you just said you knew him.”

With annoyance Reggie lifted his hand to his temple, pressing with his fingertips. “No sir,” he said slowly, evenly, as if manually summoning his reply. “I told you I knew who he was. It’s not the same thing.”

“How?”

Reggie turned toward Barbara. “I know him only through the newspapers and through my colleague here, Mrs Renfrow.”

“She communicates to you about this man?”

“Well, not really.”

Barbara volunteered, “In Mexico, we spoke about him.”

“Mexico?”

The policeman closed his book, looked back and forth between them. “Is that true?” he asked Reggie.

“Well, yes, a little.”

“Then she has communicated to you about this man.” The policeman turned to Barbara. “If you’ll excuse us, please, I think we’ll need to talk privately.”

“There’s nothing to say!” Reggie exclaimed, loudly enough that it set off an echo underground.

The conversation was slipping out of control, and though Barbara didn’t enjoy watching, it was the diversion she’d hoped for. Do me this one last favor, Reggie, she prayed. Won’t you? The officer told Reggie that the questioning would take only several minutes of his time but Reggie rashly responded that he did not have several minutes: he had nothing whatever to say.

"But I have plenty to ask," the officer told him dryly.

"That's not my problem."

"This way, please."

"It's nobody's business!"

"We'll see, sir." The officer gently touched his elbow, pointing with his notebook toward the staircase.

Reggie jerked his arm away. "This is ridiculous, I have no obligation to you." He looked at Barbara. "Help me out a little. Why don't you say something?"

"You'd better not argue with him," she said.

"Come on," said the officer.

"For Christ's sake, you don't even know my name."

"*You* are the one who doesn't understand," the officer replied. Now a distinctly annoyed tone entered his voice. "I already know who you are, Mister." He waved to another policeman to come over. "I know quite a bit about you, in fact, what you've been doing. *Both* of you. Either you join me directly, Mr Linton, or we'll have to use a more formal procedure. You follow me?"

"I *work* here. That's all I do. Period."

Reggie refused to go up the staircase. Barbara was embarrassed by the turn of events, yet knew that she had consciously lit the spark. "Hey Stan," the officer called, and a third policeman approached. "It's a 321." Stan nodded grimly.

They came slowly toward Reggie, closing in one step at a time. "So you want to play rodeo, eh? That's what you want? That's what you'll get." Reggie looked around him, shaking his head. Suddenly the policemen converged, one high, one low, one tackling him around the middle. In seconds Reggie was pinned on his belly on the ground, hands cuffed behind his back.

"He's telling you the truth!" Barbara protested as Reggie squirmed, but when she tried to come closer a policeman blocked her. Another officer who was restraining Reggie looked over his shoulder, his face flushed red.

"Mind your own, why don't you? I don't enjoy this. This shouldn't have been necessary."

So Reggie was carried off like a roll of carpet, jostling and swearing as they bent him one direction, then another, to fit him up the spiral staircase. He's only making it worse for himself, Barbara thought sadly. She hoped he would not do something even more foolish in an interrogation room. It was dangerous to take out his anger about her on them.

She turned back to the caverns, watching the light dance and flicker off stalactites and the Special Service agents disappear into the crevices. Bullhorns squawled her husband's name. "Renfrow—Renfrow!" Now she should make her move while they were busy, before anyone detained her again. Nervously her fingers flicked her hair behind her ears, then she strode straight for the staircase. Round and round she twisted, up. She worried about the grilling Reggie must be getting in the police van. And as she left the museum through the service exit, she worried about the men below so boldly exploring in search of her husband. They didn't know the history of the place. She didn't trust them not to get lost.

Seven

JAMES PRESSED HIS ear to the iron door's peephole, listening, though this could be dangerous, for guards and even other prisoners had been known to play cruel surprises with pencils. But he wanted news. Probably everyone on the block was doing the same, whenever they heard footsteps.

He'd been transferred back to his cell from the infirmary to make room for the riot's wounded. Today a total lockdown was in effect. James was still very sore, with a bandage winding round and round his abdomen. Walking was difficult; he hobbled laterally as if doing a curious, slow-motion dance. Upon his return, he eased himself with a little doglike *yip* onto his bunk, surprised not to be greeted by Mr Nice Guy. Where was that doofy fellow? As he fingered his bandage, hoping he had torn no stitches, he began to worry.

He fell asleep while praying, and slept as if dead.

The next day the lockdown was lifted at lunchtime.

When he danced out of his cell toward the dining hall, annoyed by a young prisoner who imitated his sidewise canter and mocked, *Wooo, James, get down!* (which, more than personally disrespectful, was nonsense, for Keepers of the Word did *not* dance), when he took his tray and joined the serving line, he was shocked at the signs of destruction, of smoke and water damage—puddles standing stagnant on the floor, tiles hanging precariously from the ceiling. Only then did the scale of the uprising become apparent. Word circulated (James did not hear it so much as absorb it through his pores) that inmates on the west wing, where the riot had started, were still restricted to their cells and would get no lunch. Meanwhile James and his cohorts were allowed cold sandwiches and Kool-Aid. In addition to the structural damage to this part of the building, there was the conspicuous presence of imported national guardsmen, standing along the walls as reinforcements to the usual guards. Many were scared-looking kids, with eyes moving from side to side and sweaty palms on gunstocks. The prisoners tried not to see them.

James helped himself to mustard, wondering who among the prisoners here today clinking silverware knew who'd stabbed him (all he remembered was being pushed on his face, then the first stab in his right side—*so hot*); maybe the one who did it was watching him now. The coward. He would find out sooner or later and when he did, he would confront that person, he would tell him that he was weak. Yes, he would discover his attacker, and he would not back down. Whoever it was would have to look him in the eye. And that person, regardless of what he said or did next—he could finish the attack, slay him on the spot—would have to answer to Yahweh.

He had other matters to settle, too, despite the pains still stabbing in his sides.

His tray full, James approached Myler's table, and eased carefully into a seat. For the first time in years, he spoke to him:

"You seen Jerry? Did he get mixed up in all the ruckus? What happened to him? Where's Jerry?"

Myler looked back at him, blinking through his wire-rimmed glasses, folding his sandwich into a triangle before biting off the corner. "Who?"

"Jerry!" James insisted. "White boy, a mush head! You know who I'm talking about."

Myler shrugged. "I thought you were his keeper."

Other inquiries proved as futile. It soon became obvious that inmates were reluctant to admit to knowledge of Mr Nice Guy or anyone else, nervous about the inevitable upcoming interrogations. It would be days, months maybe, before the various versions of the previous night got around and James could piece together a reasonable sense of what'd happened. "How many dead?" he asked.

This was the only question no one refused, though their answers were not all the same. Surely they were exaggerating.

"Tell the truth!" he exclaimed, and listeners, embarrassed, ashamed and exasperated, shrank from him.

After lunch, back in his cell, James listened at the door each time the guards' steps came closer. When his trained ears recognized the six-step trudge of three people approaching, he thought: Jerry, is that you coming back?

The steps came closer, closer.

Then passed by.

James hobbled back to his bunk. He sat on the metal edge and for a moment couldn't even muster the concentration to pray. He sank his teeth into his palm. Eventually he managed, "Help me, Lord. Oh help me!"

When Mr Nice Guy had been in the cell with him, he had never felt more crowded upon in his life. Now, he had never felt more alone.

Eight

SHAKING HIS HAIR back, Garson shifted his Cherokee from first gear to second: it growled and lunged forward, a burst of power. He let out a whoop. This was it! Lord Godalmighty. Hot damn Madam. Holy shitski on a stickski. He shot over into another lane, powershifted into third, tromped on the gas and *whished* past one car, two cars, then cut back to the right. Like riding a stallion! Better! Oh, the tingling of the steering wheel beneath his palms, that beautiful vibration. He squeezed the curve deliciously, hungrily, wanting more, more, letting up only for an instant to reach over and turn on the radio because he felt like singing. The radio burped only a few seconds before he snapped it off again, because he didn't want to share the song. He desired his own.

Cal-li-forn-ya
Here I come!

he sang, several times, because he didn't know the next line. Then he tried

Ari-zony
Here I come!

and

O-re-gony
Here I come!

He didn't know where he was going.

But he was ready! He was answering the call. Everything was in place—his gas campstove, sleeping bags, and twenty-four bottles of Coke in a cooler, not to mention a stock of booze, the rye and schnapps and sloe gin packed away in a wicker picnic basket and wrapped in red-checkered napkins he'd taken from his mother that morning ("I got my reasons," he'd told her. "Whyn't you mind your own business?"). It was, incidentally, a *perfect* Spring morning: fresh, sunny, with spangled shadows cast by new leaves in the trees. While he'd loaded the Cherokee, the birds had been singing their little feathery asses off.

A road atlas lay spread open across the seat beside him. His rendezvous was at a rest stop. Wow! Just looking at that blue- and red-veined network of interstates, the **X** he'd scratched into the paper with his fingernail, set his pulse racing.

"Thank you, God," he whispered.

Then he thrust his hand between his legs. From a two pound bag of corn chips, he extracted a fistful which he eased into his mouth. Slowly he munched, sucking the chips into a pasty goo. Soon he began to sing,

This land is my land,
This land is my land . . .

He pressed the accelerator, watched the needle spasm upward. Fourth gear now. All at once his exit sign loomed over him. He reacted, jerked the wheel, screeched onto the ramp, curved above the road and found new access on an even larger highway, a wider expanse, a fat paved ribbon stretching before him.

Today was his, yes it was. And tomorrow. The future! Oh, what happiness! The poles whizzed by. Yes, he could see. America was his.

Nine

BARBARA LINGERED IN the women's restroom, washing her hands twice, trying to drown her thoughts in the roar of the blow-dryer. *Nobody'll see me in here. It's safer.* With her forefinger she pressed lightly at the pouches under her eyes. She was taking chances now, more than she ever would've dreamed.

A city bus had brought her to the Municipal Aquarium but she'd ignored the entrance, its poles sporting various colored fish flags, and ventured along the brick paths winding through the flower beds behind the building till she came to the employees' parking area. She threaded through the cars and at the other end arrived at a sloping, weedy vacant lot. A rabbit darted out and bounced away as she crossed, approaching an even steeper dirt embankment where the horizon suddenly dropped.

She looked down on a surging freeway. Cars and trucks hummed and rumbled, the air shimmied up from the concrete canyon, fumes rose to caress her face.

She hooked a thumb under the strap of her purse, then began to scrabble a zig-zag path down the slope, clods and gravel spraying under her feet and setting off tiny avalanches in front of her. She went faster and faster in an effort to keep her balance. At bottom, arriving at a run on the shoulder of the road, she skidded to a stop. She paused to take off a shoe, shake out the pebbles.

So far so good.

Cars shwooshed by. Down the highway at a distance of twenty yards, she saw the red brick rest stop.

Ten

WHEN GARSON ARRIVED and didn't see her, he felt a momentary panic. Wasn't this the right place? But it had to be. He didn't see her car—a blue Dodge, as he recalled—or Jerry's old van. Maybe she was late. Or had changed her mind.

At this last thought his temper flared. Had he, yet again, been misled? Trifled with? Abused? Shit upon? Why should he take it? Yeah, why —

Just then Barbara came out, shielding her eyes from the sun, peering towards his vehicle. "Hot dog," he said, grappling with the door handle.

He jumped down to the asphalt and ran around the nose of his Cherokee to greet her. He reared to a sudden halt right in front of her, shielding his mouth with his hand. Now he wished he hadn't eaten all those barbecue-flavored corn chips.

"Hey!" he called into his palm, trying to sound casual. "Glad you got in touch, Barb! Where are your wheels?"

She was still unsure how much to tell him. For the time being, she thought, she should keep it simple.

"I left my car at a friend's," she said truthfully. (The way she figured it, when the police found her car near Reggie's, they would assume a connection and continue to distract themselves with him for a while. Reggie could say nothing that would cause any harm. The police would have no idea that she was going to play her wild card instead.) "Those your wheels?" she inquired.

The hand dropped from Garson's mouth, revealing a grin. "Uh huh." He strutted two steps to the right, waved his arm. "You could say that."

"Well let's go."

"Sure. *Sure*. Let's!"

He opened the door for her, and though she declined his assistance in climbing up, he lingered to watch. Nice. Then he ran around and bounded in on the other side. When he fired the engine and made it roar, his heart roared with it. He felt as if his clothes might begin to ripple, the material suddenly burst and his shirt would hang on him in shreds. Yet he managed to cock his head coolly to one side and inquire, "OK then, bosswoman. Where to?"

"South, Garson. We're going south."

"South it is!"

He put the Cherokee in gear and banked speedily through the exit. They melded into the traffic. He noticed her looking in her mirror. A minute went by in silence, then two.

Barbara leaned back in her seat and began to breathe more easily. So far so good. No longer was she just a step ahead: now she was two steps ahead.

As Garson watched her out of the corner of his eye, as the silence prolonged itself, he felt increasingly uncomfortable. And a little alarmed when she sank down in her seat and closed her eyes as if to doze. He wanted to talk.

"South—where south?" he asked. He cleared his throat. "Not west? I sort of liked the idea of going west. That's what I'm set up for, you see. All my stuff is western stuff."

Barbara opened her eyes. "Fine. Not just south, but west too. How does New Mexico sound to you? Southwest."

"Southwest," Garson nodded, relieved. "Sure." He increased his speed, changing lanes and passing a line of trucks. But he barely noticed his surroundings, the median strip or the flashing reflectors of semi trailers, for his mind was occupied by an image of himself in copper mountains sitting on a boulder, wearing a chain of turquoise and bear teeth across his bare, bronzed chest. Behind him jagged trees reached like claws for the sky and in front of him ran a misting stream in the middle of which, drenched by spray and meeting his gaze, bathed an Apache chick.

Barbara was thinking that if they made good time, driving all night and into the next day, maybe they could get near the Mexican border—then she would be almost safe. She would withdraw money with her cash card along the way, emptying her account. That would give the police, when they checked, a southward trail. By then, though, she would've disappeared, gotten away from Garson, and left not a trace: out of the country, they would assume. Wrongly, for she intended to double back north and find Jerry. Just as a test, she turned to Garson and asked,

"What do you suppose Jerry is up to now? Don't you wonder about your old friend?"

Garson's reverie was rudely interrupted. He scratched the back of his neck, surprised that she'd brought *him* up. After all, here they were, together at last.

"Well, the way I look at it is this," he told her. "What's past is past. And I don't care what anyone says," he added. "Sometimes he was a groovy dude."

Barbara looked at him, incredulous. She pointed to the radio. "You mean you haven't heard the news? You haven't turned on a television, seen any reports?"

Garson didn't know what she was talking about. He'd been so damn busy packing and getting everything ready on such short notice that he hadn't had time for TV or anything else.

So Barbara informed him about the uprising and breakout, told him an abbreviated version of police suspicions related to the fact that her husband was still at large. Or at least missing. Everyone was looking for him.

"Holy shit, I bet Jer masterminded the whole thing!" Garson broke in. "That son-of-a-gun!"

Barbara laughed with him, but her expression froze when he continued:

"It's gonna be perfect, just you and me. I got a tent and sleeping bags we can zip together and loads of food and everything. The whole country is waiting for us, from sea to shining sea! And as for the past, well—I don't mean it unkind, he's my friend like you say—but fuck Jerry, forget him. You know? He's got out now, he's doing all right."

She couldn't restrain herself:

"Garson, Garson! He's *not* doing all right. He's in danger! That much is obvious."

Garson puffed his lips, staring straight ahead.

"If the cops are after him, Barbara, a person shouldn't get mixed up in it. Trust me."

Never had she found him more loathsome. But she had to keep her composure. Now of all times! It wasn't just the authorities or traitors like Garson who threatened Jerry. He'd been abandoned or dismissed by people who didn't understand what he was about—and even those who did understand, like herself, had been untrue. Weak.

But that was over, she told herself. Now the time had come for something better. The time had come to . . . to do what he would do!

Except she would have to be more devious:

"I'm counting on *you* now," she said, smiling at him.

Garson actually blushed. A new silence descended as he continued driving south. Exits and motels whipped by, and soon they were speeding through open country, past fields of rolling black dirt, with silhouettes of farm machinery crawling on the horizon. Barbara was turning over her plans in her mind, including images of Garson, left alone at the roadside, steaming, when his voice intruded:

"Feel under the glovebox."

She hesitated, then reached forward.

"No, not in it, *under* it," he told her.

"There's a pouch or something here—"

"My guns," he said.

She jerked her hand away.

"No—no way! I don't want that. You hear me? That's not what I meant. No guns, Garson. You hear me?"

Garson looked out his side window. Now, was that nice? It was hard not to find her manner irritating. Raising her voice, and telling him what to do, right in his own vehicle.

"No guns?" he asked her. "Well, when there's trouble it usually takes more than sweet talk, Barbara, don't you think so? Reach your hand under the seat."

"I don't want to! I told you, I'm not having any guns!"

"I heard you, I heard you!" Garson was trying to control himself, for this time she had yelled directly in his ear. "It's *not* a gun. I promise. Reach under the seat."

"Slow down, you're driving too fast. You want us to get pulled over? Now that would really be smart, wouldn't it?"

Garson began to pant. Now she was telling him how to drive! "I'll slow down," he said, evenly, deliberately, his concentration stacking itself up like a tower of cups and saucers, "when you reach under the goddamn seat."

She shook her head, No.

"Don't you bully me," she said.

He trembled for a moment, then suddenly everything inside him tilted crazily and crashed in a heap. He stomped on the accelerator and the Cherokee jolted forward, a surge of power.

"You DO it! You do what I say!"

"Cut it out!" she cried, thrown back against the seat.

Normally, ceding to such a command was the last thing she would do. But this situation wasn't normal. As the speedometer climbed past 90, approached 95, and they passed cars and trucks like in a video game, she simply had to choose. Why risk her life in a stupid argument? And why risk the police? With a show of waving her hand she reached under the seat.

"Okay! It's wood," she called above the rising whine of the engine, groping. "You hear me? You satisfied?"

"You see?" Garson let off the accelerator, and the Cherokee's engine seemed to sigh as it slowed. "No gun. Hickory, Kentucky hickory. You won't find a better baseball bat." Garson threw back his hair and laughed. "The All-American way!"

They eased into the normal flow of traffic while Barbara thought: I can't take 800 miles of this! No way! She tried to restore some calm, and reason with him.

"We're aiming for another kind of method, you see? We won't need guns or baseball bats. Nothing of the sort. Because there's not going to be any of that kind of trouble."

Garson listened, not particularly interested. He hadn't even mentioned his briefcase and its chains. Just to change the subject to something more important, he turned and remarked, "You know, you look awfully good in a seatbelt."

Barbara stopped mid-sentence. For a moment she didn't understand. Then, looking down, she realized he was referring to the way the strap entered between and accentuated her breasts. When she looked up again he was smiling. Inwardly she groaned—maybe outwardly, too, it was hard to tell, for suddenly she was just one big groan. Still he kept smiling. Of course, Barbara had heard lame remarks before but this one, from his wet lips, ranked. If there had been a Revolting Prize, she would've nominated him for it. In seconds, scenarios were played out in her mind, each more disagreeable than the last. She could remind him that he was acting like a fourteen-year-old, and risk his getting angry again and perhaps driving recklessly, imposing new demands. Or she could simply unfasten her belt, and risk his laughing at her, maybe driving recklessly, too, in order to tempt her to put it back on. How could she win, or at least maintain? That was the trick. Within the next 20 miles, she speculated, he would try to put his hand on her knee, or touch her some other way. Oh, to be stuck for hours and hours with this person—the most unappealing male on the planet!—in order to do the right thing by Jerry. Purgatory, she thought. Is this purgatory?

"Just keep going south," she told him, hunching her shoulders.

"How long we gonna drive tonight?"

"All night. We're not stopping anywhere."

"All night?" He leered at her. "I might get tired."

"I can drive. You can crawl in back and sleep."

"Gee, I don't know about you driving this. You ever handle one of these things?"

"Of course I can drive it!"

Garson winced at her tone. She was so snappy. He sighed, reached down, pulled out a bag of corn chips. He offered her some, she took one, then he left the bag on the seat between them. Fuck, he was willing to share. Even happy to do so. Why was she so moody? A guy busted his ass. Pulled out all the stops. And look what happened. Struggle. Just struggle. What a world, really.

They chewed without speaking. Garson turned on the radio, and when the music broke for news at the top of the hour, the prison riot figured among the lead stories. Men were still at large, the radio reported.

They looked at each other, but said nothing.

Dusk began to fall. Barbara braced herself for a long trip. Still, she was determined to stick to her plan. She thought: going south so I can meet him north. Crazy, this life. I go and go till I come all the way around.

Eleven

HE WALKED BESIDE The Angel in the field, his head buzzing with exciting new schemes while he savored the sunshine on his face. The sound of crickets rose here and there in the tall grass, which changed its hue as it bent in the wind. The slope itself seemed to breathe.

"Isn't it—" he inhaled with his surroundings, "delish?"

The Angel cast him a sideways glance.

"The trees!" exclaimed Mr Nice Guy as they approached a muddy creek. "Look at those leaves, the way they shimmer. And they're sticky underneath, this time of year. Dogwoods especially. Or is it soft maple? See that blossom there? It's called bee balm. Did you know that? When I was a kid I used to picture it as what bees rubbed on their tiny shoulders when they were tired after a long day's work of going from flower to flower. Happy little suckers!" He bent to pick up a flat stone, then threw it in the creek. Mr Nice Guy used a whipping sidearm. "One-two-three-four-five-six. I used to be pretty good at skipping. Been a long time though. You get better results if you put a spin on it. How 'bout you? Are you good at skipping? How are you when it comes to the old Ducks and Drakes?"

The Angel was staring at him. His lips moved slowly and he lifted a finger. "*You*—"

Mr Nice Guy picked up several stones, and began to juggle them. In the sunshine, with the breeze wafting under his nose, it felt great. He experienced a prickling sensation under his scalp.

The Angel's voice cut through the air:

"Now I remember you. You were at my trial. You were the one who—who was *laughing* at me."

"No, not laughing, definitely not laughing!" Mr Nice Guy protested. "I just wanted to make you feel—"

The Angel lunged for him. Mr Nice Guy backpeddled, stones falling around him. Fury shone on The Angel's face as he grabbed Mr Nice Guy's shirt, his fists gathering up the material under his chin; The Angel's eyes seemed to swell and rim with yellow malice. Mr Nice Guy wriggled and pulled until his shirt ripped, its buttons raining on the ground. He whirled and took off running away through the high grass. The Angel followed close behind. "I'll get you, fucker, I'll pound you! You can't do that to me!"

"Hang on!" Mr Nice Guy called, "don't worry!" but he didn't look over his shoulder, or slow down.

They passed into a beanfield, running down the rows; Mr Nice Guy jumped one row, then two, his shirttail flying behind him; he darted toward a stand of spindly trees but The Angel stayed with him. He jumped a little washout and ran straight into the ditch and then into the creek, sinking up to his knees. The Angel came crashing out of the brush and splashed after him. They staggered through the rushes, then up into the weeds of the facing bank.

There was a fence. Suddenly changing his mind, and his strategy, with an inspiration Mr Nice Guy stopped and spun round. He would surprise him. They could talk this out, couldn't they? Panting, a splitting ache coursing up his side, he said, "A first impression can deceive —"

With a roar The Angel hurtled, his feet leaving the ground. During the brief interval that he was in the air Mr Nice Guy, who didn't have time to get out of the way, was struck by the calmness and clarity of his perceptions. Despite his fear—real as the oxygen bubbling in his veins—he felt ready. He might as well have been pausing in the park in his sweatsuit, watching seed pods from an oak tree twirl down at him through the sunny beams. In that instant, as The Angel leapt toward his throat, he was anticipating a future beyond running or reasoning: he was pondering What Next. *I need a new name.*

The Angel crashed into Mr Nice Guy's chest. They tumbled down, spinning with the impact. The Angel held on as they rolled in the grass, and his besmeared face appeared to Mr Nice Guy along with the sky and the earth, round and round.

"Auyyy, that hurts," Mr Nice Guy managed, struggling to get free. This was no good. Flailing, with the heel of his palm he caught The Angel directly on his puffed-out purple. The Angel cried out and momentarily released his grip. Gasping, hearing himself pant and groan, Mr Nice Guy rose to his knees. He forced himself to his feet and stumbled forward, still bending at the waist, his hand clasping his chest. The Angel was trying to get up, too. Mr Nice Guy staggered ahead, jerkily, feeling light as a scarecrow, weaving from side to side on the edge of the field.

He half-climbed, half-fell over the fence and landed with a crash in a patch of sweetcorn. He rose again and continued, blood pounding in his ears—the sound of another crash—but he didn't turn, he just kept moving. *Barbara, look who's back.* He came out of the corn, broke into a full trot. Now he was in strawberries.

EPILOGUE

Underground Nice

SOME POLICE INVESTIGATORS think he left the country long ago. Others, supposing that he was in the caves, believe that he never emerged. The depths were too treacherous. The truth is that if you look down from on high you can see a circle of cabooses around a lake in a forest. At the Billy Hare Lodge, a new couple is working as caretakers.

It's not a soft job, even in the slow periods. By the time you finish maintenance and repairs on the last caboose of the circle, it's time to start all over again. Such are the seasons.

Yet there's still room to dream. Although he soon found out that sapodillas didn't stand a chance in this climate, and that despite its pleasures, there was no real money in popcorn or an affordable method to bring the price of dew down, to his delight he discovered a local pine resin that showed great promise as chewing material. When mixed with fresh water lichens, the preliminary tests were astounding, whether you were talking about taste, masticity, or afterbreath. Most of his free hours were devoted to these experiments.

In these new circumstances, and under his new name, there was no question of reviving Home-Made Services, even in a country version, or of launching World Services JR. But he didn't mind. People would just have to decide and do those things for themselves, he thought. But at the same time, his situation didn't stop him from determining and carrying out personal schemes, though his status as a fugitive rendered them more complicated, necessitating secret planning and recourse to disguise. It took daring, but soon sorties were made into his home state, for guerrilla niceties.

His ailing mother was the first target. The out-of-the-blue delivery of the fattest Persian cat she'd ever seen caught her completely by surprise. The furry beast promptly took up residence on what little was left of her lap. In a moment she guessed at the source, her heart gladdened, and she knew that even if she could not see him now, he was near. She was not really alone, and her will strengthened to live on, till the next surprise. And that Christmas, and each Christmas thereafter at the penitentiary, James Davis received an unmarked, anonymous package which, after inspection and X-rays by the authorities, was delivered into his hands. Inside he found, mysteriously, a popcorn ball. The first time, James turned it over in his hands in wonder, shaking his head. He lifted his eyes and thanked his Maker that his old cellmate was still alive; that night, falling to his knees, he asked that Jerry might—finally, somehow—become smarter.

It also happened that Garson fell to his knees, but that's what 14 cans of beer will do to a person. Sometimes, as he crawled into his sleeping bag in the Nevada desert (the government surplus bunkers rented real cheap), he remembered his old boss Jer, how he used to help him out, but more often he thought of Barbara, in various postures. He speculated, wistfully, that she could've known a frontier life.

And actually, she wasn't far from it. The transition of going underground proved hardest for her. Particularly at the beginning, she was sometimes bored out of her mind. She loved Jerry, and had determined to be with him, but that on its own didn't suffice. She rarely thought of Reggie, except with regret over their clumsy parting, and she would've been relieved to know that he'd quickly recovered from his run-in with the law and was becoming quite a success, trading in futures. (Reggie, for his part, recalled her much more often, though she wouldn't have recognized herself in his mind's eye.)

No, for Barbara in the end, Jerry and Reggie, individually or together, were not the issue. She required her own peace, and at the very least needed to be looking for something; and what aided her in this new life was the discovery of "water billies." This was the local name for the lake's austere gems. In these waters, at these temperatures, the shells and their occasional deposits were tiny, hardly bigger than a grape seed—in the end nature was modest—but they were beautiful, perfectly smooth, of a lightly clouded yet lucent blue. The first time Barbara found one, she was intrigued; the second time, she was hooked. Jerry didn't have the patience to look for them; but Barbara could spend many hours sifting through the shells for what they might contain. It was never-ending, yet sometimes rewarding, and those were exactly the qualities she craved. A labor of love. According to an old story, once you'd collected a handful—she was far from that yet, and couldn't guess when her time would come—you were supposed to throw them back into the water. She found it hard to imagine anyone choosing to do so, after all the effort it took, but that was what locals said gave the lake its special cool glow, like the puddle of a melted star.

Many evenings she and Jerry sat on the steps leading up to the caboose and looked out at the lake. The birds were beginning to sound sleepy, the insects thrummed. "You know," said Jerry one time, "even if the border's close, I hope things never get so hot that we have to scoot. I like it here. This is nice country." Barbara tossed a shell, *plip,* into the water. She reached for another, and replied, "It surprises me, honey, but I hope so, too. I want this to last." Another time Jerry didn't say anything, because he'd botched his resin mix and his teeth were stuck together. Still, when he got it right and the juices flowed, conversation lasted long after the light had disappeared, and his usual topic of plans while she picked at her shells began to make room for other subjects, for talk of the past.

He spoke to her with wonder of all the things that had happened. Sometimes Barbara joined in, but usually she kept her memories of these times close to her, and pondered them in her heart.

[redacted]